REA

**DO NOT REMOVE
CARDS FROM POCKET**

DEATH OF AN INNOCENT

DEATH OF AN INNOCENT

Roger Ormerod

St. Martin's Press
New York

Library of Congress Cataloging-in-
Publication Data

Ormerod, Roger.
    Death of an innocent / Roger
Ormerod.
        p. cm.
    ISBN 0-312-04297-3
    I. Title.
    PR6065.R688D438   1990
    823'.914—dc20   89-77923
                                          CIP

First published in Great Britain by
Constable & Company Limited.

First U.S. Edition
10 9 8 7 6 5 4 3 2 1

1

Amelia had always made little of having been up at Oxford. It was only a middling degree, as she put it, in nineteenth century literature. Nothing to boast about. What brought the subject up was a phone call from her college friend, Olivia Dean, whom she had never mentioned.

'Richard,' she said, after she'd returned to her chair the other side of the fire, 'I'm sure I spoke about her. We were great friends at that time, though we've rather lost touch.'

'Hmm!' I said. 'So how come she's managed to trace you?'

'Well of course! She's got her researchers. Must have.'

'Researchers? What's she studying now?'

'Haven't you heard of Christobel Barnes? And Lovella Treat? I grab every one of their books as soon as they come out.'

I tried to remember. She certainly did a lot of reading. 'So?'

'Olivia's both of them. She writes romantic fiction. Christobel Barnes is the Regency stuff, and Lovella Treat the modern.'

'Lovella Treat. I rather like that. I suppose they're packed with sex, and that sort of thing.'

'Well. . .' She looked past my shoulder. 'Shall we say Georgette Heyer would've blushed – and Jane Austen fainted right away.'

'I think in Jane's days they swooned.' I was filling my pipe, keeping my eyes down. 'And why did she set her researchers to hunt you up, my dear?'

When she didn't reply at once, I looked up. Amelia was frowning, though making even that appear attractive. She knew how I hated becoming involved with other people's affairs, and was deciding how to put it. In the end she nodded to herself decisively.

'I wrote and told her at the time about my new husband. We were really very close in the old days, Richard.' That in a slightly defensive tone. 'So she knows you were a Detective Inspector, and she might well have seen bits in the papers. . .'

'It's unlikely. But she's got her researchers, as you say. She's probably assembled a complete file on you. Maybe you're the heroine of several of her books.'

'I'll assume you mean to be flattering, Richard, but I'd prefer you to be serious.'

'Serious, is it? You told her I'm no longer in the police, I suppose?'

'Yes. Now you're making assumptions. She knew, anyway.'

I was being cynical. Out of the blue, there we were with an old friend suddenly needing some sort of assistance. That was how I'd guessed it to be. The snag was that whenever I became involved with this sort of thing, it spelt trouble. And Amelia knew it. She even discouraged me at times. Still. . . this Olivia Dean sounded interesting. Lovella Treat, indeed! Whoever could invent such a pseudonym was worth attention. Nevertheless, I grimaced, not to seem too eager.

'I'm assuming there's some difficulty with which she wants your assistance and encouragement.' I was choosing my words carefully. 'And I'm assuming she expects me to go along with you.'

'Something like that.'

'Did she say what the trouble was?' I asked vaguely, not too encouragingly.

'She's had a burglary.'

'Ah!' I raised one eyebrow at her. 'And the police – what do they say?'

She flicked an invisible bit of dust from her skirt. 'I gathered she hasn't reported it.'

'Umm!' I commented.

It was November. I was safely married, had retired a little early, and was rapidly becoming domesticated. There was a lot of terraced garden to look after, which kept me reasonably fit, though it hardly exercised the mind to any degree. Nevertheless, I was quietly contented, and had relaxed into the routine.

And I was bored to hell. The garden at this time of the year no longer required my full attention, and the two cars were tuned to perfection. I was due to go screaming up the wall very shortly. I considered Amelia blandly.

'What did she ask you to do?'

'Go and visit.'

'When?'

'She suggested tomorrow.'

Lovella Treat, I thought, savouring it. 'We'd better pack a couple of cases,' I suggested. And, because the weather wasn't being too kind, I added: 'We'll use the Granada. Where is this place, anyway?'

'She's got a house overlooking one of the waterways on the Broads in Norfolk. I wrote down the address.'

I nodded. It was settled. I was feeling better already.

From Boreton-Upon-Severn to Norfolk was going to be a decent run of about 180 miles. Across country. That meant it would mainly be on ordinary roads, with not much motorway driving involved. At that time I anticipated the visit would entail no more than an amicable chat and the necessary unofficial advice, so the expectation was that we would be back the next day. Amelia said she'd gathered that we were expected to stay at Mansfield Park, as her friend coyly called her house, so I explained our absence to Mary in those terms, and we got away early.

Mary Pinson is not really our housekeeper, as she has a legal right to residence, but she looks after us, and is always anxious about our welfare. She said: 'Now watch out for yourselves,' and waved us away.

I was driving. We normally shared, but it was misty as we descended to river level to cross the Severn, and the weather forecast was for rain. Amelia hates driving in the rain. We settled down to do it in one long, unbroken journey.

We got the rain. It pelted down. We also got a puncture in the rear nearside tyre. Punctures are rare these days, and this was a slow one, but due to the wet surface I detected a change in the roadholding and had to stop. I changed the wheel, getting thoroughly soaked, and was naturally not vastly pleased when I at last got back inside.

But I was not actively annoyed, though Amelia assumed I was. I could always tell when she makes such assumptions; she taps her fingers on her knee, impatient with herself for being unable to do anything about my distress. She has never understood. As a serving officer in the CID I had gradually developed a mental skin, protecting myself from misery. Countless hours of waiting, cold, wet and unable to detect an end to it, had gradually inured me to discomfort. It's a question of philosophy. I was prepared to sit, damp and steaming, behind the wheel, and drive on.

'We'll look for an hotel,' she said, 'and have lunch. You can change in the men's room.'

'I'm all right.'

'We can hardly arrive at Olivia's with you smelling of wet tweed.'

'True,' I agreed, equably enough I thought. 'We mustn't have that.'

She was silent as we drove on. Silent for quite a while. Then she said abruptly: 'You didn't want to come, did you?'

'If I hadn't, you'd have had to change the wheel yourself.'

'You're not giving me an answer, Richard.'

I turned my head and grinned at her. 'I can't wait to meet somebody who writes under the name of Lovella Treat.'

'That's not an answer, either.'

If you ask me, it was she who was in a bad mood. I guessed at the reason. It was because she feared this was going to be a paltry and futile visit, which could in some way denigrate her friend in my eyes. But how could it be paltry, when Olivia had taken considerable trouble to contact her – and me – yet hadn't even reported the burglary to the police?

We found an hotel. We had lunch, after I'd changed. A very pleasant lunch. Amelia was able to assume I was now more pleased with life. She became her usual relaxed self.

'She must be earning a fortune,' she said over coffee.

'Sure to be.'

'I mean. . . dozens of bestsellers.'

'So she turned her degree to good use,' I commented. 'I suppose she did get her degree?'

'A double first.' She nodded, indicating a reflected pride.

8

'Oho! A clever woman. In your subject?'

'Yes. We shared the same tutor.' She was speaking with her cup poised in front of her face. 'Shared most things, really. Clothes, books, notes. Even boyfriends.'

'Ah yes. All those available young undergrads. I'd have thought there'd be plenty of choice.' I cocked an eyebrow at her. 'Unless you also shared the same taste in men.'

'I suppose we did.'

'Then perhaps I shouldn't have come. She might take a liking for me. I'm not sure I can keep two women happy.'

'You're making an assumption there,' she said, but she was smiling. Yet that could have been because of her memories, because she went on: 'We were both wild about Philip, I remember. Tall, slim and handsome. Doing economics, I think.' She rested her chin on her hand, her eyes going out of focus. 'Dear Philip.'

'And neither of you got him?' I asked, to keep things moving.

'Oh, *she* did. In the end. They were married. . .oh, three or four years after we graduated. She'd sold a book or two by then, and he was doing her research, I believe. It was probably more convenient. . .' She allowed it to tail off, musingly.

'It's he who traced you, then?'

'Probably. Clever Philip. You'll like him, Richard.'

This was perhaps doubtful, when I had to consider that she might well be more interested in meeting Philip Dean again, than in a reunion with her dear friend Olivia.

We went out to the car. It had stopped raining. She suggested that she should drive the rest of the way. 'You're so much better at reading the map, Richard.'

But that wasn't the reason. There is a certain psychological satisfaction in driving towards a past lover, best savoured from behind the wheel.

'You're driving a little too fast,' I suggested a few minutes later.

'Nonsense, Richard.'

She had the seat hitched well forward, and mine was well back. I was able to grin to myself without giving offence. I concentrated on the map, and located what seemed to be the nearest village to our destination, about fifteen miles north of

9

Norwich. We were on the A11, and I told her to keep going until we hit the outer ring road of Norwich, and I'd tell her which turn-off to take.

It was a gloomy afternoon, not certain whether to settle down to a quiet period of mist or to venture into a spell of drizzle. We were running on dipped headlights, but Amelia made no suggestion that I should take over the wheel. Merely, her speed was reduced. The poor visibility made me uncertain of direction signs almost until it was too late to act on them.

We located the turn from the Norwich outer ring road. Twice I missed the proper turnings, but eventually we ran into the village I'd been looking for. I got out and enquired. The street was quiet, the shop windows ghostly in the misty half-light. Shoppers were rare. I could hear the engine clicking after she'd switched off.

I was told at a newsagent's that we had driven past the turn-off for Mansfield Park. We were to go back about half a mile and take a turn to the right, where, as far as I could recall, there had been nothing but water and reeds on either side of the road. We went slowly back. The turn-off was there, over what could have been a dyke or bridge, and along a narrow causeway, which was not designated on the map. Now it was nearly dark. Amelia had the main heads on, and they just managed to pick out the sign fastened to a post: Mansfield Park.

This time it was certainly a bridge we crossed, because the car juddered and I heard the thump of woodwork beneath the tyres. The drive became gravel. There was a fall-off on both sides. Amelia concentrated.

The lights ahead were spread in the mist, and gradually the house took shape. It was wide, but seemed not to be deep, and the whole front and the sweep of the parking drive were floodlit. We drew up on cobbles and Amelia switched off the engine. For a moment we sat, and she breathed out with a sigh. Somewhere a dog bayed, the deep bell of a Great Dane. Holmes would have been in his element.

Then a door opened in the centre of the sprawl of stone wall, light spilled out, accompanied by a bounding dog, and revealed the figure of a tall, gangling man, who called half-heartedly after the dog into the darkness but made no move to follow it. So

10

our welcome was a wet nose against my side window and a slobbering sound. Before it jumped up and started to remove our paintwork, I said quickly, 'Me first,' and thrust the door open against the weight.

I have a way with dogs. You have to be firm. 'Down, boy.' As I could see he was. But he upped, with his great paws on my shoulders, nearly having me on my back, the initiative his but his temperament fortunately amiable.

'He wants to make friends,' called out the man, waving vaguely as though to disperse the mist. 'It's Amelia, isn't it? And Richard. Come along in. It's cold out there.'

This was perhaps his apology for not coming out and holding doors open and the like. The dog, at the sound of his voice, went galloping past him into the house, presumably to tell the rest of the household we'd arrived. Philip called out: 'Leave your bags, I'll get 'em later.' There was something defensive in his attitude.

I thought Amelia slammed her door a little too hard. In the floodlight her face was shadowed heavily, but it gradually assumed a smile as I stood back to let her lead the way.

'Philip,' she said, 'how nice to see you again.'

She held out her hand. He reached forward so that he took both, then he held her away from him theatrically and observed her with pleasure, his head to one side. 'You look wonderful, my dear. Not changed a bit.'

'Idiot,' she said. 'It's been over twenty years.'

'So it has, so it has.' His eyebrows bobbed up and down. Then he released her and turned to me. 'And this is your husband. Richard, isn't it? I'm Philip Dean.'

'Richard Patton,' I said, and we shook hands, smiling at each other, he with a manic delight, as though my presence signalled the end to all his concerns.

He was naturally about ten years younger than me, being Amelia's contemporary, but he looked more than his age. He was as tall as me, but couldn't have been much more than half my weight. At that time, he was was wearing only a shirt and trousers, but they managed to hang on his frame loosely, the belt drawn tight to take up the slack at his waist. It was clear that the shirt collar, if fastened, would be too loose, and now it revealed

11

hollows in the skin of his neck. His face was heavy, the bone structure strong, with a wide mouth, the forced smile lifting folds of skin that normally fell towards his chin. His eyes were blue and bright. Intelligence burned from them. And something else. Stress? Even fear?

He backed into the hall, which I could see was no more than a passage, and said: 'Olivia will be free very shortly. Come through, and we'll have a pot of tea. I'm sure you'll be exhausted. This weather! But it's November, after all. . .' And so on, useless words, promoted by nerves.

He explained that where we had parked the car was, in practice, the rear of the house, as this had originally been the frontage of a row of five attached cottages. But they'd run them all into one residence, and the main hall, into which he now led us, was the full width of what had been the central cottage. Here there was a transformation, the hall being square and spacious, panelled in pine and with a few pictures to break up the surface areas.

'You'll want to wash up and freshen yourselves,' he announced, flinging open a door into a living-room, which, possibly in honour of Christobel Barnes, was pure Regency. I'm no expert, but the furniture seemed genuine. Books lined one wall, not one of them with a bright, modern dust cover. The fireplace was stone, wide, a fire burning in it, with the Great Dane and two Spaniels sprawled on the hearth. They lifted their heads, but were too relaxed to do more than beat their tails on the rug. The window overlooking what he called the front of the house was uncurtained, and though it was unmistakably an opening french window and double-glazed, it was nevertheless in a Regency style.

'Do make yourselves at home,' he said. 'I'll get Doris to rustle up some tea. Then I'll fetch your stuff in, if you left the boot unlocked. And I'll. . .' He backed out of the room, not a perfect host by any standards. Perhaps he didn't get much practice.

Amelia had walked over to the wall of books. 'Richard,' she said, 'these must surely be first editions. All of them. Regency and Victorian romance. Just think.'

I'd gone to make myself known to the dogs, always a useful insurance against future misunderstandings. 'I'm thinking.'

12

'And all this stuff. . .' I looked round, and she meant the ornaments, the *objets d'art*, the exquisite porcelain displayed on low tables and in a china cabinet against one wall.

'I noticed.'

'It's all genuine.'

'I'm sure it is.'

'You're not looking.'

'I did so as we came in. It's a burglar's delight. And don't forget, this is what's left. I wonder what was taken.'

I straightened up. Amelia looked beautiful in that setting, a little mist caught in her hair, her eyes bright, and the whole picture set perfectly against the array of splendid antiques.

'You've got no romance in your soul,' she said, not too seriously. 'Your mind's set on business – now isn't it?'

'I'm remembering why we're here.'

'There's time for that. Relax. Make yourself at home.'

I shrugged, smiling.

She walked round the room, idly picking up pieces of porcelain I wouldn't have dared to touch, and glancing at their bases. 'It's genuine stuff, you know.'

'I'm sure it is.'

She walked some more, then she came to a halt in front of me. 'He's changed, Richard.' Her tone had changed, too. There was concern in it.

'It's twenty years,' I reminded her.

'All the same. . . there was always a bounce to him, a kind of eagerness to get on to the next important objective in his life. And somehow, he always gave the impression that *you* were it. The very centre of it. There was a sort of casual elegance about him. Proud, dogmatic, and charming with it.'

'He doesn't seem to have lost that.'

'It's not the same. He's having to make an effort.'

My hands were dirty, with the smoking I'd done on the journey. I wished he'd shown us where we could wash. I hadn't noticed any dogmatism and pride in him. I said nothing. Philip had seemed almost resentful of our presence.

'He was all lined up for entering politics, or trying the diplomatic service, I remember.'

13

'Perhaps he hadn't the drive.'

'Or perhaps he was too open and sincere,' she said supportively.

'No use in politics, then.'

'I never thought he would be,' she admitted thoughtfully. 'He could never stick to anything for long.'

'Such as his women friends.' Then I wished I hadn't said it, catching Amelia's sideways smile.

'He seems to have stuck faithfully to Olivia,' she murmured.

As though it might have been a stage cue, she made her entrance. Olivia Dean, having cast aside Christobel Barnes – or perhaps it had been Lovella Treat – flung open the door, and maybe a flush of one of them still commanded her because it was a heroine's entrance, centre-stage, theatrical and brimming over with emotion.

'Darling!'

'Livia!'

Then they were in each other's arms, then banging cheeks, standing back to observe what the ravishing years had destroyed or matured, and if there was a dry eye in the house it was Olivia's.

Having come directly from her den of creation, the muse was still with her. She had mentally rehearsed her entrance and greeting, and had now carried it through so that it was firmly recorded for posterity. But now it could be discarded, and she was all down-to-earth practicality in a moment.

'You've put on weight, Mellie.'

Mellie? There'd never been any hint of such a corruption of Amelia.

'But not you, I see. You're working yourself to a frazzle, Livia.'

'I do six hours a day. Say stockbroker hours. It's not painful. Did Philip offer you a drink? Oh, there he is. Philip, didn't you offer them a drink?'

'I asked Doris to put a kettle on,' he told her mildly, grimacing an apology, shrugging his shoulders at me. Then he emerged fully from behind her and said: 'What'll you have? We can cover most eventualities.'

'Unless,' Olivia said severely, 'you forgot to get in the sherry.'

14

Then she turned to Amelia. 'It's still sherry before dinner, I assume, Mellie?'

'Sherry,' she agreed, and to me Philip raised his palms and tucked his lower lip between his teeth, like a naughty boy who's forgotten to call in at the shops.

Later, I realized he was addicted to these comic, self-denigrating gestures and expressions. They were intended to convey that his inadequacies were vastly overrated.

The two women were now in excited discussion. Twenty years to be covered in a few minutes. With a glass of Amontillado in my fist, listening half-interestedly to Philip's explanation that the new book was promised for the 1st of January, I was able to consider Amelia's friend with interest.

I had attempted not to frame a mental picture of a writer of women's romantic fiction, but I hadn't really succeeded. There had been an expectation of someone svelte and lissom, with large and captivating eyes and a luscious mouth. One whom a man might expect to be sultry and passionate, tingling on the edge of a collapse into emotional outbursts and sentimental sighs. Of course, I was wildly wrong.

Olivia Dean was a short woman – two inches shorter than Amelia – stocky and widely-beamed, firmly planted on capable feet. She was at that time wearing her writing costume, slacks and sweater, and looked at the same time relaxed and competent. She had square features, with that squashed-up hint of trials and tribulations resolutely faced and trampled underfoot. At that moment she was excited and voluble, but her mouth wasn't far from being set and uncompromising. She was a woman who knew what she was after and was determined to get it, whatever had to be sacrificed. She wanted to be the world's premier romance writer. If she destroyed herself in doing so, she would leave behind a monument to achievement. And an epitaph: she knew what she wanted.

And yet – wasn't there a hint of humour, albeit turned against herself? What else would explain 'Lovella Treat'? It suggested, even, a small self-contempt, to be hinted at. A modesty, perhaps, an underlying lack of self-confidence, like a not-quite-anonymous gift to charity, a plea for recognition.

I was aware that Philip had stopped talking. When I turned

15

to him he was smiling, head cocked. My turn. Say something, Richard. Charming place you've got here? But no, I hadn't yet seen much of it.

I said: 'Amelia didn't tell me. This burglary of yours – what exactly was taken?'

His smile remained, but it was no more than a shape for his lips. His eyes were empty.

'Well, that's the worrying thing, you know. Nothing was taken.'

2

They gave us a corner room, at what they called the front. There had been a change in the weather – a variation in air pressure or something – so that the rain had ceased and the mist was held down as a thin layer. The moon, with a halo, gave enough light for me to view the prospect from the low and narrow window. Beneath us was a paved area, on which I should, no doubt, have run the car. At the far side of it there was a low wall with an opening in it, beyond which the ground seemed to slope into the mist. I guessed that the gradient ended at the water's edge, because the tips of wet reeds caught a reflection of the moon, and just visible there was the roof and half the wall of what could have been a small boathouse.

We had eventually been shown up here by Philip. There was an attached bathroom, so that bedroom and bathroom occupied the top floor of the original cottage. I couldn't change for dinner, because my wet suit was still on the rear seat of the car, but I felt better after a shave and a bath, and inside the bathroom I could hear Amelia splashing about. I stared out at the flat grey view.

They had done what they could with the upper storey, but nothing could disguise the fact that it was poked up beneath the roof. The ceiling was low, and the rafters at the outer wall protruded through the ceiling down to the top of the window. The floor creaked. Although the furniture was modern – two single beds, a bedside table, dressing-table, two wardrobes – and the decoration done in light and flowery pastels, the room still carried a taint of poverty. In the 1700s the tenants had used it as somewhere in which they could fall exhausted on to pallets, beyond caring about the oppression of the room. The tiny window would never have been opened, and their lives would have been governed by sunset and sunrise.

I turned away. I was thinking myself into depression.

'We haven't heard much about this burglary,' I called out.

'After dinner, Richard. Don't be so impatient.'

'Did I tell you what Philip said?'

'Two or three times.'

I hadn't been able to extract any more information from him, as we'd been drawn into a group of four, and as most of the chat had been about university days, I'd found myself odd man out.

It was therefore with anticipation that I followed Amelia down to dinner. Over the meal, still nothing of what mainly interested me. Olivia was now firmly in charge. She spoke of foreign royalties, and the loss of revenue caused by the strength of the pound. She spoke of the possible serialization of one of her recent books. By the time we'd emptied two bottles of wine, the atmosphere was light and amusing. She had us laughing at her scandalous remarks about the recent Romance Writers' Convention they had attended in Copenhagen.

'All fritter and posture,' she commented, her mouth suddenly sour. 'No sense of occasion, no serious responses.'

'It was,' murmured Philip, 'a social get-together. A bit of fun.'

'It was a flop,' she told him decisively.

Philip caught my eye. His eyelid flickered and he dipped his head. I felt, uncomfortably, that I was being drawn into some sort of conspiracy against his wife, even a betrayal. But though I watched him when he was watching her, I could detect nothing but admiration.

Amelia chattered in response. I recognized her mood. She's an alert detector of atmosphere, and something was making her uneasy and nervous.

I had no time to ask her about this, as, with the coffee, we split up. It was not so much a withdrawing of the ladies, leaving the men to their brandy and cigars, but the simple fact that Amelia and Olivia went to two easy chairs on one side of the room, and

Philip led me to a similar arrangement on the other. It could have been planned. For us, it was brandy and pipes. I waited. He eventually offered an apology, when I could see no need for one.

'Olivia,' he said, sitting back, 'should now be in one of her writing sessions. Eight to ten every evening. Drag her away from it, and she's disorientated. Her time machine goes haywire – like jet-lag.'

He was quite serious, but I could see nothing to justify this remark. Olivia was an ordinary housewife, gossiping with an old friend. Or so it appeared to me.

'She'll suffer for it later,' he told me, as though he'd read my thoughts. 'In her workroom she's lost, gone into a strange land, dictating away. Ten o'clock, she'll come out and say, "Brandy, Philip," then she'll click back to normal.'

'It sounds grim work for her.'

There were now none of his little mannerisms of mock apology. I realised these occurred only when he was dealing with Olivia. 'Dealing with' was about it. She sounded terrible to accommodate. He tapped his pipe stem against his teeth, in between a smile.

'It's all right when you get used to it. Two hours in the morning, two in the afternoon, two in the evening. It's a rule. She says she has to treat herself as an office worker. She dictates. The plots come in her head and she just makes notes of what she wants in each chapter, then she dictates. To a tape recorder. There's a young woman in the village who comes up every morning and takes the cassettes away, types up what there was, and brings it back the next day. It's like a word factory.'

I wasn't sure what he was trying to tell me, certainly something, because his eyes were bright and never left mine. So this was not idle conversation.

'It must be a great emotional strain,' I murmured, to indicate I was listening.

He shook his head gently. Greying, gingerish hair tumbled forward on to his forehead, and he leaned forward, elbows on his knees, hands clasped in front of him. His smile was no longer pleasant. There was a hint of distaste in it.

19

'She would tell you otherwise,' he said softly. 'There's nothing emotional about it. She's a pro. She says that with pride. It's all a matter of knowing what to do. She knows what is necessary to create characters, and she can see clearly all the emotional conflicts that occur when she puts her characters together. She knows what words to use to describe those emotions. They're not hers personally. She can write a torrid love scene in practical and excruciating detail, and still she'll be unmoved. She can kill a character in tragic circumstances, and never shed a tear. She knows how to do it. She's a wonderful woman,' he finished, using minimal pride.

I nodded. Looked down at my hands. Looked up. 'Her sense of humour redeems her,' I suggested.

'I've known her enjoy a good laugh.' He blinked. 'How d'you mean?'

'Lovella Treat.'

'Oh. . . that!' He sat back and laughed, a hushed affair, but he enjoyed it. 'That was me. I suggested that. She said it was fine, and it ran off the tongue. She never did see the joke.'

'So it was intended?'

'A corruption of Love is a Treat. Yes. Intended.'

So the sense of humour was his. But the joke had been aimed at his wife.

'And you?' I asked. 'How do you fit into this book-writing machine?'

He clearly didn't want to be considered as a cog in any machine. He was a separate aspect in the business. His voice dropped a note or two and became sonorous, an economist's voice, designed to impress.

'Me!' he said, waving a hand negligently. 'I'm her accountant, her manager. It would be disturbing for her to have to get involved with figures and facts. She says she wants something, and I get it for her, from publicity to a bigger advance, foreign sales, a new car.'

'Don't you ever get a break?'

'Oh yes. Between books. We go to our place at Antibes. She can wind down. Me too. Anonymous. No encroachment. We look for locations, me with a camera to record them. It's not

20

all go, go, go. I have. . .' He stared at his pipe bowl, 'as you'll realize, six hours a day.'

He made a mockery even out of his difficulties. I guessed that for a full twenty-four hours a day he maintained sentry duty on this empire, resisting anything that might intervene and destroy it all.

'Sounds harrowing,' I observed, wondering whether he was asking for sympathy. If so, he'd got no chance. He had an equal share in all the goodies. 'And no possibility of retirement,' I said with sympathy.

'Eh?'

'Writers don't retire. They just run out of ideas.'

He gave another of his soft, breathy laughs. 'No fear of that. She's only got half a dozen, and keeps doing variations. It can go on for ever.'

I couldn't understand, then, the challenging tilt of his head. I abruptly changed the subject. 'Was that a boathouse I saw from the bedroom window?'

He was startled. 'Well. . . yes.'

'A boat in it?'

'Oh, certainly. A dinghy, with an outboard. She said, one day, why didn't I buy myself a boat. So I did.'

'Use it?'

'I potter around. In the summer, you understand.'

His little retreat from the pressures. 'Certainly in the summer.'

We were running dry. Conversation lapsed. I couldn't understand what Amelia had seen in him. Yes, I could. Be fair. He had charm and grace, and a sense of humour I could go along with. Dry and deceptive. Yet still there had been nothing said about the burglary. He resented its intrusion as he did ours. It was an indication that his defences had been breached.

Then the women were coming to their feet, so we joined them.

'Doris goes home at eight,' said Olivia. 'I wanted the house to be quiet and empty.' Then she led the way to the kitchen.

This, like every other room, occupied the whole lower floor of one of the original cottages. So it was a large kitchen, but now thoroughly and hygenically modernized. Doris had left it clean

21

and sparkling. There was not even a lingering smell of cooking. I wondered why we'd been brought in here.

Olivia had seemed to be relaxed, but now I could feel her tension. She moved restlessly, one elbow clasped in her other palm, a cigarette poised in front of her face. Without any preamble, she launched into a prepared narrative.

'Last month, October, we went to Copenhagen on an International Romance Writers' Convention. As I've said, a dreadful waste of time. About the beginning of the month. When was it, Philip?'

'The tenth.'

'Thank you, dear. The tenth, for a week. We locked up securely. There are valuable items in this house. You'll have noticed. But we have an alarm system, connected directly with the police station. We're a bit isolated. When we came back, we'd been burgled.'

She made it a dramatic statement. Although she had intended her speech to be flat and unemotional, at the end her voice hadn't been steady.

'But I understand that nothing was taken,' I said equably. 'Philip told me.' She shot a quick, angry glance at Philip, but I gave her no chance to interrupt. 'So strictly speaking you've had a breaking and entering, not a burglary.'

'Thank you for that information.'

'In case you needed to use it in a book,' I explained.

'My readers don't care about such details.' She was edgy with impatience.

'And you're sure nothing was taken?'

'Do you think. . .' She controlled herself, glancing at the floor. 'We went from one end to the other, top to bottom, every room. Not a page of manuscript disturbed, not an ornament moved. Nothing.'

'But you didn't inform the police, I understand.'

'When nothing was taken?' she demanded, her voice strident. 'And when the alarm never even went off!'

'It's a point,' Amelia put in quickly, covering her friend's lapse in manners, embarrassed by it.

But I'm immune to aggressive display. I went on steadily. 'So how did he get in?'

'We don't know.'

I looked from Olivia to Philip. He shrugged. She, her lips mobile, was struggling for control.

'Then I'd better find out,' I said, 'before we go any further. Have you got a torch, Philip?'

'There's one here,' he offered, opening a drawer.

'Thank you.' I tried it. The batteries were fresh. 'I'll have a general look around, if you don't mind.'

Philip nodded. Olivia, obviously believing I didn't accept one word of it and was humouring them, turned away. All three sat at the table. Philip suggested tea or coffee. No takers. They sat, as I began in the kitchen still wondering why we'd been brought there.

I was aware that they believed me to be a bit of a fool. I had come there – oh yes, been asked, but the result was the same – and the expectation was that with my experience I would utter a magical incantation, and it would all go away. The trouble was that I didn't know what was to go away, and I didn't know any magic words.

So I stood on a kitchen chair and solemnly inspected the edges of the windows and the outside door. Although the upstairs windows had apparently been impervious to improvement, all those downstairs had been modernized, though in a tasteful fashion as befitted the prevailing period. The windows were double-glazed, each separate leaded diamond. The alarm system was modern and recently installed.

There are a number of cunning devices to trap anyone attempting to rob places like museums and art galleries: infrared rays which must not be interrupted, pressure devices in the floors, even heat detectors that can pick out a heavy breath at a hundred feet. All of these can be circumvented by an experienced crook. And all were far too exotic for a house this size. The system installed was a double one, which would have baffled any local initiates and most of the city professionals. One circuit set off the alarm if the current was broken, one if it was made. And the wires were carefully hidden. Nothing had been interfered with in the kitchen. No one had entered that way.

'Central switch?' I asked, replacing the chair.

'In the front hall. A cupboard behind the hallstand,' said Philip, in the same brisk tone I'd used.

'You checked it, of course?'

'Of course. It was switched on, and hadn't been tampered with.'

'You're certain of that?'

'That I hadn't forgotten to switch it on?' he asked sourly. 'Yes, I checked. I'd have to. The front door lock activates the whole system as you go out. If you forget the main switch, the key turning in the front door gives a warning beep.'

I grinned at him. He was proud of all this; one of his personal special defences. 'So anyone with a spare key, or a copy – '

'No,' he interrupted curtly. 'The security company told me that was impossible.'

'Anything's possible to an experienced crook, if the prize is big enough.'

'For God's sake!' he shouted. 'You're talking about a top pro. So why wasn't the house stripped? Down to the last Meissen. There was plenty of time, damn it.' Then he blushed at his own anger.

I was well aware that no alarm system would deter an experienced burglar. But there was in the background the strange fact that nothing had been taken. 'I'll just take a look in the other rooms, and upstairs,' I told them soothingly, and left them alone to brood. I heard Amelia say something brightly, in an attempt to break the mood.

I was away for twenty minutes. When I walked back into the kitchen they were sitting round the table solemnly, as though conducting a silent seance. Three pairs of eyes turned on me.

'It's as I thought. All the windows and doors are secure.' Philip was about to burst in, but caught Olivia's eye and clamped his lips shut theatrically. I went on: 'But the trapdoor into the loft wasn't wired. How any reputable company could miss that, I don't know. I've been up into the loft. He removed a few roof tiles, quite a job, that'd be, 'cause they're old and weighty. He broke a few laths, and got into the loft. You'll need to get it seen to, by the way. He had to crack one tile to get started, and he's put 'em back as well as he could. But with the laths broken it sags, and you're getting a bit of rain in. That was how he did it, and once in, he could've taken his time. The fact that he appears to have wasted it – as he seems to have done if he's taken nothing – '

'You don't believe that, do you?' Olivia demanded, lifting her firm chin.

I shrugged. 'It's your home. If you say nothing's gone, then that's that.'

'Nothing,' said Philip gloomily.

Then what the hell's going on? I nearly shouted. Instead, I took a seat at the table and tried not to catch Amelia's eye. I sensed she was on their side in this.

'He would come here,' I said quietly, 'in daylight, wearing overalls and driving a van, with ladders. Anyone seeing him – which is unlikely, I'd think – would assume you were having work done on the roof. He would have to be somebody who knew you were going to be away for a week. He'd have time to take it leisurely, and with a van to load stuff in. . .'

I looked up, inviting a reaction. Blessedly, Amelia was silent, realizing now that I was placed in an awkward situation. We were guests. I could not say out loud that I thought they had to be lying. One of them, anyway. Olivia said it for me.

'How many times do we have to tell you that nothing was taken! Call us liars, and have done with it.'

'It's just. . .' I smiled in apology, 'that if nothing was taken, and if you couldn't see how he could have got in, how the devil did you know you'd had a burglar?'

Olivia clamped her lips into a thin line. There was a glint of satisfaction in her eyes. She'd planned it as she would a chapter, with a lead-up to exactly this.

'Show him, Philip.'

Philip's embarrassment had been growing. She'd let it go on too long. He got to his feet with relief, skittering his chair back. The kitchen cupboards reached to the ceiling. Up at the top were the items rarely used. He grabbed his chair before it toppled, put it down in front of the cupboards so that he could stand on it, and reached high to one of the top ones. What he brought down was a biscuit tin. This he brought over to the table, put it down, levered off the lid with his thumb, and brought out a clear plastic bag, its top tied in a knot.

25

Why this had not been brought out earlier I couldn't imagine. Perhaps it lacked climax and demanded a build-up. I looked from face to face, not wishing to reach out an eager hand.

'So?'

Olivia did the talking. 'This is what really upset us. We were being told: I have been here. A kind of gesture of contempt. When we came in here, with our first thought a cup of tea, there was a mug, face down on the draining-board, a spoon, and three tea bags lying in the sink. Those,' she said, pointing at the bag. 'He'd. . . he'd made himself a mug of tea. Three mugs! How dared he. . . how. . .'

It was Philip who took it on. Still on his feet, hands on the table, he managed to convey a hint of authority. 'I mean, it hit us. Somebody had been in. He'd made himself free with our kitchen. It was quite appalling. I thought. . . better keep them, and I put them in that bag. Foolish, but I had to do something. There was some idea that the police would want to see them – but that was before we found out that nothing had been stolen.' He glanced at Olivia's lowered head. 'My wife was. . .' He hesitated. 'She was very upset.' And so had he been, judging by the tense and jerky way he was speaking.

She lifted her eyes to me. 'Of course I was damned-well upset. We don't use tea bags. He'd brought his own. Go on. . . open it up. They're Earl Grey. A burglar! His own Earl Grey!' She stopped, her fingers going to her lips.

Amelia reached past me and took the bag, in which the tea bags were a brown blob, barely visible through the now misted plastic. She had sharper nails than mine. Philip had tied the knot tightly. At last she had it open. She peered inside. She sniffed, then she handled it to me. 'Earl Grey,' she said definitely. 'You can still smell the Bergamot oil.'

I sniffed. In spite of being a pipe smoker, I too could detect it.

'All right.' I glanced sideways at Amelia. 'Tie it up again, my dear. Keep in the smell. Right!' I looked round me. I don't suppose my smile was very convincing. 'The position is that you decided not to call the police. With only the tea bags to show for it, you didn't think they'd believe you.'

Olivia lowered her eyes, and Philip launched into what was

clearly intended as a long statement. 'I mean, if the tea bags meant anything to them – '

'You nevertheless assumed they wouldn't believe you, and that they'd go away with raised eyebrows, and chuckle in their own time.'

'Not exactly – '

'So in the end you decided to try it on me. And, surprise, surprise, I do believe you. We now know there was a break-in. The roof proves it. So why not – now – contact the police? They wouldn't be pleased that there's been this delay, but they'd still like to know.'

'We don't want the intrusion. . .' Philip began, but this time it was his wife who cut him short.

'We may have seemed. . .well, lacking in politeness,' she admitted. She had herself well in control now. 'But you didn't appear to be sympathetic. I'm sorry, but you were sceptical.'

'Until I found the hole in the roof?' I made it a question.

'But we do not – do *not* – want the police involved.'

'There's still the strange fact that nothing was taken,' Philip explained anxiously. Olivia tutted him to silence.

'There's a possible explanation for that,' I told them. 'Sometimes a collector, of, say, porcelain, will hear of a piece possibly existing somewhere, which would complete a collection. He'll hire a professional to steal it for him. That pro will be well briefed. He'd know exactly what he was after, and if it didn't turn out to be here after all, he'd leave with nothing.' I spread my hands. For all I knew, that could well be the answer.

'Well. . .' said Philip, almost ready to accept it, but frowning all the same.

'I don't believe,' said Olivia flatly, 'that he'd leave empty-handed.'

'Come, my dear.'

'I do *not* believe it,' she repeated. 'There's too much tempting stuff here.'

'Very well. Then what do you expect me to do about it?' I was determined to get something positive from them.

'Find him,' said Olivia flatly. 'You'll know how. You're no longer in the police, so you can. . . what's the phrase?. . . lean on him. Yes, I want to know what he came for.'

27

'But Livia,' said Amelia brightly, 'hasn't it occurred to you – he would have had time to photocopy what there is of your new book? Pirate it. It would be valuable.'

Olivia gave a bark of flat amusement. 'Nonsense, Mellie. Quite apart from the fact that I was only in chapter two at that time, a complete version would have been useless to anybody. I don't flatter myself I'm a great writer. It's the name, the reputation that I won't deviate from what is expected. It's fairy tales for grown-ups, like children who like to hear the same story over and over. It's my name on the cover that matters.'

She came to her feet and smoothed her skirt over her hips, as far as it could be smoothed. Now she was all decisiveness.

'I'm relying on you, Richard. Now, would you like another drink before we retire? No? I'm off to bed, then. Breakfast will be early. Seven-thirty. I like to be at my desk at nine. Good-night.'

And because there was something in her eyes remarkably like tears, which she wished to hide, she stumped out of the kitchen.

I scooped up the plastic bag. Philip was trying to recover the situation, but he couldn't keep his hands still, one sweeping back his hair, one plucking at the edge of the table. 'Well,' he said, 'I suppose it's left to me. We won't discuss a fee, but I'll make sure. . .' He scanned our face anxiously. 'Out-of-pocket expenses, then? Yes. You'll have to trust me on this. Now, I'm sure you'd like a nightcap. No?' We must both have shaken our heads at the same time. 'Then, if you'll excuse me, I'll have to get to Olivia. I'll wish you good-night.'

He followed his wife through the door, not managing quite such a dramatic exit.

Amelia looked at me. I was probably grinning, because it all seemed very amusing to me. But not, apparently, to Amelia.

'Well!' she said.

3

In the morning, breakfast was a silent meal. It was as though the burden had been hoisted on to my worthy shoulders, and the whole problem could be put in abeyance. Philip fidgeted, his anxious attention on us, but quietly. Olivia was sunk in dour contemplation of something mysterious, from which she emerged only to shake my hand and kiss Amelia's cheek. The inference was that we would not be expected to be around when she once more appeared from her den. No invitation to stay on for a few more nights was made.

We headed out to her car, Philip and the dogs watching from the door. The wind was whipping in over the mere, the reeds bending to it. The sky was purple. I managed to turn and smile and wave, during which Amelia claimed the driver's seat. Apparently she intended to savour the leaving as she had the arriving. Two doors slammed together, Philip's back door and mine.

For a few moments Amelia sat silent behind the wheel. Then she burst out: 'She's so changed, Richard!' It could have been an accusation or an excuse.

'It's been twenty years.'

'Even so. . .' She turned to me, her eyes wide. 'She was so alive! Enthusiastic – emotional. In tears because a boyfriend had dropped her, the next day in ecstasy because another had smiled at her. And now. . .' She shook her head, unable to accept it. 'She works too hard of course.'

'I don't think it's that. Not entirely.'

She wasn't listening. 'We were so close, and now. . .' Then she burst out violently. 'How dare she! To put me in such a situation. Put you, rather.' She placed a hand on my knee. 'Of course, she can hardly hold you to a promise she's forced on you.'

I took her hand and held it. 'I didn't promise anything.'

'Then we can leave it there and do nothing?' Yet she clearly didn't want to do that.

'I'm not sure I can drop it so easily,' I said. She withdrew her hand. 'Look at it like this. They say nothing was taken. Of *course* something was. The man had a full week to work on it, and clearly he was prepared to take his time. He must have got his instructions from somewhere. And so – he wouldn't leave until he'd found what he was after. One of those two people in there knows what that was. Not both, I shouldn't think. One is trying to keep it from the other. And the other one, sensing it, is very uneasy indeed. You'll notice that our illegal visitor, spending all that time in the house, resisted the temptation to take even one small item of valuable porcelain or a picture or a rare first edition. That means he was being careful not to leave a valid charge that the police could throw at him. Yet he left a definite trace, which could well lead straight to him. But not for the police. Oh no. For someone like me. He's waiting. And in the house, there, someone is also waiting, for exactly that to happen. Heaven help us, Amelia, I'm supposed to recover this whatever-it-is. I've virtually been given an open cheque to buy it, if necessary. Out-of-pocket expenses, Philip called it. He's as subtle as a house fire.'

I stopped, to give her a few moments to think about it. She took a deep breath.

'You should have been a barrister, Richard. So lucid! But I've got a nasty feeling there's a punchline you haven't got to.'

'Just a thought. If it's so important, this thing nobody admits was stolen, then I'd be expected to return it, sight unseen, wrapped if it's wrappable, or in a package or whatever, and never know or care what all the agitation's been about.'

'You'd do that?'

I laughed. 'Can you imagine it?'

She reached forward and started the engine. 'No. You're far too nosy. So what do we do? Norwich, and find an hotel?'

'No. That'd be the city force. I've got an idea this'll interest the county people more. Let's try Cromer way, and start from there.'

She negotiated the causeway with care. The wind buffeted the car. 'You're not going to involve the police?' There was surprise in her voice, protest.

'Minimally. Head for the coast, and then north. Where's the map?'

We were soon driving along that portion of the coast road which is open to both the north and the east winds. Any rotten weather around, and they got it.

I had picked the name Cromer out of my memory, but in practice we didn't reach there. We were heading north up the coast road when I spotted an hotel up ahead, set back a little from the road. Amelia slowed. This, at least, might add a flavour to our visit, I thought.

It was called an inn, and had been one of those post-houses on main connecting roads, where the horses were watered and changed. It was a genuine beam and lath-and-plaster building, seeming to lean outwards, but still in business. We turned into the courtyard, beneath a low beam that would never have allowed room to a high chaise. It seemed deserted. It was the off-season, so was likely not to be heavily patronized, except for the public bar part of it. I got out on to the cobbles and tried a door, which opened.

There was a short passageway, then a deserted lobby with a half-circle of desk formed out of slab oak, and a bell that I had to ping. It fetched me the manager, and yes he could find us a double room, and would we be requiring meals? I was indefinite on that, not knowing what we were going to be doing.

As soon as we'd unpacked and settled in our room, I sat on the edge of the bed and got busy on the phone. They were modern enough for that. What I wanted to do had to be discreet, so I tried my home patch, where my old friend, Ken Latchett, was now an Inspector. I needed a Norfolk contact, somebody who'd be willing to part with information without asking too many awkward questions.

'Inspector Latchett?' they asked at the desk. 'I'm afraid he's on leave. Would anybody else do?'

'Is Tony Brason still with you?' This was tentative. After the tragedy that had struck his marriage, Tony, then a constable, had plunged head on into a conflict with his Chief Inspector. I hadn't heard the outcome, so perhaps he'd been dismissed, or even promoted. But it seemed that the latter applied.

'Sergeant Brason's available, sir. Who shall I say's calling?'

'Richard Patton.'

'Hello there, Mr Patton. And how are things with you?' he asked cheerfully.

This took a minute or two to dispose of. It was pleasant to discover I still had friends there. Then: 'I'll put you through.'

'CID,' said the familiar voice. 'Sergeant Brason. Who's this, please?'

'It's Richard. Didn't he say?'

'Richard! Great to hear from you. . .' And more of the same. He sounded chipper, on top of things. Again, more chat, until eventually I got round to it.

'A favour, Tony, if you would.'

'Ask away.'

'I'm in Norfolk, near Cromer. I've come across something strange, and it's not sufficiently criminal to get rid of with a simple report to the local police. I need a contact. Somebody discreet in the country force. Somebody who won't ask questions. Not too many, anyway.'

'Let me think,' he said, thinking while he said it because he went straight on. 'I attended a special course on terrorism. There was this Detective Inspector on the county force. Yes. Should suit you fine. Name of Poole. Very smart and bright. Inclined to be friendly,' he said pensively.

'I'll phone – '

'No, let me do that, Richard. What number are you on?'

'We're at an old posting inn called The Bull, near Cromer. It's 5182913. Room 7.'

'We? Amelia's with you?'

'Yes.'

I thought I heard him chuckle. 'Wait for a call,' he said. Be seeing you. Give my love to Amelia.'

We hung up. 'We wait,' I told her. There's always a lot of waiting involved. It was nowhere near lunchtime.

'What're you up to?' she asked.

'I'm trying to get a possible trace on our burglar.'

'That's optimistic, surely.'

'Not at all. He deliberately left his tea bags.'

We waited. It was impossible to consider a stroll along the coast road or across the scrub grass to what seemed to be low cliffs. Quite apart from expecting a phone call, the wind thumped against the window and I could see in the distance the spume whipped from the tops of the waves.

An hour. The phone rang. There was someone waiting for me in the lounge. I said thank you, I'd be down.

'That was quick. He's come himself. D'you want to. . .' I raised my eyebrows, wishing really to be alone on this.

'No,' she decided. 'See him yourself. You'll be on your own ground.'

'On *his* ground. That could make it awkward.'

Taking my packet of tea bags, I went down to the lobby, which was deserted, and discovered the lounge, dim with its tiny windows and its low, beamed ceiling, in which there was only one person, a woman, sitting quietly smoking. I half turned away before I realized that she was getting to her feet.

'Richard Patton?' she asked. 'I'm Melanie Poole. Tony phoned.'

I felt I had to apologize for my initial reaction. 'I'm sorry, I didn't expect – '

'A woman? Tony didn't tell you?' She laughed, a deep and throaty sound. 'His bit of fun, I suppose. Disappointed, Mr Patton?' She cocked her head.

No, not disappointed. Somewhat discomposed, perhaps, by her poise and confidence, and the fact that she seemed too young to be an Inspector. Not yet thirty, I guessed. But they were all younger, now, in the force. She'd probably come in on a good degree, and had a mind like a man-trap, never letting go. Her informal dress was almost a challenge, a rejection of the authority she wielded. Jeans and a T-shirt, with a blouson over it. Flat-heeled shoes and a commodious shoulder bag. Even in the flat heels, she stood five feet ten, slim with it, but with a solidity of stance that indicated she would expect no nonsense from anybody. She had her hair cut short, auburn, practical. A redder shade than Amelia's. No ear-rings, not much make-up, but her bone structure was so fine that she didn't need any. She had high cheekbones, a pointed chin, a wide mouth, and eyes that danced, probed and seemed to vary from grey to blue and back again.

All this I put together later. At the moment, I was too busy countering her probing query, wondering how to answer.

'Disappointed?' I asked. 'Shall we say disconcerted. I expected a man. I could perhaps have bluffed my way through it with a man. But now. . .' I pursed my lips and shook my head.

She smiled, a gamin sort of smile. She couldn't control it. Either you got the lot, or nothing.

'Candour could in itself be a bluff,' she said. 'You're trying to disarm me, Mr Patton.'

'Only if you came armed, Inspector. I'm wondering why you came at all. I expected a phone call. Nothing more.'

She lowered herself to the settle she'd occupied. 'It intrigued me.'

I saw that we were getting along far too well. Not two colleagues, but man and woman. I wondered whether Tony had mentioned Amelia. So I shrugged, tried to look as though annoyed with Tony, and said: 'It's too dreary down here. Why not come up to our room?'

She was on it like a flash. 'You're not alone?'

'My wife. Amelia.'

'I'd love to meet her.' She came to her feet in one smooth, lithe movement. Her smile told me nothing.

On the way up to room 7, I asked: 'What was it that intrigued you? I didn't tell Tony what it is.'

'What Tony said about you – that was what intrigued me.'

Amelia had the door open before we even reached it. I introduced them. Melanie topped my wife by five inches. They smiled at each other. Amelia said she'd ordered coffee. At my expression, she added: 'Tony phoned. I guessed you'd bring her up.'

With pride, I beamed at Inspector Poole, who produced her smile again.

There was only one chair, so I sat there and the other two sat side by side on the edge of the bed. The coffee arrived. Good, it saved a pause in the proceedings. The scene was almost informal. It was by no means all questions from me. Melanie Poole threw in her own, briskly, as necessary.

I produced the tea bags. She untied the knot, looked in, and sniffed.

'Mean anything to you?'

She looked up. 'Yes. But I thought he'd retired.'

'Who?'

'The man I'm thinking about. Tell me where you got them.'

'They were left behind at a house that'd been illegally entered.'

'Where?' she pounced.

'I'd rather not say.'

'If there's been a crime – '

'Nothing was stolen.'

She was suspicious. 'Nothing?'

'So I've been assured.'

'But you don't believe that any more than I do?'

I agreed, smiling. 'I don't believe it.'

She tapped her teeth with a finger nail. 'Tell me whatever you feel you can trust me with.' Her eyes were big and round and mocking.

'A friend of my wife phoned us at home. She and her husband were worried. They'd had a break-in, but they tell me nothing had been stolen. There was also no sign of forced or unforced entry. So I looked around, and discovered how he'd got in.'

She nodded. 'The roof?'

'Yes.'

'It's his speciality. Damn him, he promised me he'd retired.'

'Promised?'

'I did him a favour. Never mind what. You were saying?'

'Then the teabags were produced. In my day, I've come across burglars who made themselves a meal, but nothing so distinctive as Earl Grey tea bags.'

'He's always done that. Sort of a game he played with us. Thought of himself as Raffles, I suppose. Nothing else was ever left. Not a fingerprint, not a footprint. And how could we take a tea bag into Court as our only evidence? No stolen property was ever traced back to him. He's always known what he was after and went for it. Discreet. Not too often. Of course, he always worked under contract – somebody wanting a specific item.'

'Which is just what I want to get my hands on – that item.'

She shook her head. The hair flew loose in auburn flames, then settled back to a sultry glow. 'Not a chance. How long ago was this?'

'Over a month.'

'Then he'll have unloaded it. Probably the day after. Keeping in the clear.'

'Hmm!' I stared at my pipe, then looked up. 'Then he might be persuaded to tell me what it was. At least.'

'Why should he? It'd be an admission.'

'Tell *me*, I said. Not you. I'm a civilian.'

'With an extendable purse?'

'To some extent.'

'And you, Mr Patton? Are you on contract too?'

'If you mean am I getting paid for this, the answer's no.'

'Then what's your interest?'

I wondered about that. I couldn't simply admit that I was quite incapable of releasing an unsolved problem, that it would nag and nag at me, giving me no rest. It was a weakness I didn't care to admit to her. Amelia rescued me.

'She's my friend. We were at college together. And she's changed terribly. You would have had to be there, at the house. The atmosphere was all crawly with tension, and she was distressed. I wouldn't want to leave her alone with it, when Richard can perhaps help her.'

'By recovering what she claims wasn't even stolen?' asked Inspector Poole, friendlily, easily, her eyes now on the warm side of grey.

But Amelia was still prickly with the memory of the tension, and came back sharply.

'If we knew what it was, we'd at least understand what the problem is.'

Melanie nodded, accepting that. 'Of course. I see your point. But Mr Patton. . .' She turned back to me. 'You surely wouldn't expect me to give you a name and address, and leave it to you?'

I rubbed the back of my neck. 'I suppose not.' But it was what I'd been hoping for.

'You suppose quite correctly, my friend. I'll make a bargain

36

with you. Clearly, there doesn't appear to be a case in this for me. If the householders insist nothing was taken. . .' She waved a slim hand expressively. 'But I'd like to know, just as much as you do, what *was* taken, and I'm willing to do a bit of off-duty work on that with you. We will see him together. No, let me finish. We'll arrange it so that he realizes you're unofficial. Then we'll see what happens. All this on one condition. Whatever you get from it, I see. If it's important, and seems to involve a crime, then I take over and you're out of it. All right?' Her face was set in an uncompromising expression.

Then she fumbled in her shoulder bag, giving me time to make up my mind. I looked at Amelia for guidance, though she would not appreciate where that arrangement might lead. It all depended on what had been stolen. Judging by the atmosphere at Mansfield Park, it could well be something very important, even the possessing of it being illegal, and involving Philip and Olivia. By agreeing, I might be landing them in deep trouble. I'm relying on you, Richard, she had said. Was I going to risk betraying that?

But I had not been taken into their confidence. I think Amelia saw that, and made her judgement on that consideration. She nodded to me. Really, I had no choice. It was that, or we were at a dead end, and might as well go home.

'I agree,' I said. 'When?'

She seemed surprised. 'Now.'

'What about lunch first?' I suggested. 'We owe you a lunch.'

She swept flowingly to her feet. 'We don't know yet who owes what to whom. Can we get lunch here?'

'Certainly we can.'

And we did. It was quite excellent, considering that the kitchen seemed to be cooking for only us and a couple in a far corner. The conversation was general. Inspector Poole had been, as I had, in the same district all her official life. So she knew what went on. She had her contacts. She was, in other words, a competent police officer. Amelia, realizing that this was for me alone, said she would go for a walk while we were away.

'In this wind!' I said.

'I like a sea breeze. Bracing, they call it round here.'

That meant you had to brace yourself not to land flat on your back.

So when Amelia had gone upstairs to put on something suitable for facing the challenge, Inspector Poole and I went out to our cars. Her little blue Metro was parked next to the Granada.

'Better take yours, I think,' she decided. 'It's coast road all the way, and yours is heavier.'

I drove the car out into the force of the wind, and at once appreciated what she meant. The car swayed and heaved, and as we hit the coast road south I was busy every second correcting our line. The sea spray was carried further inland than I would have believed, and I had to leave the wipers working.

'Is it always like this in the winter?' I asked.

I didn't think I would get used to driving in apparent rain, when the wind had taken the clouds inland and left the sky clear. Bright, sharp sunlight winked in the spray on the glass.

'His name,' she said, 'is Harvey Cole. As I said, he's supposed to be retired. In any event, he seems to live comfortably off his past crimes, and of course he's never been in any way violent or destructive. Even without the tea bags he left behind, you could always tell one of his jobs the moment you walked through a front door. Not a mark, not a scratch anywhere. If he spilled his tea, he'd clean it up carefully. Very considerate, he's always been. You'll like him.'

I couldn't spare a sideways glance. The wind was lifting the wipers away from the glass. 'And you? What're your feelings?'

I felt her shrug. 'I admire a true professional. Harvey's an artist in his own line. It's just a pity it had to be illegal, it puts us on opposite sides of the law. We never once got anything on him we could take to court.'

I drove in silence for a couple of miles. The road was never far from the sea, and there was at no time any protection from the wind.

'How much further?'

'Another four or five miles. We turn inland at Happisburgh.' She pronounced it Haysborough. 'You'll spot the lighthouse.'

That was my marker. I saw it long before we reached the village, a white finger with a red band.

'Past the garage and turn right,' she instructed.

There was a garage, an hotel, and what looked like a block of holiday chalets. I turned right, and instantly there was silence. The wind that had slapped and thumped at the side of the car was now behind, urging us forward quietly, our own speed depleting the force of it. The road was narrow, but well signposted. Around us there was nothing but flat distance. I saw areas of reeds.

'Is this part of the Broads?'

'Not really. They're a bit further south. All this is probably swampy. Not enough water to float a boat in. Turn left at this fork, then right again. He's got a cottage called Honesty.'

'You're joking.'

'Not at all. It's named after the weeds in his garden. Blue flowers and round seed pods.'

'I know it. Can't wait to meet him.'

It was a stone-and-flint cottage with a thatched roof. There were certainly enough reeds around to supply a new roof, if this one blew off. But it seemed firm. I wondered how he would get in through a thatched roof, and decided to ask him. We drew up. There was a tiny gate in the fence, but a wide opening to one side. A drive, rough-looking, headed towards a garage, outside which a car was parked. It was a BMW, one of the 500 series, I thought.

Harvey Cole had seen us arrive, and had the door open as we walked up the path.

'Well!' he said. 'Inspector Poole, as ever was.'

'May we come in and talk, Harvey?'

'Yes, and make it sharp-like, I can hardly hold this door.'

We walked past him into the narrow, dim hallway. The cottage was simply designed, two rooms, one each side of the hall, and probably two more behind them. A modest home for a successful villain. He led us through to the room on the right. From this window he had seen our arrival.

The room itself dispelled any illusions. He lived in quiet and muted luxury. The walls were the original base blocks, and undecorated, solid, on which his pictures were splendidly displayed. I didn't need to check that they were originals. In his china cabinet there was a set of porcelain, which would

39

most certainly not have been stolen. A professional doesn't waste his working hours on his own home. It's the plumber whose taps always drip. His easy chair, to one side of a large fireplace, now with a large fire whipped to fury by the wind, was a leather-studded recliner. His carpet was something foreign and exotic. I was probably walking on a year's salary for an Inspector.

But he'd been sitting at the window. He had an embroidery frame set up, and had been working on a tapestry. Seeing my interest, he explained.

'It's a set of covers for the seats of my dining chairs. Just the hobby for a retired man, don't you think?'

'You're not retired, Harvey,' said Melanie Poole severely. 'You're a liar.'

He raised his fluffy white eyebrows at her and smiled gently. 'Come now, Miss Poole. Strong words.'

She relaxed. 'I've brought somebody to meet you. Richard Patton. This is Harvey Cole, Richard.'

He took my big paw in his small hand, and I felt the strength in his fingers. His smile was still easy and relaxed. 'A new Sergeant you're breaking in? Introducing him to all your treasured friends?'

'He's not in the police, Harvey. We just want a few words with you.'

For a moment he stood there, his eyes going from one to the other of us, considering, deciding. I could now observe him and try to weigh him up. He must have been in his sixties. His hair was a careless shock of pure white, his face still smooth and pink and placid, but his chin had a firm set to it, and his bright brown eyes, so light they almost appeared yellow, were wide and full of mischief. He was short, around five-four, with the slim build of a professional jockey, but also with a jockey's muscle tone and balance. His movements were smooth. Nothing sudden. In a stranger's house, it would be necessary for him to move discreetly.

'I'll put the kettle on,' he said at last.

'No, Harvey. Don't trouble. How can we talk, if you're in the kitchen?'

'I've got some nice tea. It's Darjeeling. You'd like it.'

She spoke firmly. 'Sit down, Harvey. It's Earl Grey we want to talk about.'

He shrugged, and went to sit at his tapestry frame, knees together and his hands on them, like a naughty boy.

'I've quite gone off Earl Grey,' he said meekly.

Melanie Poole found an upright chair in the corner. One of those requiring a new seat? She banged it down in front of him. I sat on the padded arm of his leather recliner and got out my pipe. There were no ashtrays around, so all I could do was play with it in my fingers.

'Now,' she said, getting down to it. 'I hear you've been naughty again, Harvey.'

4

I had had the impression that she was going to introduce us, then leave the rest to me. It was my interview, wasn't it? Apparently not. But I said nothing. My turn would come.

He was looking at her with wide eyes, all innocence. 'How could you say such a thing!' he complained.

'A month ago,' she said briskly, 'around then, a house was entered. It was your style, Harvey. We have three used Earl Grey tea bags. Your MO, too. What d'you say to that?'

'Where was this?'

She didn't know the answer to that, and tossed a glance at me. I shrugged. It was my secret for now.

Harvey said: 'Well then. . .' He smiled blandly.

But already the message had been put across. I was the one who knew, and I hadn't told Inspector Poole. Therefore – I was not police.

'I'm asking the questions,' she told him. 'Something very valuable was taken – '

He was missing nothing. 'Valuable? How valuable? What was it?'

'You tell me.'

'How could I possibly know that, Miss Poole, if I wasn't there?'

'You were there. There's nobody else in the county – probably in the whole country – who works as neatly and cleanly as you.'

'Flattery, now!'

'Nor anybody who's got such a smooth tongue. It was your method of entry, and your careful attention to leaving everything exactly as it was. You were inside quite a while. A whole

42

day on it, and probably you stayed the night. That's *you*, Harvey. The tea bags are you. Earl Grey. Your signature.'

His hands were resting relaxed on his knees. Always watch hands. His expressed only innocence, his fingers together. Nothing twitched.

'Tea bags!' he complained. 'I'm always getting that thrown at me. If I've used them in the past – and I'm not about to admit that – then somebody else has picked on it. They're trying to set me up.'

She flung herself out of the chair. I thought it a little too theatrical. There was also too much anger in her voice.

'You make me mad, Harvey. Here you are, all comfy with your cottage and your expensive car, and probably with a nice portfolio of gilt-edged, and you play games that could land you inside. You've never been to prison, have you?' He shook his head mutely, lips pursed. 'You wouldn't like it. There's always a last job; you don't seem to realize that. The last one before we put you away. You told me you'd retired, and now this!'

'You mustn't upset yourself, Miss Poole,' he begged her unhappily.

'Parkhurst instead of the Caribbean, or wherever you swan off to on your holidays.'

'I prefer a nice, quiet cruise.'

'Oh. . . you're hopeless.' She turned to me. 'You'll get nowhere with him, Richard. I know him. He can keep this up for hours.'

I got to my feet, smiled at her, and said: 'Reckon I wouldn't.'

'I'll see you to the door,' Harvey offered, but making no move.

'We'll see ourselves out.' Melanie marched out of the room and into the hall. I caught the door as it swung, and glanced back. I raised my eyebrows – his nod was minimal. I closed the door behind me and marched towards the wind outside.

We got in the car. He waved to us through the window, a needle dangling silk in his fingers.

'Well?' she asked, as I started the engine.

'I didn't get to say much, did I? You went a bit over the top, I thought.'

She grimaced. 'It wasn't all an act. He really infuriates me. I *like* him, Richard. I'd hate to have to arrest him. And you?'

43

'I got the signal. He'll see me alone.'

'When?'

'No words were exchanged. A raised eyebrow and a nod. But he spread his fingers on his knees. Eight fingers.'

'Ah!' she smiled. I put the car into gear, and we headed back into the wind. 'So it was fairly successful, I'd say.' She sounded complacent.

'It achieved what we came for. He knows I'm not police. He knows I've told you next to nothing.'

She was silent for a while. Spray hit us a quarter of a mile from the coast road, and the wipers flapped madly. The car was heavy, and seemed to lack power.

'You'll show me what you get?' she asked at last.

'That's what I promised.'

She was silent again. I turned north on the coast road. It was just as bad driving north as south.

'I want to make it quite clear,' she said, 'that everything I've done up to now is unofficial. On my own time.'

'No report?'

'Nothing on paper. But if this thing, or whatever, that he's stolen in any way relates to a crime – '

'Other than the fact that it'd be proof of his own crime?'

'You're making that a condition?' she asked sharply. 'It's a bit late to throw in new conditions.'

'Come *on*,' I said. 'You don't want to touch him, and you know it. And yes, I realize that if a serious crime is revealed, then you'll have to go all efficient and official on me.'

'As long as you understand that.'

'Of course. I was ahead of you.'

We said nothing more, each of us considering how best to play it. There was no more discussion. I drove into the courtyard of the inn, and she got straight out of the car, heading for her own.

'Say goodbye to your wife for me,' she shouted into the wind.

I nodded, reached over to lock her door, and got out to watch her drive away. A gust seemed to catch her car and twitch it, but she had control at once.

Amelia was waiting for me in the lobby, quietly and patiently.

44

'How was your walk?'

'Richard, I couldn't *stand*. It took my breath away.'

'I'm told you get used to it.'

'I'll bet. And how did it go?'

We were mounting the stairs. After the wind noise outside, the silence was like a blanket.

'We made contact. He's got something to offer, or to say. I'm seeing him later, at eight.'

'Oh!' she said. 'What a pity. Dinner's served at eight.'

'I didn't think of that.' I stood aside for her to enter the room. 'Oh well, I'll have to miss it, I suppose. In the interests of justice and peace of mind – '

'We'll have to miss it, Richard. We.'

'You want to come?'

'Well. . . just consider. You're in your role as an interested citizen. All unofficial. Wouldn't it look better if you take your wife along? And besides, I hate being left on my own, and out of it.'

I kissed her. Held her back and grinned at her. 'Then by all means come along. We can get fish and chips somewhere on the way back.'

'I doubt that. I did get a bit of the way along the sea front, and everywhere is dead. Not just closed. Shuttered.'

'Ah!' I thought about it. 'We'll ring down for sandwiches.'

At five o'clock we did that. We got them, plus a tray of tea, at five-thirty. Delicate, frilly sandwiches. They left me still hungry.

We set out at seven-thirty. The wind had blown itself away. The sea whispered and the stars were bright. On the east coast, the night sky is black. The still air felt much more cold than the wind had.

I now drove the journey with confidence, knowing I only had to keep an eye open for the lighthouse. If there's one thing you can't miss at night it's a lighthouse. We were watching the flicks of light, every five seconds, from over a mile away.

When I drew up in front of it, the cottage was welcoming, lights all on at the front and the grey smoke from his chimney just visible against the sky. He had a brass pixie for his knocker. I tapped, and he opened.

'Ah, here you are. Oh. . . I wasn't expecting. . .'

45

'My wife, Harvey. Amelia, this is Harvey Cope.'

'Come in. Come in. I'm pleased to meet you, Mrs. . .Patton, wasn't it? My memory. . .' He squeezed his brow.

'Yes,' she said, smiling, at once captivated by him. 'You don't look a bit like a burglar, I must say.'

He laughed out loud, throwing his head back. 'I *am* glad you came. The Inspector's a friend, but you can't have a laugh with her.'

'That's true,' I agreed. 'Amelia wasn't keen on being left on her own.'

This time he was showing us into the room on the left. It was his dining-room.

'My wife didn't either. She would get worried, and in the end I had to take her along. She'd sit in the car or van, or whatever I was using. Behind the wheel. For a quick getaway, she always said. But of course, that never arose.'

'You must miss her terribly,' Amelia murmured.

'Well. . .no.' He ran his fingers through her hair. 'I'm afraid I gave you the wrong impression. She's at our place on the Côte d'Azure. We always winter there. Now. . .I was doing a cheese omelette with chives and a side salad, followed by strawberries and ice cream. It's nearly ready. All I'll need to do is pop in two more eggs. If you'll just excuse me. Make yourselves at home. There's sherry on the side, there.'

He slipped out of the room. We looked at each other. 'Not look like a burglar!' I said.

'It slipped out. He's nothing like I expected.'

I went over and poured us sherries. It was a fine madeira, I thought, not a sherry. The room was beautifully furnished. The four chairs, for which he must have been doing the seat covers, were surely Hepplewhite.

Nothing about this evening was what I'd expected, either. I'd imagined a short, crisp discussion, and a rapid departure. But, without his wife, the poor chap was lonely. He wanted company. He'd even put on a white shirt, black slacks and a dark jacket.

'Here we are!' he cried, sliding into the room.

We sat down to dinner. The food was excellent. The straw-berries, he told us, had been sent to him by his wife. He was a

46

born conversationalist, picking up a new subject at the barest hint of silence, his agile mind ranging in all directions.

We finished with brandy, then we sat on, amongst the scattered plates and dishes, and got down to business.

From his inside pocket he produced a yellow envelope, the sort of thing you get your prints in from the developers. For a moment my heart sank. Surely he hadn't uncovered a secret horde of porno photographs!

'What've you got there?' I asked tentatively. His hand was still on the envelope. It lay flat on the table surface. There couldn't have been much in it.

'First,' he said, 'I'd like to know more about your interest in this. I don't think you're a private investigator. . .'

'No,' cut in Amelia. 'Of course not. The house – Mansfield Park – where I assume you found that envelope, is the home of a college friend of mine, Olivia Dean.' He nodded and she went on: 'She was worried. They'd had a burglary, but she told us nothing had been taken.'

'Did she now!'

Amelia gestured, and I took it on from there.

'I'm ex-police. Mrs Dean thought I could help, though you'll understand it wasn't clear how. I'd better tell you now that if what you've got there is evidence of a serious crime, I'll have to hand it over to Inspector Poole.'

He thought about that. 'I wouldn't like that to happen. The evidence would point straight back to me. But. . .' He shook his head. 'For the life of me, I can't see that it can be evidence of *anything*. I'll tell you what we'll do. A bargain. You can look at what I've got here, and if you think you ought to hand it over to the police, then there's no deal. You're friends who've visited, and that'll be the end of it. You'll simply walk away from here with nothing.'

'No deal?' I asked. 'I never suggested there could be a deal.'

'I think you might. Agreed?'

How could I refuse? I nodded. He slid the envelope across to me. Slowly, because I didn't know what might be in there, I slipped out the contents.

My first impression was a sense of anticlimax. There were two glossy coloured photographs, apparently identical, and taken by someone used to handling a camera. They were sharp and crisp, and in complete detail.

The detail was not pleasant. In the left foreground was a sloping, muddy bank, on which the photographer must have been standing. Or maybe just in the water. There were reeds and algae. Lying amongst it was the body of a woman. I say woman, because the blond hair was spread and distributed across the algae, and seemed too fine and luxuriant to belong to a man. It was not possible to see her face, which was down in the water. She was turned with her left shoulder beneath the surface and her right shoulder protruding, the right half of a green anorak or combat jacket clear of the water, and she was wearing blue jeans. Short heels of black boots were just visible.

I stared at them side by side, eyes flicking from one to the other, and it was some time before I spotted the difference between them. High on the breast of the right side of the jacket was a round, yellow disc. It was there in the one picture, not there in the other.

Silently, I turned them round and slid them across to Amelia. I heard her sharp intake of breath, but blessedly she said nothing. I was marshalling my thoughts. What I now said would be of importance, and I had to assemble it in the correct order.

'Harvey,' I said, 'I'm going to try to set out a scenario on this. If I go wrong, I'm sure you'll correct me.'

He inclined his head. There was no sign of his smile now, and his eyes were fastened on me unblinkingly. Intense. He was a clever man, sharp. I had to try not to insult his intelligence.

'You're retired,' I said. 'Miss Poole wasn't wrong about that. But I know what it's like. At first you relax. There's all the time you could wish for in which to enjoy your retirement, and all the world left to explore. But after a while you get a bit itchy. You miss it, and there's all that experience and expertise going to waste. You feel you're not keeping up with developments. So you allow yourself to become involved again.'

'A fellow sufferer,' he murmured.

'Yes. You see, I know. You allowed yourself to become involved with the odd little job, provided it seemed to offer interest. And this one did. Someone asked you to get into

48

Mansfield Park and recover this envelope with these photographs.'

'Go on. I'm admitting nothing.'

'Then I'll guess. You'd think about it before you'd take it on. There was just the hint of a smell of blackmail about it. There's a lot of it about, I expect, that we never hear of. Minor stuff, perhaps psychological, perhaps financial. Bigger stuff, as big as murder, perhaps. But if murder's involved, it's not a very good idea to try blackmailing the murderer. He might be prepare to do it again. Or he might take the easier course of resorting to an expert to recover the evidence. Am I making sense, Harvey?'

'You make a reasonable case.' He was not conceding one iota.

'And this, to you, would sound like just that sort of situation. Recovering photographs. What photographs, you'd ask yourself. It would certainly offer a hint of interest. And yet – and you may not have thought of this, Harvey – if a murder happened to be involved, and there was no likelihood of the murderer getting the chop, then maybe it would serve the bugger right to be blackmailed. I don't get the impression you'd have any sympathy for a crime of violence.'

'I have always,' he admitted, 'had a hatred of any form of violence.'

I smiled at the brandy in my glass. 'D'you mind if I make a guess at what happened?'

'Help yourself. I'm not saying anything for now.'

'Of course not. Right. So you got into the house. What you were looking for was slim and easily hidden, but therefore more difficult to find, I'd guess. But the information was that you had a clear week. No doubt that information came from the client?'

He smiled, but said nothing.

'So you took your time, and you eventually found it. Taped under a drawer somewhere perhaps. . .' With raised eyebrows, I made that a question, but he didn't fall for it, sliding adroitly round it.

'I'd have thought,' he suggested, 'more likely in one of the books, with pages cut out of the middle.'

'That sounds likely. And she'd have a complete collection of her own books, which would certainly be there for show, not for opening.'

'You'd make a very good burglar, Richard,' he conceded. It was an accolade, though he spoilt it a little. 'If you weren't so bulky.'

'A drawback,' I admitted. 'In any event, you found the photos. And what would they mean to you? I'm still guessing, Harvey. Care to help me out?'

'Not really. I'm enjoying this.'

'All right. I'd say you realized you had nothing particularly sinister. The photograph of a young girl – apparently young, apparently female – who had drowned. From the picture, it would be impossible to say that murder was involved. Accident. Suicide. Both possible. So – how can this picture be used for blackmail? Someone found the body, and before reporting it took a photograph. A bit sordid, but not criminal. Perhaps there was some intention to sell it to a newspaper. That sounds unlikely. I suggest you sat there, in that house, and puzzled over it. Drank a mug or two of tea, and gave it some consideration.'

All through this I had been using the word 'photograph'. Singular. There must, though, have been two separate ones taken. I was testing him out, but he didn't react.

'You make me out to be quite a thinker, Richard. What did I decide? I'd like to know.'

'It was a month ago this happened, but you've still got the envelope. You decided you'd like a second opinion. If you deliberately left your trademark, the Earl Grey tea bags, you could reckon on somebody coming along in due course, somebody like me, feeling their way. You haven't delivered the goods to the client. There was a chance that you would find out more, and then decide whether or not to hand the whole thing over. It could be better to allow it all to go back to where it came from.'

'And perhaps not be out-of-pocket.' He smiled thinly.

'We mustn't forget that. And you've held on to them for a month. . .'

'No hurry,' he observed, 'if the client had been told it would be necessary to wait for the opportunity.'

'He – the client – *gave* you the opportunity. He told you when the house would be empty.'

'That's a flat assumption,' Harvey shot back at me.

'Yes, Richard,' put in my wife. 'You're making a lot of assumptions.'

Amelia likes to be helpful. She could see I was working hard to persuade Harvey to part with the envelope. She realized I needed a boost.

'Not at all, my dear.'

'Yes you are. Listen to you, assuming what Harvey did and thought and how he acted and why. It's a bit of a presumption, I must say.'

'He hasn't objected.'

'Nor would I, if I heard you making a fool of yourself.'

'In what way,' I demanded, 'have I made a fool of myself?'

'He could well have gone there for something else, and come across this envelope by accident.'

'They said there was nothing missing.' I reminded her. 'And I'm not at all sure I can rely on your friend and her husband. And *there's* the photo, under your nose, and you can't say it's a normal sort of photograph to take – '

'Of course not.'

'It *means* something.'

'Of course it does,' she said with scorn. 'But not a murder. Nobody could read that meaning into it.'

'I didn't *say* that,' I protested.

'Oh. . . didn't you? I must have missed something.'

Then I understood. Harvey wasn't going to part with his treasure unless he was sure it wasn't going to land him in trouble with the police. Amelia had seen a way in which to convince him. I looked at Harvey and raised my shoulders. He grimaced. His eyes had been darting from one to the other of us. He changed it to a smile.

'I take it you've lost interest,' he murmured.

'Not entirely. I'm still intrigued.'

'To what extent?' he asked quietly.

'Two hundred.'

He laughed. 'The fee mentioned was a thousand.'

'If you hand 'em over you'll never know what harm you might be doing. If this *is* evidence of blackmail, you've already put an end to it.'

51

This was specious argument, but he seemed to miss the weakness.

'Two-fifty,' he said briskly.

'Three hundred, if I get the name of the client as well.'

'Come on now. . .' He pursed his lips, shaking his head.

'I'd have to make a few more enquiries, and if I find there's nothing serious going on I could hand this envelope over, intact, to your client. And get my money back.'

'With seven hundred profit!' He laughed, clearly delighted with the bargaining.

'Which I'd send to you. Otherwise, you'd be out-of-pocket, and I wouldn't want that to happen.'

'Richard Patton,' he proclaimed, 'you'd make a fine blackmailer yourself.'

'Wouldn't I! Not a good burglar, though.'

I didn't dare look at Amelia as I drew out my cheque book. I was going to be overdrawn. 'A cheque do you?'

'I can't handle credit cards, and you'll not have brought the cash. A cheque, then. If it bounces, I'll be round to collect. When you're not at home.'

With my pen poised, I looked up into his eyes. He was not joking.

'His name and address?' I asked.

'It was at a boatyard I met him. Ruston and Sons, they called it. They might live there. He's a son, the only one I think. Mark Ruston. It's a boat repair place on Salhouse Broad, next to Wroxham Broad, where all the yachtsmen hang out.'

I wrote the cheque. He took it from me without glancing at it and put it in his inside pocket. I took up the yellow envelope. It had a pocket each side, so I put one photograph in each, and slipped the envelope in my own inside pocket. We got to our feet. Business was completed. I was aware that I'd bluffed him, that I'd lied to him by implication, and tried not to be disturbed about it. When he shook hands there was a twinkle in his eyes that warned me of something, but I ignored it.

'Call again,' he said.

'Unless you call on us first.'

'Ah, but that wouldn't be by invitation. It's been very interesting meeting you, and your wife of course.'

He showed us to the door. Just before it closed, he said: 'Remember me to Inspector Poole.'

We sat in the car, me behind the wheel. The temperature was falling rapidly and the windows quickly steamed up. I started the engine, did a three-point turn, then drove out of sight of the cottage before I stopped.

'Now what?' Amelia asked. She sounded a bit short with me.

'I've stopped to warm up the engine and clear the windows.'

'I meant, what have got for your money? Nothing.'

'Oh, I don't know. We have two photographs, which may or may not refer to a crime. Certainly, there's a dead woman. The two pictures aren't the same, because the yellow sticker's there in the one and not the other. So some sort of fiddle was done by the photographer. That suggests to me something like an alibi being rigged, and you don't rig alibis unless there's something serious happened.'

'You're surely not saying – '

'What I'm saying is that your friend, with or without her husband, could well be involved in blackmail. No. . .make that possibly. These were stolen from Mansfield Park. Challenge Harvey on it, and he'd deny that. He'd say he'd found them, or something. But *we* know they came from there. Don't we?' I tried to press her into an admission.

She was reluctant. 'I suppose so.'

'So. . . these photos are either the ones received by a blackmailed person, or copies of the ones sent by the blackmailer. It's one or the other.'

'Nonsense! Ridiculous!'

The engine had reached full temperature. I turned on the heater and the fan, and drove away. 'Which would you rather have?' I asked.

She didn't reply.

'Now we'll have a word with Inspector Poole,' I told her.

'Now?' It was a protest. She wanted more time to assimilate it and accustom herself to the proposition.

'We can hardly avoid it. She's waiting at the garage on the coast road. Didn't you spot her little Metro?'

5

It was no longer necessary for me to watch signposts in order to get back to Happisburgh. I drove on dipped heads, the lights slicking the tarmac, and made for the lighthouse. Amelia was silent for a while. I knew what was troubling her, apart from the involvement of her two friends, and waited until she got round to it. In the end she spoke in almost a weary voice, as though she was tired of working things out.

'I don't know what's got into you, Richard. I really don't. You promised Harvey Cole – and I must say I liked him – you made him a promise that you wouldn't take the things to the police. Now you're going to let him down. You *are* going to show them to Inspector Poole, aren't you, even though you've said there could be murder involved.'

'She's waiting for exactly that.'

'You promised him! It's not like you. Specious and plausible, that's what you're being. I don't like you in this mood.'

'I promised him what?'

'That you wouldn't give anything away to the police unless there was nothing serious involved. You persuaded him there *wasn't* anything serious.'

I smiled to myself. 'In which you were of great assistance, my dear.'

'It was what I thought you wanted.'

'I did.'

'To cheat him with!' She said passionately. 'Now you say it *could* be serious. Where are you heading with this, that's what I'd like to know? Do you really know what you're doing?'

That was the point – did I? I knew what I wanted to achieve,

54

but was far from sure how to do it. 'In effect, I promised Harvey I wouldn't hand Inspector Poole anything in which she would have to involve him. I don't intend to let him down. I also promised Miss Poole something – to show her what I've got. Now all we've got to do is persuade her that there's no case in it for her, and everybody will be happy.'

She muttered something. I said: 'Pardon?'

'I said, I'm far from happy.'

'A bit of a crafty wriggle, and we'll be home and free.'

'Home?' she asked hopefully.

'It's a saying. I think we're a long way from home.'

Where the side road met the coast road at Happisburgh there was the now dark and silent garage where I'd seen Melanie Poole's Metro parked. I drew in beside her. The only light was from a distant street lamp, the intermittent flicks of the lighthouse, and what leaked from the windows of the nearby hotel. She'd been waiting a long while. It was nearly ten o'clock. I could just detect her face when she climbed out and stood beside us. I was set, and pinched with cold.

'You got it?' she asked

'Yes.'

'You certainly took your time, I'm frozen.' Light flicked across her face.

And fed up, and about to be disappointed. I didn't say that, only tried to sound cheerful. 'We'll try this place for a drink. You'll soon get warm.'

'Very well.' She hesitated. 'Is it something you can show me in a public bar?'

'Quite innocuous. You'll see.'

We hurried into the warmth of the public bar, which was half empty but even so was not sufficiently private. I had to allow for the possibility of Miss Poole losing her temper. We went through to the lounge and found a corner seat. I sat them down behind the table, and fetched beer and two gin and tonics.

Inspector Poole had forsaken her casual look, and was smart in green slacks, a darker green jacket, and a white shirt. Her hair seemed brighter in artificial light. There was now some make-up on her lips and cheeks, and small ear-rings, remarkably

55

resembling handcuffs, swung from her ears. We sat, the two women on the bench seat, myself on a stool. I hate stools; they make your back ache. Melanie sat back and reached for her cigarettes. She offered one to Amelia, who shook her head. I leaned forward.

'Without any direct admission from Harvey, I got this from him,' I said, my hand inside my jacket. 'In court he'd claim he found it in the street.'

She waved smoke from in front of her face – or it could have been in dismissal of Harvey's optimism on that score. 'I don't really want to see him in court, but. . . Is *that* all?'

This was on sight of the yellow envelope. I opened it and whisked out one of the photographs, the one that included the yellow disc stuck to the breast of the anorak, and slid it across the table to her.

'Is this *all*?' she repeated, a touch of anger in her voice, that she'd wasted so much time on it.

'What do you make of it?'

'Are you trying to tell me that a top man like Harvey Cole had been employed to steal a picture of a dead girl!'

'I'm not trying to tell you anything. Harvey sold me this envelope – sold, Melanie, so that the contents are mine – and it's not my fault there was nothing in it but evidence of somebody drowned.'

She looked up into my eyes, hers an ice-cold blue. 'You're trying something on, Patton.'

'*Look* at it, and stop arguing,' I said, equally cold, though in fact her anger and her sudden distancing of herself from me with the curt use of my surname I found in some way comforting. I didn't feel so bad about what I was doing.

'I've looked. A drowning. The fact that some ghoul or other chose to take a picture isn't necessarily relevant.'

'Unless,' I suggested, 'it was her murderer, recording her death.'

'Tcha!' she barked in disgust. But at least she returned her attention to it. She was silent. I spoke softly.

'You said "girl". So you recognized what it is. You knew in a second.'

She didn't raise her head at once. I waited. When she did look up the anger had gone from her eyes and her voice was soft with sorrow.

'I went out on this one. There was the question of identification. She wasn't. . .' She glanced at Amelia. 'Wasn't recognizable. And though she must've been in the water for a week or so, there'd been no report of a missing person that fitted. We found out later that she was supposed to be at college. At home, they assumed she was there. At the University – Birmingham, if I remember correctly – they hadn't missed her. But we got there in the end. She was nineteen. Her name was Nancy Ruston. That's without an aitch. Her family does boat repairs. . .'

Her voice faded off. She'd been talking too much. The death had affected her. Perhaps they didn't get too many in Norfolk. I didn't dare to look at Amelia, no more than a glance at her hands. At the sound of the girl's name, her fingers had twitched. The liquid was still moving in her glass.

I gave it a few moments, the time it took to empty half my glass. I tried for a casual tone, the detached voice of a man who's seen far too many dead bodies.

'This was. . . when?'

'What? Oh, early on in the year. May. Yes. The season hadn't really started.'

'So – that photograph was probably taken where she was found, not necessarily where she'd gone in the water?' In the holiday season she wouldn't have remained unspotted for a week or so.

'It certainly looks like it. I seem to remember. . . yes, see there, that's a yellow bog iris. They were growing on the bank. It's where she was found.'

'Which was where?'

She looked at me sharply. 'You're asking a lot of questions about this, Richard.' So I was back with my Christian name. 'Now you know how things are. It was an accident. The inquest verdict was one of death by misadventure. There's nothing in it for you.'

'For me!' I raised my eyebrows at her, looking all naïve I hoped. 'It's not for me. Amelia's friend's upset because of a burglary that she says is abortive. What am I going to do? Nothing? Or take her a photograph I can't explain?'

She pouted at me. 'I don't care what you do. For me, her death is a closed file. There was no evidence of foul play. On a Friday, just over a week before she was found, she borrowed a car from a friend in Birmingham. We never discovered why she was in Norfolk, when nobody was expecting her. We never even found the car, which was the only point at all suggestive. But not enough to justify keeping the file open.'

I nodded. Fair enough. So Harvey Cole need not be involved. I asked gently: 'But where was she found?'

'You're very persistent.'

'He always is,' Amelia put in.

'And?' I asked, still at it.

'She was found in the River Bure, a mile east of South Walsham. She could have drifted down either the Bure or the River Thurne, which meets it just north of there. As I said, she'd been in the water a few days. The river's pretty deserted just there, in May. Schoolboys found her, out looking for anything going, I suppose.'

'So that photograph doesn't change a thing?'

She skimmed it back at me. There was blue ballpoint ink on her shirt cuff. 'I've got a dozen like that.'

I stared at the wall behind her. There was a faint glow of satisfaction, that I'd steered her clear of Harvey and now had an open field. Yet there was a vague uneasiness.

'You're certain of the time she'd been in the water?'

'You know the pathologists are pretty accurate on that. We were given five to eight days, probably nearer five.'

'It *was* drowning, I suppose?'

'Of course.'

'And she was found on a Saturday?'

She looked surprised. 'How d'you get at that?'

'A guess. Schoolboys. May. It sounds like a Saturday or a Sunday.'

'It was a Saturday. The 14th of May.' She cocked her head. Her tone was sarcastic. 'Anything else?'

'No. I don't think so. Oh. . . where did she live?'

She moved in the seat impatiently. 'I told you. The family had a boatyard, it's on Salhouse Broad. I hope you don't intend to go worrying them.'

'I shouldn't think so.'

She rose to her feet. 'Then I'll just buy you a drink . . .'

'Thank you, but no more.'

'I'll say good-night then.'

'Good-night to you, Inspector. It's been nice meeting you.'

She nodded. Amelia smiled. Melanie stalked off through the public bar, purposeful and annoyed.

Amelia sat and stared at her glass. She still had half her drink left, so I went into the bar and got myself another half of bitter, giving her time to mull over what had been said, and for the pain in my back to ease. When I returned she was still frowning and silent. I slid on to the seat beside her.

I said: 'Penny for them.'

'They're not worth a penny. Richard, you weren't really honest with her.'

'Wasn't I?'

'That idiotic look of innocence of yours! You know what I'm talking about. You showed her only one of the pictures.'

'I offered her the one I thought she'd recognize.'

'The one with the yellow charity sticker on. Yes, I noticed. But how did you know *that* was the one she might recognize?'

'She didn't point out any discrepancy.'

'It was six months ago. She might not have remembered it in any detail. Now be sensible.'

'Of course she remembered. The point is, she didn't point it out.'

'But why did you show her *that* one? Why not the other? Why not both – come to think of it?'

I hid a smile behind my glass. 'If she'd seen both, that would've been evidence of something suspicious, and she'd have wanted to know more. Perhaps from Harvey. Which would involve your friends, Amelia. I had to guess which photo showed the girl as Melanie saw her, when she was found. The odds were that it was the one with the sticker.'

'Odds were!' she said scornfully. 'It was a guess.'

'Not exactly. Look at it like this. Some sort of fiddle was done with what seems to be a charity sticker. It was either taken off or put on. Obviously, the intention was to change the evidence. Right? So. . . take off a sticker, and that's a negative action. It

59

says nothing. Put one on, and that's a definite statement. It says something.'

'Such as what?' she challenged.

'Such as the fact that she probably died on a Saturday involving a charity collection, which would make it the Saturday before she was found.'

'Call her by name, Richard,' she said testily. 'Nancy Ruston.' She frowned over the name, then shook her head.

'Very well.'

'And you could easily be wrong, anyway. The intention of the person who changed the sticker – '

'And who obviously took the pictures.'

'That too. The intention could have been just the opposite – to hide the fact that she died on that Saturday.' She smiled hugely at my expression. 'And suppose the body of Nancy Ruston was found by the police *without* a sticker. Think of that. What then? I'll tell you what, Richard. Inspector Poole, not being in any way foolish, will have spotted the difference in the picture you showed her – and just imagine what she'll be thinking about you at this very moment. She would realize you've tricked her, and she'll keep her eyes on you, like a hawk, from this moment on. You could well have made a serious error, Richard.'

'Oh, I don't think so.' But I wasn't as confident as this sounded.

'And Harvey Cole,' she continued, piling it on, 'don't you think *he* noticed the difference between the two? He didn't say anything. I wonder why!' And her eyebrows lifted, putting fine creases across her forehead in an expression of naïve enquiry.

'Let's get out of here,' I suggested.

There was a car parked in the darkness of the side road from which we had arrived. I didn't notice it until its lights flicked on and the BMW slid across the road and stopped beside us.

Harvey Cole climbed out. He said: 'Well?'

'I've seen her. She seems satisfied.'

'You showed her what you'd got?'

'She was in a bit of a huff that there was nothing in it for her.'

'I thought so, from the way she slammed her car door. You showed her the photographs?'

60

'One of them.' I wished not to tell a direct lie.

He smiled thinly. 'Which photograph, I wonder.'

Then he got back inside his car, swung out, and headed for home.

'There!' said Amelia as we settled again in the Granada. 'What did I say!'

'You're usually correct, my love.'

'You know what, Richard? I think you're getting yourself all tangled up in this, and before long, no amount of words and your theories will rescue you. D'you know what we ought to do now?'

I wished I had a clear picture of that. 'Tell me.'

'In the morning, we should go back to Mansfield Park. You produce the envelope and the photographs and tell them you've been able to recover what was stolen, get your money back, and then we leave them to sort it out between themselves.'

I sighed. Oh dear. . . and what sort of domestic crisis might that precipitate!

'That's a distinct possibility,' I said neutrally.

Then she dropped the subject, and was silent. She knew when to leave me to sort my own thoughts into some kind of order. The coast road slid beneath the tyres. It was a perfect night for driving. I needed only a corner of my mind for the car, which in any event recognized the road now.

But was it really so easy as she suggested? One of those two had known nothing about it, of that I was certain. And what it was about was murder, of that I was equally certain. There is no necessity to play about with corpses and fake a time of death, if that had been the intention, unless something as important as murder is involved. Was I – we – going to lay that in their laps, for one of them to see that the marital partner was involved in such matters? Amelia and I had been asked to help. To break up a marriage, with death and violence in the background, was not much in the way of help.

All right. I could pretend to complete ignorance, could seal the yellow envelope in a plain brown manila one, and say: 'I paid three hundred for this. Open it, and tell me if it's worth it.' In this way I would display a complete lack of knowledge of the contents, and be able to march away in complacent triumph, possibly with a cheque for £300 in my pocket. Chickening-out, they call it in the USA.

I couldn't imagine myself doing that. I had at least to discover more about the background, something hopefully more palatable to put in front of them.

Such as what, for heaven's sake? Two photos relating to a crime had been stolen from Mansfield Park. On contract. Yet what did that show? Even if they were evidence of a faked alibi, and thus would provide a lever in a blackmail attempt – who sent them to whom? The photographer, arguably the blackmailer, would naturally send to the victim a copy of each print. But would equally naturally keep a pair of copies for himself. So, was one of the occupants of Mansfield Park, if not both, the sender or the receiver?

One could argue, though, that the most likely person to hire a professional burglar to recover blackmail evidence would be the victim. We knew who Harvey's client was, a person called Mark Ruston, more than likely either the brother or the husband of the dead girl, Nancy Ruston. As I'd not met him, I was in no position to decide if he could be a murderer. But I had met Olivia and Philip. Did that make them, or one of them, a blackmailer?

That was a completely unacceptable proposition.

I could now understand why Harvey Cole had been sufficiently nervous of what he'd uncovered to be willing to unload the responsibility.

As we turned into the courtyard of The Bull I said: 'I don't think we can do that.'

She was half asleep. 'Pardon. Do what?'

'Drop it all into your friends' lap, and sail off merrily for home.'

'I was hoping you'd say that.'

'You suggested home.'

'I said we ought to do it. In this case, I believe it's one of those situations where "ought" doesn't come into it and "must" takes over. What we *must* do is find out more about it first.'

I took her arm, squeezed it, and headed for the side door, behind which there was a dim light. The front had been in darkness as we'd turned in. The door was unlocked. There was a card dangling by a string from the inside doorknob. On it was written: 'Please lock up when you return.'

In the off-season they caught up on their sleep. The Bull, apparently, slipped into a gentle death after eleven at night. We turned into the lobby. It wasn't completely dark. One corner light was on.

Philip Dean rose stiffly and awkwardly from a green velvet easy chair, which he'd clearly found uneasy. He was embarrassed, his hands fluttering, his diction not quite steady.

'I wouldn't have blamed you if you'd walked out and gone home. Amelia. . . Richard. . . I really must apologize for Olivia's attitude. She tends to be short and abrupt when she's working on a book. It upsets her routine, missing an evening session. I simply had to explain that.'

He was breathless at the end. It had been a prepared speech. Amelia put a hand to his arm. 'Don't worry about it, Philip.'

'I was sure you'd have left.' He gave her a miserable smile. 'But all the same I rang around, and found you're staying here. Which means. . .'

He hesitated, waiting for a lead, but I didn't give him one, simply stood there discouragingly quiet, and forced him to go on. Which he did, bubbling it out.

'I meant what I said, Richard. About the out-of-pocket expenses. I mean, if they should arise. I was thinking – you know – if you managed to locate whoever did it, I'd be prepared to pay whatever's necessary to recover. . . the. . . the situation.'

Considering he had not admitted there could be anything physical to recover, he was placed in an awkward position.

'Of course, Philip. I'll bear that in mind. If the occasion arises.' I cocked my head sideways, smiling at him man-to-man, forgivingly. 'You *did* say nothing was stolen, though.'

'Well. . . actually. . .' His eyes searched the shadows. 'Really, you know, there *was* something. When we said we searched the place top to bottom, that was me doing the searching. When she's writing, she can't be distracted. And there were. . . well, a couple of Meissen figurines she's particularly fond of. I didn't tell her. She hasn't noticed. She gets lost in her books. And I'd hoped to. . . to get them back before. . .'

He'd gone on too far for the truth, which is easily reached. Lying requires decoration.

'Before she finishes the book? And looks round with seeing eyes?'

He'd spotted my deliberate sardonic tone, and blinked. But he was forced to agree. 'That's about it.'

'We don't want her upset.' It was her magic pen – or voice – that kept the shekels rolling in. 'Take long, do they, these books?'

'They're very big. Yes.'

'But the burglary was a month ago. Longer than that for a book?'

'Three to four months, easily.'

'So we've got plenty of time,' I encouraged him.

'What?'

'You'd been to a writer's do at Copenhagen,' I reminded him. 'She said she'd done only two chapters, and it's only a month since then, so she won't spot any missing figurines for a month yet. At least.'

I looked to Amelia for approval of this transparent item of logic. She was staring at me as though I'd gone mad.

'Why don't you come up to our room, Philip?' she rescued him with sympathy.

'No. Really. I must be off. She'll be wondering. . .'

Unhappily he turned away. I followed him to the side door. He paused, and clutched at my bicep.

'Richard, I meant what I said. Pay anything. . .'

'Anything?' He never seemed to finish a sentence.

'Within reason.'

He slipped out into the darkness and I locked and bolted after him. I couldn't find the light switch for the stairs, so we had to manage with the feeble light we left on in the lobby.

'You didn't have to tease him, Richard,' she said severely.

'Tease! Good heavens, I was using my best technique for shaking a bit of truth out of him. Tease! I can imagine, at the station, interrogating a villain for hours, and the sergeant saying I shouldn't tease him!' I threw back my head and laughed.

'Hush, Richard. People are asleep. And he's not a villain.' She glanced at me. 'Is he?'

64

'He's a rotten liar, I know that much. He's either very nervous because he knows what was stolen, or very nervous because he's afraid to find out what it was. He's too much on the defensive, and his fortress has been invaded.'

'Fancy ideas get us nowhere.'

I opened our door. 'It's confirmed the decision that we need to know more. And, I suppose, it guarantees a bit of relaxed sleep.'

I needn't have worried on that score. They were quite correct about the beneficial effects of the bracing sea breezes; we both slept as though unconscious.

6

We were taking our morning stroll along the coast road. It was nine o'clock. The weather was fine, brisk and sharp, with a sea breeze in our faces we could just about live with. We were well wrapped up, me in anorak and scarf with my tweed hat, Amelia in the coat she'd thought to bring and a nylon scarf over her head.

The district seemed deserted. Nobody else shared our eccentric inclinations. On the far horizon a ship stood still, no smoke, no apparent movement. Rarely, a car slid quietly past. For a while a dog followed us, then got tired of it and inspected a shelter.

'What day is it?' I asked.

'Wednesday.' Concentration nearly broke her step. 'I think.'

'Hmm!'

We walked. We turned about and began to return to the inn. The sea was whispering to itself way out there.

'I'll be running out of clean underwear,' she decided. 'I didn't expect to be here for long.'

'We'll buy some. There ought to be some shops.'

'Yes.'

'Charge it to Philip. Out-of-pocket expenses.'

She made no answer. The wind shifted into our faces again.

'What say we go and look for that boatyard.' I suggested.

'Why not? But it's November. I bet it'll be deserted.'

'Oh, I don't know. Somebody mentioned repairs. They must do all that out-of-season.'

'You and your logic!'

There seemed to be no point in going up to our room. I was beginning to hate the sight of it, anyway. We got in the car and I turned out into the road.

'Which way?' she asked.

I stopped, not having thought of that, and we consulted the map.

The indications were that here we were about twenty miles north of the Broads. Salhouse was a village just south of Hoveton. So it would be south to North Walsham, then on to Coltishall and Wroxham. I looked out for the right-hand fork from the coast road.

For a while I thought we must have gone wrong, because there wasn't much sign of open water, and the greenery wasn't particularly sparse. With confidence, we followed the map, and suddenly there was all the water you could wish for. This was clearly a yachting centre. There were certainly shops, though a large percentage, which clearly catered for the yachting and boating trade in the summer, were now closed.

We parked. Amelia went away to search for her necessities, and we agreed to meet at the car in half an hour. I decided to stroll around and ask questions, and try to find the location of Ruston and Sons.

We had not actually reached Salhouse Broad. The river Bure, here, does quite a bit of wriggling about before it heads off in the general direction of the east coast. Water runs downwards, and in that area it has some difficulty in finding anything other than level. The result is two Broads, north and south, one on the outside of a larger curve, the other in the inside, further south. Or so it seemed. There was a large-scale map in a frame outside one of the closed boat charter places. The waterways were clearly marked. With a boat you could find your way to Salhouse Broad with reasonable ease.

There were, however, no motor vessels available for hire, and as I'd never been in a boat in my life (well, fancy that, I thought in surprise) I was not about to contemplate it.

To reach the village of Salhouse we would have to drive south and tackle a complex of lanes. I went back to the car and stood smoking as I waited for Amelia. She appeared, hurrying.

'All right?' I asked.

'Yes, thank you. I can last another week.'

'Bring any for me?'

'You didn't ask.'

'True.'

'But I did get you a map of the district.'

We got in the car. She said; 'We have to find the village of Salhouse. It's south from here. This is really Wroxham Broad.'

'I know. We could have managed it in a boat from here.'

'Oh – lovely. I used to adore boating.'

'Fortunately, there aren't any for hire.'

We headed south. Of course I got lost. I always do. But eventually we found the water before we reached the village. It was surprisingly surrounded by trees. But searching for Ruston and Sons seemed almost impossible by car. The road obstinately refused to stay near the water, and performed a series of exasperating contortions in order to keep us away from our objective.

'There!' Amelia cried suddenly.

The sign was very nearly deleted by time and weather. It indicated a turning to the left, directly into the trees. We tried it, encountering rutted mud. The car slithered and lurched, and we emerged alongside a wooden fence in very poor repair. The driveway ended, with the nose of the car nearly in the water. In the fence to the right was a double gate, one wing of it open. I hesitated before turning in. There was no sign of activity, but the open gate indicated some sort of presence. We turned in. I decided to pretend to be somebody with an eye open for a yacht or something. It would have to be an ignorant somebody, because I knew none of the jargon.

I saw at once that the yard itself was extensive. It fronted the water, with slipways disappearing into it, and further along there was a crane for hoisting. There were several large, iron-clad sheds set well back. We got out and looked round.

Salhouse Broad, if this was it, in this light and at this time of the year, wasn't appealing. Reeds lined it, making the perception of an actual border difficult. It didn't seem broad to me. Out there, waterfowl were screeching and honking. Something took off in agitation from over on the far side. A migrating flock crossed high in a V.

Then I realised that the screeching was not from the birds; it was too continuous, and came from the nearest shed. The double corrugated iron doors were open. Followed by Amelia, I wandered inside.

Wearing goggles, a young man was kneeling in shirt sleeves and overalls, sending sparks cascading with a rotary hand-held sander. I didn't recognize the metal structure he was working on. There was a hot smell of carborundum.

It would have been impossible for him to have heard me, even if I'd shouted. The rear portions of the shed were deeply shadowed, but the shapes visible appeared to have no relationship to yachts or boats. I tried to sort them out as we waited.

He seemed to reach a point where it was necessary to stop and consider progress. The sander was switched off, and died into fluttering silence. He lifted his goggles, rubbed his eyes, then noticed us. The metal was red hot, and died to black as I watched it.

I smiled. He may not have been able see it. 'You'll be Mark Ruston,' I said.

'No I wouldn't. Who're you? You'd better see –'

'It's Mark I wanted to have a word with.'

He came to his feet easily, with all the smooth efficiency of a twenty-year-old. Now I could see he was about five feet six, and slim with it, a handsome youth with a thin face but wide, generous mouth that I could detect through the grime. His eyes, protected by the goggles, were set in white circles, in which their dark blue seemed to glow. There was no mistaking his interest. He tossed fair hair away from his face.

'Mark's in the next shed. It's the wrong time of the year for buying, and anyway this is a repair yard.'

'I know.'

'What d'you want to see him for?'

None of your business, young man, I nearly said, but his interest seemed genuine and there was no challenge in his voice.

'Just a word,' I told him. 'This and that. You one of the sons?'

'Not me. Larry Carter. Short for Laurence. I just work here. As I say, he's next door.'

'Then I'll leave you to it. Thanks for your help.'

69

He hesitated. 'Any time.' It was, I thought, not simply a casual acknowledgement, more like an offer.

I walked out into the daylight, where Amelia had been waiting. 'He's next door.'

'I know,' she said. 'I heard.'

The whine of the sander working up to full revs came from behind us. We walked on to the next shed.

This one was much larger, its huge doors closed, but with a wicket door in one of them. I pushed it open. Inside this one there was plenty of light. In the middle of the floor, spots were centred on a thirty-foot yacht on a cradle. It was stripped of all rigging, and sat there, its full complement of lines exposed. As I've said, I know nothing of these things, but I can appreciate the flow and swell of curves, the beautiful proportions, the perfection of shape. I wondered for a moment how they'd got it in there, but then decided the crane I'd seen was probably mobile.

The man working on it, in contrast to Larry Carter's efforts, was doing nothing that involves noise. There was only the quiet, tuneless whistle with which he accompanied himself. A man contented in his work. Who could ask for more? From behind he seemed stocky, his hair black and thick in his neck. He, too, was in shirt and overalls. There was no heat in the sheds; they bred them tough in Norfolk. There was an impression of strength in his shoulders, his arms were well-muscled, and his hands were huge. He was working with what looked like a trowel, and, like a bricklayer, had a hod in the other hand, loaded with a white, smooth paste.

Amelia was just behind my left shoulder. I moved in close to him, interested. In that thrusting, slim prow there was an uneven hole, backed by a sheet of something from inside the hull. Into this hole he was spreading his paste. At his side was a tall table, and on its surface were cut sheets of fibreglass reinforcement. He was working smoothly, but fast. Paste carefully layered, sheet of fibreglass, paste, and so on. I knew what he was doing. I'd used the same method on an old car I'd once owned.

Patiently, I waited, but suddenly he realized my presence. He jerked his head round.

'Who're you?'

'Are you Mark Ruston?'

'Bugger off!' he said. His eyes, shadowed by heavy eyebrows, were more angry than the situation warranted.

'I can wait.'

'Gerrout of here. This bloody stuff sets. I can't talk to you.'

'I'll wait,' I assured him.

For a second his gaze held mine, then he returned to his work. 'Please yourself.'

I stepped back a yard to indicate willing co-operation, but I noticed that I'd upset his rhythm. No longer were his movements smooth and precise. He fumbled, and his trowel went awry. He wasn't whistling now.

At last he finished. He turned, and plunged the trowel into a pungent can of liquid. 'Y'see! If I've ruined the job, you'll answer for it. That's epoxy resin. It don't let you waste time.'

'I'm sorry.'

'I should think so, too.' But he had calmed, and was looking better for it. There was a blunt, heavy sort of handsomeness to his face, a strength that some women might admire. His nose wasn't much, a kind of afterthought with the last bit of clay tossed on, but his chin was square and his mouth, relaxed now, was a pleasant shape. From behind he'd seemed older, but I now saw that he was about the same age as Larry Carter, twenty or twenty-one.

'What d'you want then?' he asked.

'I was given your name –'

I got no further. The anger again flared. His arm jerked out, a finger pointing in the general direction of the wicket door.

'You gerrout of here.' He seemed to be fond of this phrase. 'I've had enough of you lot, pesterin' and creepin' round. It's been six months, damn it!' He seemed to notice Amelia at last. 'And who're you?'

'My wife,' I explained. I turned to her. 'This is Mark Ruston, my dear,' because he hadn't denied it.

'Pleased to meet you.' She nodded, having no more idea than I had where we were heading.

I tested out the water with a tentative toe. 'You seem to think I'm from the press. . .'

'No. Let's see your warrant card.' He held out his huge hand.

'I'm not from the police, either.'

'Then who the hell *are* you? Not that it matters, as long as you sod off. I'm not sayin' another word.'

'Not even about your sister?'

This was a guess. He didn't correct me and say she'd been his wife, so it was the right one.

'Ya see!' he shouted. 'Told you! Why can't you let it drop?'

'As I said, I'm not from the police, and I don't represent a newspaper.' I was interested that he'd asked for my warrant card. So Inspector Poole, or her officers, had pursued the question of Nancy's death with some degree of thoroughness. She hadn't implied that.

'What, then?' he demanded. But there'd been no need for him to carry it on. He might reasonably have lost interest. Yet interest, or suspicion, was certainly still there.

'I have something I thought you might be prepared to buy.'

'Buy? You'll be lucky.' But his eyes had been bright, and now slid sideways. 'We don't buy vessels, we repair 'em. You'd better see my father.'

That was really rather quick thinking, when his first reaction had pointed in only one direction.

'I was given your name. Yours personally.'

'I'm not in the market, whatever it is.' He was waiting for my lead.

'A figure of a thousand pounds was mentioned.'

He stared, then he threw back his head and gave a bark of laughter, which bounced hollowly from the roof. There was no trace of humour in it. He returned his gaze to me. I was surprised to see that he was genuinely puzzled. Or I was slipping. He seemed actually to be seeking guidance. He knew very well what I was talking about, and yet he was baffled.

'Let's just say I've taken over the transaction.'

'What transaction?' he demanded. 'What bloody transaction?' he suddenly shouted, his temper breaking a very short rein. 'A thousand! You trying to be funny? Or what? Where'd I get a thousand? You're just plain crazy. You know that! Goddamn crazy. Gerrout of here!'

That phrase again. But this time it wasn't merely a suggestion, it was a definite command.

'All right,' I said placatingly.

'There's nobody got anything I want,' he continued at full blast. 'And as for a thousand! Ha-bloody-ha.'

'Sorry to have troubled you.'

'Don't just stand there. Get out. Out!' Then his voice shook the roof, bouncing around up there. 'Get away from me.'

Nothing was right. I couldn't continue with it because I was confused. His fury was too real to be an accompaniment to innocence. Half of it was acting. But his whole reaction did not fit with what I knew. Or understood, I corrected myself. Where had I gone wrong? What had I misunderstood – or misinterpreted?

There was no point in trying to continue with it. With a shrug, I turned away, just in time to see the outside doorway shadowed by another man.

'What the devil's going on here?' he demanded.

This was a voice that didn't need to be raised in anger. It was deep and sonorous, a voice of command. He had the bulk to back it up, as tall as me, with wider shoulders but slimmer at the waist. In his forties, I guessed, so ten years younger. As he advanced into the pool of light surrounding the yacht, it was obvious this was Mark's father. The same heavy brows, the nose, the strongly-boned face, but blunted by an extra twenty years of wear and tear, creased by responsibility and worry. A bear of a man, but with no aggression. He carried his bulk and strength with confidence. He was a man who was not often opposed.

'Who are these people, Mark?'

Then he stopped and stared, advancing slowly. His voice changed. It became tentative and warm. 'It can't be. . .' Then he was certain it was. 'It's Mellie!' His voice rose to a great shout of pleasure.

'Mellie – after all these years! My dear. . .'

He held his arms wide, his hands extended. I'd heard that nickname before; it carried a tang of Oxford. Amelia moved forward towards the invitation. It was there in her voice, too. Excitement and pleasure.

'Malcolm! Isn't this. . .'

73

She said no more. His hands had taken her by the waist and he'd lifted her up without any apparent effort and kissed her on the lips.

I can do that too, the lifting, but she says she doesn't like it. It hurts. She didn't say that to him. What she did say was sheer genius, considering she'd had only seconds to assess the situation. But I didn't realize that at the time. My mind was disorganized. Coincidences like this just did not happen. As it turned out, I would have been better occupied in working out why it need not have been a coincidence. But I was already discomposed by Mark's reaction, and was slow in deciding how to handle his father's.

What Amelia said was: 'We were in the district, Mal, and heard about the terrible thing. . .' And left it there. It was enough. An excuse and a lead-in, all in one breath.

'Oh God, yes,' he said, instantly sobering. 'We haven't got over it yet. But you must come along to the house. Meet the wife. She'll be so pleased. I've often spoken about you.'

He was clearly a man of little imagination. I glanced at Mark, wondering how he was taking this. He hadn't taken it at all. Nothing made any sense to him, either. His eyes were dull, and he'd retreated into a secret self.

'And this is your husband? I might have guessed. She always liked her men big. And handsome.' He lifted his head. 'Haw!' he laughed. It could have been construed as an insult, but not intended to be, I was sure.

He took my hand and shook it, nearly tearing my arm out. I couldn't see why they'd need a crane with him around.

'Richard Patton,' I said.

'I'll call you Dick.'

'I'd rather you didn't. I only come running to Richard.'

He eyed me. We now knew where we stood. Then he dismissed me, turning to his son.

'You finished that job, Mark? Wash up, then come on up to the house.' It was said kindly, but was nevertheless a command.

Then he led the way outside. Or rather, he led me, ushering Amelia with an arm around her waist, which I was sure she didn't need, and I certainly didn't.

'Is that your car?' he asked. 'You came in the wrong entrance.'

'We didn't know, did we Richard?'

'We didn't know,' I agreed.

'Well. . . leave it there for now.'

'Right. I'll do that.'

I only then realized that I'd not heard the sander for some time, when only two metal walls stood between us. It rasped into action as I thought it, and as I realized that only one metal sheet need have been between an interested ear and the scene around the yacht.

As Malcolm led the way, I could see that the boatyard spread further than I'd thought. Beyond the crane there was a properly constructed staithe, as they called it around there, where vessels with a deep draught could lie alongside. At the further end, too, was lying all their winter work, a multitude of small boats, a few motor launches, an adapted canal longboat, all with scrapes and holes, and heaven knew what damage to their innards.

'They come here,' he boomed, casting his voice back to include me, 'from the cities. Never on water in their lives before, and they take control. Learn all the rules, and forget 'em in a day. Putter along gently the first couple of days, then they think they know it all. Clever city types, who're used to standing on their brakes. Only boats don't have any brakes. It's a great big laugh. We watch 'em from the house. Bumpety-bump. All work for us in the winter. Insurance work, too, so you're sure of your money.'

But only a few months of work a year, I thought, and that necessitating no more than one paid employee. I said nothing, strolling along in the rear with pipe smoke trailing behind me.

'They come through here,' he went on, 'to get to Salhouse Broad. What you see over there is called Hall Fen. It's all marsh, till you get to Hoveton Broad. There's no way out from Salhouse, so they have to come back again, and if they didn't bump somebody going in they can have another go coming back.'

He laughed his haw sound again. I felt he was trying to encourage himself.

The house was behind a row of trees and on slightly higher ground. We had to climb a flight of stone steps through the trees.

It had the appearance of once having been a farmhouse. The

building was uninspiring, being four-square and with no relief to the block effect, built of red brick with plain sash windows. The only decorative effect was a handsome pantile roof. What outbuildings I could see might have been farm sheds, but were now, no doubt, either garages or store sheds. A firmly-surfaced drive headed off to the right through the trees.

'You'd have done better to have come in from Horning,' he told us.

'We didn't have much to work on,' I said. 'Ruston and Sons, Salhouse.'

'I'm one of the sons. My brother died, so I'm Ruston now. Should change it to Ruston and Son, I suppose. I was hoping it'd be Ruston and Company. But Nancy died.' There was a shadow in his voice, then it cleared. 'Angie'll be in the kitchen. Come along.'

He used the side door, which opened into what had clearly been a farm kitchen, with space to work, and maybe to feed a whole bunch of farmworkers. They hadn't done much to modernize it. The black iron Aga cooker had been retired, but was still there in its recess. It had been superseded by a black gas cooker, at which Mrs Ruston was working, and, before she spotted us, cursing softly to herself.

'This is my wife, Angie,' he said, the pride in his voice a little forced. 'Angie, this is a college friend of mine, Amelia. . .' He hesitated. '. . .Patton, and her husband.' He grinned at me. 'Richard.'

She made no move, her hand continuing to stir something that smelt like stew. She just inclined her head. 'Pleased, I'm sure.' Yet she appeared doubtful.

He clearly felt the atmosphere was a little too stiff. His voice became jocular. 'I must have mentioned Amelia to you. We used to call her Mellie then. . .'

'Oh yes. Of course. *That* Amelia.' She managed a smile. 'Malcolm's a fool. He makes his college days sound like one round of jolly japes.' I was sure the old-fashioned wording was used deliberately. 'Never any work done. You'd think he went there to enjoy himself.'

'One needed to relax,' Amelia said evenly, refusing to be provoked.

'It's no wonder he didn't get his degree.'

'Now Angie. . .'

'All I ever hear is Amelia and. . . who was it, Malcolm? Oh yes. . .Philip and Olivia something.'

Perhaps Malcolm had not been so important to Amelia as she had to him. Certainly, the name had not struck an immediate chord in her memory.

He turned to us. 'You can stay to dinner I hope?'

It was not a perfectly timed remark. We smiled. I smiled, anyway. I didn't dare to glance at Amelia. We were not committing ourselves. But his wife shook herself free from whatever had been upsetting her, and put in: 'But of course, they must stay. It's only beef stew, I'm afraid, but there's plenty to go round. And steamed jam pudding to follow. Do stay.'

'Thank you,' said Amelia. 'We'll be pleased to.'

I went to look out of the window, while Amelia and Angie launched into conversation designed to make themselves acquainted. There was talk of how bleak it must get here, in the middle of winter, and Amelia was lectured on the wildlife that made existence pleasurable.

Now that she was more relaxed, Angela Ruston was a very personable woman. She had the slim figure of a younger person, though she must have been about the same age as her husband. Her hair was showing no sign of grey, and was pure, glistening black, and apparently free from any sort of treatment other than with brush and comb. She had an almost gypsy beauty, with dark eyes and a heart-shaped face. But behind those eyes, even behind the shadow of her earlier mood, there was a suppressed passion that Malcolm had not perhaps fully exploited, and the lines around her mouth, even on the upper lip, indicated a long period of discontent, even suffering.

She was a woman with a short rein to her temper, I thought. Those eyes would snap with fury at the touch of any tender spot in her emotions. And so much of her was raw, and would not heal.

'You can see from here,' said Malcolm, at my shoulder, 'that the water's not very wide. It's fen the other side. Full of wild fowl.'

He had interrupted my fanciful thoughts, and jolted them

into another channel, though no less fanciful. I had a sudden yearning for the seclusion and peace of these surroundings, all the unspoilt beauty hidden away in this corner of England. I'm a townee. I feel lost without streets. So why was I so caught by this solitude?

'Nancy loved it,' he said softly. 'She knew the waterways from end to end. When it came to it, they took her life.'

Did they? I wondered. Were they not, perhaps, assisted in this?

7

What he had said confirmed a point that had been worrying me. Nancy Ruston had been a woman of the Broads. Now he'd said she loved them, knew them, and was no doubt perfectly safe with them. Undoubtedly, drownings did occur. It would've been surprising if they didn't, with all those amateurs playing about in boats. But not to Nancy. Death by misadventure, my foot!

The two young men came in to dinner. Apparently Larry Carter was treated as one of the family in this respect. As Angie had said, there was plenty to go round, and say this for her, she had a fine touch with beef stew. The steamed roll of jam pudding I had not encountered for years.

We talked. The atmosphere was cheerful, and everybody managed to put in a word or two. Inevitably, the general trend was towards college reminiscences, though it began to be evident to me that Amelia and Malcolm were carefully omitting to mention Olivia. My growing conviction was that Olivia, decribed as highly emotional in those days, which probably meant over-sexed, had played the field. And whereas Amelia – I had to allow myself to believe this – had concentrated unsuccessfully as it turned out on Philip, Olivia had spread her interests to include Malcolm. Perhaps?

'If you'd only concentrated on your books,' commented Angie, returning to a well-worn theme.

'Now Angie. . .' He turned to me to explain. 'My father had this grand idea of reaching out – building our own craft, and perhaps making a name in the yachting world. He thought I could learn engineering and design. What a hope! I couldn't design a matchstick.'

'And besides,' put in Mark, 'there was the question of capital. Grandad knew that. You can't refit a place like this for boatbuilding without a lot of money.'

'Dad was a dreamer,' Malcolm said fondly.

'Like you,' his wife said with some contempt.

'What's the matter with dreaming, for heaven's sake?'

'You can't live on dreams.' She turned to Amelia. 'You wouldn't believe. Nancy was a young girl. *This* was her life, what you see out there. The fens, the wildflowers, the wildlife. And what you see in here. Why couldn't he have left her alone!' Then she bit her lip to silence, and bent her head.

'She wanted to go to college,' said Malcolm in a chilly voice.

Amelia spoke quickly. 'What was she studying?'

'Can't you just guess!' Angie was bitter. 'Fantastically stupid, that's what I think of these modern high-flown ideas. Whoever heard of a woman yacht designer!'

'Oh, ma!' Mark groaned.

'And don't you come oh-ma-ing me,' she snapped, turning on him. 'A girl's place is in the home. And God knows I need some help with this mausoleum.'

Malcolm slapped both palms on the surface of the table. 'She could have designed some lovely yachts.'

'Perhaps that was all she was good for,' she murmured. Then, abruptly deflated, she looked down at her empty plate.

But Malcolm glossed over the awkwardness. 'Nancy was born to the water, and she had a feeling for it. All she really loved was the feel of the wind in her sails. Yes. . . all right. . . so she loved the wildlife, too. It was all part of it. Take her away from the water, and she'd. . .' He stopped. Taking her away from it might have saved her life.

And Angie, more perceptive than I'd have thought her, jumped to her feet and said: 'I'll make some coffee.'

Mark, facing me and next to Amelia, looked after his mother with burning eyes. Amelia murmured something about helping, but Angie restrained her with a touch on the shoulder. Larry, beside me, muttered to himself: 'Nancy was the water-girl, Nancy was the dream.'

Startled, I glanced at him. No one else had heard. He was looking across the kitchen and out over the water, and his eyes were the soft blue of the sky.

When I returned my attention to the others, the conversation had turned towards the Broads and its shipping. They lived with it and on it. Malcolm lapsed into his ultimate interest – his boatyard.

'We're getting a genuine old wherry in,' he told me with enthusiasm. 'A complete refit. The best contract we've had in years. I can't wait to get my hands on it. . .' And so on.

I listened, nodding. So far, I'd discovered little of my own main interest: Nancy. Carefully, I drifted him towards the subject, by way of the plans for yacht designing and expansion.

'Nancy had the brain for it,' he insisted quietly, as though trying not to upset his wife with further mention of the girl. 'Don't ask me where it came from, with me a dead loss at college, and Angie. . .well, Angie's a farmer's daughter. Her fingers are deep in the soil. But Nancy was different. She was adopted, you know.'

'I didn't know that.'

'Oh yes. It's true.' As though I'd questioned it. 'We had her from birth. Pretty well that. They told us her mother hadn't even seen her. Angie'd wanted another child, you see. After Mark, the doctor said no hope. So we did this. Adoption. And there was the same fifty-fifty chance, because we'd arranged it before. Just like a real birth, you didn't know what you were getting.'

'I think they can tell, these days,' I observed.

'This was nearly twenty years ago. I think Angie might've preferred another boy.' He contemplated his knuckles on the table. 'Maybe I would've, too. I mean – help in the yard. It's a bit of a laugh, really. Fate's joke. In the end Angie was glad she was a girl, for help in the house, and me. . . well, I loved Nancy, and knew I'd got better than any boy. She wasn't just going to be a help in the business, I could see her as the life-blood of it. That's about all there is to it.'

I wondered whether his dreams would have been realized, had she lived. To emerge from college as a confident and expert design engineer, or to drift, as the indications were, into a passionate defence of the environment in which she'd been brought up? Norfolk, not yet exploited for motorways and concrete and fumes, must certainly be under threat. From such materials as Nancy Ruston, champions for the ecology are bred.

Beside me, Larry must have heard every word, but had said nothing. He was quietly smoking, not even talking to Mark. But I had the impression that Larry, of all of them, possibly had more empathy with Nancy, had been closer, and probably knew her best.

We sat over coffee. The chat became empty, with large gaps. The memory of Nancy was intruding. When Mark spoke up abruptly it was in a truculent voice, one that had been restrained so that now it emerged with too much force.

'They never found out what she was doing in Norfolk. You'd have thought they'd have done *that* much.'

Malcolm explained to Amelia, apparently assuming it would be she who was most interested. 'It was May. Near the end of term. We couldn't understand why. . . why. . .'

Amelia smiled at him. 'I'll bet you've never been far from here, Malcolm.'

'I've been to Oxford, and lots of times to Norwich.'

'Not the same. Why on earth did you send her to Birmingham?'

Nobody had mentioned Birmingham, but Malcolm didn't seem surprised that Amelia knew it. He went straight on.

'Because they offered the appropriate course,' he said simply.

'If you'd never been anywhere but around here,' she told him, 'and you'd always lived on open air and water. . . oh, Malcolm, can't you imagine! She'd be stifled in Birmingham. She'd hate the noise and the bustle and the confusion, the skyline, the smell, the air, the water. . . everything. And it was May. May here – it must be beautiful. There could come a time when she just *had* to see the water and the great big sky you've got here. . .' She waved her arm. This was Amelia, letting her romantic imagination flow free.

Malcolm, who couldn't imagine Birmingham, was not impressed. 'Not like her. Set her to something, and she carried it through. The best thing they came up with was that she'd had some sort of message. To meet somebody.'

'But who?' demanded Mark. 'And where? Damn it, she could've gone in the water pretty well anywhere, and ended up where they found her.'

'Mark!' his mother said sharply, rebuking his lack of taste.

'Well, it's no good waffling round it,' he protested. 'The police know nothing, and we know nothing. So what's the point?'

There was a short silence, into which, because it was becoming awkward, I spoke quietly.

'You said this was at the beginning of May.'

'She was found,' Angie said with tight-lipped disapproval, 'on Saturday the 14th.' She nodded. 'If that matters.'

Not to be discouraged, I continued: 'I believe that was a flag day.'

'A what?' Mark asked. 'What're you on about?'

'Flag days, we used to call them, when they were little flags with pins in. Charity collections. Nowadays they use little coloured discs with a kind of rubber glue on the back, to stick to your coat. I suppose you get the same things round here. Mind you, the beginning of May doesn't seem the best time to pick. I mean, all the holiday people wouldn't be around. They're the ones with the money. Just a thought, though. . . how would you collect from people on boats?'

I looked round, raising my eyebrows in polite enquiry. They all seemed to consider I was slightly insane. Including my wife, perhaps.

'What on earth are you talking about?' asked Angie.

'Collections. Did you have one on *that* Saturday? The day she was found. Or around about then.'

Frowning, Angie agreed. 'The *previous* Saturday, yes. I was in Wroxham myself, selling them.'

'Were you? What was the charity?'

'The Wildlife Protection Society. Nancy's favourite. She'd asked me to do it for her.'

'Ah yes,' I said. It figured, as they say. 'What colour were they?'

'What the hell does it matter?' demanded Mark with unnecessary anger. 'I was doing the same thing. Selling 'em in Potter Heigham.'

'So what colour were they?'

'They were damn well yellow. That suit you?'

I smiled at him, trying to cool him down. 'It does. Thank you.'

I had talked myself into a trap, having seen an opportunity to become better acquainted with the background to the yellow disc that had been on Nancy's anorak. But I would've had difficulty in explaining my own knowledge and interest.

Malcolm was eyeing me with suspicion. 'What's this all about?' His voice was a deep growl.

'Why. . .don't you see!' Amelia chided him. 'Richard was trying to find some reason for Nancy being in the district. Perhaps she travelled here to take part in the collection –'

'They'd have the same collection in Birmingham.' Angie lifted her chin in challenge.

I smiled her down. 'They'd have very little interest in wildlife in Birmingham, I'd guess. Their own wildlife consists of car drivers.'

I was past the worst. Malcolm allowed himself a laugh, though there was no force to it. 'Like our summer sailors!'

'Precisely.'

'Then she could've done that, I suppose,' he accepted. 'But she'd have surely let us know.'

'Yes,' Amelia commented. 'Then it remains a complete mystery.'

We all contemplated this. Mark scraped back his chair. 'Better check on that fibreglass job, I suppose.'

'I hope it's sound,' his father grunted.

'If it's not, you can blame him.'

He meant me. I beamed at him. He said: 'You coming, Larry?'

'In a sec'.' A shadow crossed Larry's face. He resented Mark's foreman-like attitude, recognizing only one boss, who was quick enough to notice and himself got to his feet.

'I'll have a look at how you're getting on, Larry.'

'The weld looks sound, but I'll need some more sanding discs.'

'I'll let you have 'em.'

And while this was going on, Amelia and I were saying goodbye to Angie, who wiped her hands on her apron and managed to smile.

'You must come again.'

'We'd like to do that.'

The result was that the five of us walked out together, Mark and Larry trailing at the rear but not saying anything.

Malcolm led the way down the steps and through the yard, pointing out the damage to the craft as he went along. The water to our right looked dark and motionless, with the sun way over on our left and declining.

Malcolm now walked in front with Amelia. I hadn't been listening to him until a name caught my attention.

'Whatever happened to Olivia, anyway?' he asked. 'I suppose she married. . .'

'Philip,' she told him. 'You remember Philip Dean.'

'Not that weed!'

'She's a writer now.'

'Is she? I don't read much.'

'Not your sort of stuff, anyway Malcolm. Romance fiction. Under two names, Christobel Barnes and Lovella Treat.'

'Well I never. . .'

Was it possible that he didn't know she lived only twenty miles away? If he did not, I hoped Amelia wouldn't tell him. But she, too, recognized the problems this might bring about, and said nothing.

'I bet she's been doing well for herself,' he decided.

She was non-committal. 'I should imagine so.'

'Old Philip hit the jackpot, then, the cunning devil.' We got his haw sound again. 'More strength to his elbow, I say.'

We reached the car. Mark and Larry hung around. Malcolm asked where we were staying, and I told him. He said we'd do better going back by way of Horning. We shook hands, then got in the car. It seemed advisable to turn in the yard, rather than back out. I did that. The three men watched stolidly. We drove away with a wave.

As advised, I turned left out of the entrance, heading roughly towards Horning. As Malcolm had indicated, in a quarter of a mile we passed his main entrance, which offered a more impressive invitation, with two gate posts, but no gates, and a recently re-painted sign: Ruston and Sons.

'So what did you make of that?' I asked.

'One thing I'm certain about – she didn't die from any accident. Nancy was completely at home with the water. She knew all the dangers, and I expect she could swim like an eel.' Amelia was using her flat, decisive voice.

'Nancy – the water-girl.'

'Pardon?'

'Something young Carter said.'

'Hmm!' She nodded to herself, as though I'd confirmed something.

'Suicide?' I asked.

She hesitated over that one. 'Didn't you get the impression she was an unhappy young woman? Perhaps she didn't want to take that degree. Perhaps she wanted to devote her life to the ecology. Heavens, Richard, just imagine! To be studying for a degree that you're taking only because it's expected of you – and all the time yearning to do some naturalist kind of thing! She'd find that depressing, to say the least.'

'You heard what Malcolm said: set her to something, and she'd carry it through.'

'That's just it. Don't you see. *Set* her to something. The impression I got was that she was a quiet girl, even withdrawn. A lonely girl. No – not lonely. An alone one. She loved going out on her own on the water. And don't forget, she was adopted.'

'What on earth can that have to do with it?'

'Oh, Richard! A great deal, I suspect. She was taken from her natural mother at birth. That implies a pre-arranged adoption. The psychologists reckon it's better like that, for the mother and the child.'

I was sceptical. 'Psychologists have been wrong.'

'You're a man, Richard. I know you can't help that, but it does mean you're deprived in a lot of ways.'

'It's a good thing I've got you, then. Carry on.'

'I intend to. You know nothing of motherhood.'

I admitted that.

'Then you'll just have to manage with your imagination. Sometimes a woman expecting a baby doesn't want it, and has every reason for intending to part with it. Nowadays, of course, abortion's easy, but we're talking, here, about twenty years ago.

86

Then, it was probably the best thing to arrange a prior adoption. But the doctors have to think about emotional disturbance. For the mother and the child. And as far as the child's concerned, the first arms to take it are its mother's. Are you with me?'

'I'll take your word for it.' I was managing still to make light of it, though my first wife and our child had been killed in a car crash.

'That's the theory, anyway,' she went on. 'And it does have a certain amount of the logic you enjoy so much.'

'It sounds logical,' I admitted.

'Yet you heard them talking openly about it. They wouldn't be doing that unless they'd always been open about it, and that means to Nancy, too.'

'So?'

'So why did they tell her? They need not have said anything. Mark must have been very young at the time, and he'd never realize. She could've grown up as their own daughter. But she was told she'd been adopted. And with both Malcolm and Mark being forceful types, and Angie probably sour and disillusioned, you can imagine what that would do to Nancy.' She gave me time to do so, but I didn't respond. She went on: 'She was a quiet girl, and meek. No – not meek. I got the impression she'd developed a quiet resistance. But withdrawn. She certainly wasn't forceful. Her caring for the environment indicates that. Those people are against force, the force that destroys landscapes and wildlife. In *that* respect, I could imagine her working up quite a bit of steam, emotionally.'

'Is all this leading to a suggestion that she committed suicide?'

'What! And destroy herself? That'd be self-betrayal.'

I smiled to myself fondly. 'So we get round to foul play?' I asked.

'Of course. What else did you think?'

'We'll phone Mary, when we get back to the hotel.'

'What on earth does that mean?'

'To tell her we'll be stuck here for a while. Quite clearly, I'm not going to be able to drag you away before we've seen it through.'

'I should say not.'

'So there we are. Now you know how I always seem to get myself involved.'

'But it's different for you,' she pointed out kindly.

'Is it? In what way?'

'For you it's a jigsaw puzzle with no picture on it. Flat and cold and with missing pieces. Puzzles drive you mad. Men are like that.'

'Not only puzzles.'

She put a hand on mine, just as I was changing gear. 'I was teasing, Richard.'

'I know you were, my dear.'

She patted my hand. I changed gear again, just to leave it there. 'Now tell me,' she said, 'what pieces you still can't fit.'

'I can't see that either of your friends at Mansfield Park could have been blackmailing Mark. I can't see that Mark could've been blackmailing either Philip or Olivia for murder. Neither of those possibilities fits, emotionally or psychologically. I could enlarge on that –'

'All right. *Touché.*'

'I also cannot understand Mark's reaction, if he'd hired Harvey Cole to get those pictures for him. I don't think Mark was acting. He's too hair-triggered with his anger to be able to fake it convincingly.'

I glanced at her. She was considering me purse-lipped, but with a devil of amusement in her eyes.

'Anything else?' she asked.

'Yes. I don't understand the reaction of Inspector Poole in dismissing what I showed her, not the way she did it. *She's* sufficiently controlled to be able to put on a convincing act. But she was furious. And make no mistake, my dear, from what we've heard – and which I'm sure she knows very well – she must be very suspicious about Nancy's death.'

'You think she's up to something?'

'She's leading us on. She's using me. She can't continue with an investigation officially, so she's hoping I'll drop on something.'

She laughed lightly. 'I don't think she'd expect to hear it from you, even if you did.'

'She'll think of a way.'

88

I pulled the car into the side of the road, and stopped.

'What now?' she asked.

'Where's the map? In some way, I think Harvey Cole fooled me completely. I want to look up the shortest way to Happisburgh.'

'He's clever. He's smooth. You'll never get anything out of him.'

I bent over the map. 'No? With my fingers round his throat, he could well change his mind.'

8

We approached Happisburgh by way of Horning, and because of this we found ourselves negotiating the minor road in which Harvey Cole's cottage was located in the opposite direction to before.

We couldn't have timed it more accurately. We observed him leaving, without being in time to stop him. As he turned out of his drive ahead of us, I was close enough to read the legend on the tailgate of his car, BMW 528i. I knew, then, that I had no chance of catching him, though I tried. There was just a chance that superior driving ability would smooth out the inequalities between the performances of the two cars. But he not only had the faster car, he had the better driving ability. On the winding side roads I managed to keep him in sight, but once he hit the coast road and turned right he was away.

After a few miles I gave it up, and slowed. There was no point. My guess was that he was on his way to the nearest airport, from which he would flit off – first class, on my money – to the Cap d'Antibes or the Côte d'Azure, or wherever his wife was awaiting him. There was, in my mind, no longer any doubt that he had cheated me.

At least, I now knew that. The trouble was that I didn't know in what way.

'He took those photos himself,' Amelia suggested.

'No, no. He couldn't possibly have been involved in Nancy's death. It's not our harmless Harvey. Whoever took them was a person who must have been. In a very close way.'

'A very close way? Aren't you jumping to conclusions there?'

She knows that when I'm annoyed my mind races away, sometimes in the wrong direction.

'All right, then. But whoever found her and stuck the sticker on –'

'Or removed it,' she cut in. 'I'm still not happy about your reasoning, there.'

'All *right*!' You can see my anger was still lingering. 'Put it like this, then. Whoever took the photographs did *something* with that Wildlife sticker. So they had a close interest in her death. A personal one. It wasn't just a matter of doing that, it was also taking pictures to prove it was done.'

'That's better. Which eliminates Harvey, you think?'

'I think he came into it exactly as he said, to steal those pictures from Olivia's house. But now – from Mark's reaction – I can't help thinking that Harvey had already handed the haul over, and been paid for it.'

'And what he gave you?'

'Gave! I paid him three hundred pounds! He'd had time, and I think he'd had copies made. There're top-class people who can make perfect copies of prints.' I reached in my pocket, produced the yellow envelope, and glanced at it. 'There. You see. Pro-Labs, it says. Some specialist firm. He simply kept two copies, guessing some gullible idiot would turn up.'

'And that was you?'

'It was me. I could kill him.' And, I recalled, I'd forgotten to ask him how he would get in through a thatched roof.

'You can always stop the cheque,' she told me.

'So I can!' And perhaps have him visit us in the night? I thought I might enjoy that.

Somewhat eased by the thought of getting a belated laugh on Harvey, I stopped the car, and we had a look at the map.

The chase of Harvey had absorbed more miles that I had realized. We were not far short of Winterton, so we decided to go there, locate somewhere we would get a pot of tea later, and in the meantime stretch our legs. It was almost like being on holiday, searching for some way to absorb the empty hours. There was a café, which was open, but it was early for food so we left the car and went for a walk. There wasn't much to be seen, and the road was quite a way from the sea, but we were able to benefit from the refreshing, freezing wind, which had encountered no resistance before it reached us.

Enlivened, we returned to the café. It was nearly sunset. We ate jam and cream scones and drank weak, very hot tea. All this irregular eating was upsetting my stomach. One time it was lunch in the middle of the day and dinner late in the evening, the next it was dinner around midday and tea in the early evening.

It was dark when we emerged from there. For three hours, not one word had been spoken relating to the death of Nancy Ruston.

'What now?' asked Amelia, when we were moving again.

'Back to the hotel, I suppose. We'll phone Mary and tell her the situation, and then. . . well, I'd like to have a quiet word with young Larry Carter. I wonder if Malcolm would be suspicious if I asked him for Larry's address.'

'I would, if I were him.'

'We'll see.'

When I drove into the hotel's courtyard there were a number of cars already there, and from the lighted windows I could tell that the bar was open. In the summer you'd get the clattering jar of the Black Country accent in there, but now, with only the locals keeping the bar ticking over, it would be the burr of the Norfolk voice that prevailed. This was a pleasant prospect. I could allow the sound to flow past and not make the effort to understand.

Amelia noticed the direction of my interest. 'I'll just pop upstairs and tidy up,' she said, 'and phone Mary. Then I'll see you in the bar. All right?'

'Fine.'

She had disappeared into the passageway before I'd locked the car, and before I'd become aware of a shadow moving from a corner of the wall. I was at once alert, aware that I now carried photos which could well be dangerous to somebody. But this person took his time, moving quietly. A tall figure, the glow of a cigarette in his fingers. There was a soft laugh from him.

'Relax, Richard. It's only me.'

The last time I had seen Tony Brason he'd been sitting, soaking wet, inside Chief Inspector Donaldson's car, solving his case for him. Tony and I had stood in the pouring rain, arguing it out between us, he furiously. But he still worked the same patch. He was 200 miles from it.

'Tony! Whatever. . . Good Lord, man, it's good to see you.'

We shook hands. I grinned at him, he smiled at me, for him the meeting being expected.

In the poor light I could detect that he was looking relaxed, better than he'd been when tension and fury had been tearing him apart. The lines had gone from his face. He was genuinely pleased to see me, and Tony was never one for disguising his feelings. Direct and guileless, that's how I thought of him.

Then what the hell was he doing here?

'Come inside to the bar,' I said, 'where we can talk. Are you staying here?'

'Yes. For now. I'm using a bit of leave that's mounted up.'

I put a hand on his shoulder and steered him towards the bar. Partly, this was to reassure myself that it was really him.

'Amelia will be delighted –'

'I saw her, Richard. I didn't speak to her, just let her go ahead. We've got to talk, you know.'

'There're no secrets from Amelia.'

He didn't reply. I thrust open the door. The old fireplace roared with heaped logs, and provided most of the light. The bar was half empty and hummed with relaxed voices. Got to talk, had we? Did I need more than one guess to decide the subject?

'What'll you have?' I asked.

'Whatever they call beer around here.'

We stood at the bar, waiting patiently.

'You made Sergeant, then?' I asked.

'It was partly that case, and Ken Latchett put in a few words for me.'

'I'd have thought it'd be Donaldson who'd do that.'

'He tried to take all the credit. There was a bit of a row, and soon after Donaldson had to go. He accepted a transfer.'

'Had to?'

'So the rumour goes.'

Our beer arrived. I looked round for somewhere quiet to sit. Tony was too relaxed, too chatty. He was covering up, and wasn't happy about it. I knew what had happened. Melanie

Poole had phoned him. He'd come along to sort me out. And he would hate that, caught between a certain loyalty to me, and a closeness to Inspector Poole at which I could only guess.

I'd have liked to help him out, but I wasn't sure how much of him was on my side of the fence. I felt rotten about it, and could only allow him to lead into what he wanted from me. So we needed a quiet table, and they were all occupied. The only one least cluttered had one young man sitting there, a corner table as though he'd seized it early and held on to it proprietorially. If there'd been a likelihood that he would shortly leave, then that would have been fine. But I thought not. He'd been waiting for me, and I didn't dare lose him now. It was Larry Carter.

He had spotted me the moment I entered the bar, of that much I was certain. Now he was viewing our approach with his head bent over his glass, looking up huntedly from beneath his eyebrows. He would speak to me alone. Or with Amelia there. With a stranger present, I'd not get one word out of him.

This was dreadful. I didn't yet know if I dared to allow Tony to hear what Larry had to say, and the thought undermined me. And I had only a few seconds to make a decision as to my approach.

Larry sat over a half pint glass he'd probably been nursing since the bar opened. When we came close his nerve failed him, and he stumbled halfway to his feet.

'Larry,' I said. 'Hello.' I reached out my free hand, putting down my glass with the other, and detained him. The pressure of my fingers was meant to imply that I wanted him there, wanted time to get him alone.

He subsided. 'Get you a drink?' I asked.

'I'm all right,' he mumbled.

'Fine.'

Tony and I sat facing him. Larry must have felt trapped. Tony's size, alone, would have seemed overwhelming. 'This is a friend of mine. Tony Brason,' I told him. 'Tony, this is Larry Carter, who works at one of the boatyards around here. I met him this morning.'

Tony smiled at him. 'Interesting work, is it?'

94

'Oh yes.' Larry was still suspicious. 'Interesting. It's just a job, though.'

'He's a lucky bloke who can earn his bread doing something he really wants to do.'

'I could be chucking it up.' Larry tried a half smile, encouraged by Tony's friendly interest. 'Nothing for me there, now.' He shrugged, his eyes fell. He wanted to talk about Nancy, and he couldn't.

Tony turned to me. 'Melanie phoned. She said you were giving her a right runaround.'

'Did she? She exaggerates.' I prayed he wouldn't mention who Melanie was.

'She thought I might be able to handle you. Now there's a laugh for you, Richard. Who's ever managed that? Except Amelia, of course.'

'You can but try.'

Larry had his ears cocked to all this. I could almost see them quivering.

'I thought,' Tony observed thoughtfully, 'that I might just be able to maintain the peace between you.'

'Melanie's a strong-willed woman.' I told him, partly as a warning.

'You never said a truer word.' He sounded complacent, and I looked at him sharply, detecting a note of pride. 'Here she is now,' he added.

'Who?' I thought he meant Melanie.

'Your wife, Richard.' He got to his feet, I followed, and Larry didn't seem to know what to do, and settled for inertia.

'Well, well,' Tony said. 'How are you, Amelia?' He took her shoulders and kissed her on the cheek.

Her eyes darted from one to the other of us. 'But Tony. . . you here. . .'

'He'd got a bit of leave coming.' I explained, though it explained nothing.

She tucked her skirt under her and sat at the table, noticing Larry at last. 'And Larry! Well, fancy meeting you here. Has my husband introduced you?'

'Yes,' he mumbled. He was poised for flight, totally outnumbered and finding himself in a tight group of friends, which

95

excluded himself. 'I was just going. If you wanted to. . .' He thrust back his glass, his intention clear.

'No, no.' Amelia was emphatic. 'Don't go. I wanted a private word with Tony, anyway. Richard, you wouldn't mind, would you, if we leave you for a while? This is woman talk. You wouldn't understand. Tony, is there another table. . .'

He lifted himself to his toes. 'Over there. A couple of seats. I'll take my beer. . . and what are you drinking, Amelia? Isn't it gin and lime?'

'Gin and ginger ale, I think.' She smiled at Larry, smiled at me. 'If you'd just entertain my husband for a few minutes, Larry. . . You're not in a hurry, I hope.'

And, Tony's hand at her elbow, she left us. She was already chattering away to him and conveying the impression she'd aimed for, of close and particular friends who had secrets of their own that excluded her husband. Woman talk, indeed!

Larry still wasn't certain about the way things stood. 'What was that about?'

'My wife's quite a clever woman, Larry. She knew I wanted a quiet word with you, so she dragged him away.'

'Uhuh?'

'She also guessed you wanted a word with me.'

'She couldn't be *that* clever.'

'Oh come on, Larry. She was there, at the Rustons'. It was quite obvious that Nancy meant more to you than just the daughter of your employer. We turned up, obviously also interested in Nancy. It seems to me we might swap ideas and thoughts to our mutual advantage.'

He looked up at me, his blue eyes shadowed with suspicion, but his expression one of hope. There was something he would very much like to load on to somebody. Perhaps I was that somebody.

'There's no reason to suppose that Nancy and me. . .' He stopped, and had to swallow.

'No?' I quoted: '"Nancy was the water-girl, Nancy was the dream."' I tilted my head at him. 'What does that mean?'

'I didn't think you'd heard.'

Now, washed and clean and clothed for an evening out, there was nothing about him that suggested the welder. No basic strength to him. Only a square jaw that hinted at stubbornness.

'Of course I heard,' I said. 'You intended me to. Any more of it?'

'It was something I wrote in her birthday card. Her eighteenth. A special one, that was.' He was becoming more animated, a flush on his cheeks.

I nodded encouragingly. 'Her majority. Her life her own from then on.' I'd perhaps expressed that badly, but he didn't notice. 'How does it go, this bit of verse of yours?'

'Oh. . .' He moved his glass in embarrassment and spoke to it, quietly, sharing it now with a third person. 'It was in the present tense then, of course. "Nancy is the water-girl, Nancy is the dream. Oh, for love of Nancy in the soft and breathless twilight and the murmur of the stream." That's all.' Then he blushed furiously, realizing he'd confided far too much to a stranger. Yet to whom could he confide anything so personal but a stranger?

'You're a bit of a poet,' I said, in pleased discovery.

'A bit of.' He seemed to realize, then, that he was handing out all the information, and me none. 'Who *are* you, anyway?' he asked 'Why should I tell you anything?'

I'd already realized that it was necessary to confide in him. It might be a risk, but I had to take it, and it would have to be the truth. I might need to hold some of it back, but what I said would have to be untarnished, or he would detect its worthlessness. He had a poet's ear and perception.

'I'm an ex-Detective Inspector of police,' I told him, keeping my voice even and unemphatic. 'Now married and settled down. My wife had an appeal from an old college friend, who'd had a break-in. The idea was that I might help. Advice, that was all. But one thing's led to another, and in the end I heard of Nancy's death, and with what I already knew it seemed to me to be very suspicious. The police are willing to accept it was an accident. I'm not so sure. Somehow, I don't think you believe that, either.'

His eyes were on me steadily, a shock of blond hair fallen over his eyes. 'Is that the truth?'

I lifted my shoulders. 'Not all of it. If I told you everything, I might be revealing confidences. Life is full of loyalties you don't care to betray. Don't you find that?'

I watched his fingers loosen their grip on his glass. He reached a hand up and swept back his hair.

'Nancy wouldn't have died like that. Not Nancy. Not in anything involving water.'

'You're thinking in terms of murder?' I asked gently, knowing that most ordinary people shy from the word.

'If you like.'

'It's not for me to like. It's what you think, Larry.'

'All right. I think she was killed.'

'Any ideas on that?'

He seemed to think the balance of question and answer had again swung in my favour. 'What was all that about – the yellow Wildlife stickers?'

'My wife explained. . .'

'No she didn't. You were after something.'

I smiled at the vigour of his attack. 'I wanted to know the date of the collection.'

'Saturday,' he said, 'May the 7th. What about it?'

I allowed a small silence to build up, wondering what he might already know about it, and afraid to push him into concealment. Then I said: 'What if I told you that there was one of those stickers on her anorak when she was found?'

'I'd say. . . I'd say. . .' He paused, his mind scanning the implications and his eyes hunting. 'She couldn't get one before the Saturday, and you don't go on wearing one after. It means – I dunno – means she was here, around here, on the Saturday. But she wouldn't come back to the Broads and not let me know.'

'But she must have done,' I reminded him gently. 'She did come back.'

He blinked. 'Must've, I suppose.'

'Because she died here, Larry.'

He looked down and said nothing.

'And you really didn't know she was here?'

'Of course not.' There was hesitation, then, 'You're trying to trap me into something.'

I thought, then, that I'd lost him. Candour, I decided, was all that would retrieve him. 'Larry, try to look at it from my point of view. The police aren't making any more advances. It's not a case to them. I'm the one trying to get at the truth, and I've got past experience to draw on. At this time, I virtually know nothing that makes any sense. So. . .ask yourself. I know nothing about you. You could have killed her yourself, as far as I know. All right! Relax. It's possible, and you're got to admit it. A lovers' quarrel. It happens.'

'We were not lovers,' he told me tensely. Why did he take me so literally?

'Just a phrase. But you really must see – I have to start from scratch. I need to know anything I can find out. From you just as much as anybody else. Am I making myself clear, Larry? Either you trust me or you don't. Make up your mind. Do you or don't you?'

There was an inch of something flat and unpalatable in his glass. Nevertheless, he stared at it for a full two minutes. Then he lifted his head.

'Yes, she must've been in the district, and no, she didn't tell me.'

'But you'd surely have kept in touch.'

He nodded. 'She used to phone me every Wednesday, or me phone her. Alternately. She rang from her digs, and me from home.'

'You live with your family?' This was no more than a mild interest, background colour.

'With my mother. Dad's dead. Ten years ago, that was.'

'And the last time she spoke to you?' I asked. 'Would that've been the Wednesday before the Saturday of the Wildlife collection?'

He nodded. His expression was empty. His mind was miles away. 'Yes,' he said absently.

'And at that time there was no mention of her coming to Norfolk?'

He shook his head impatiently. The impatience was with himself. 'I'm trying to remember – exactly. You don't understand. There wasn't any talk about coming to the Broads, or I'd have fixed up to meet her. Yes. . .' He met her my eyes brightly. 'I've been trying to remember. . .looking back. I'm beginning to. You know, fitting it together. That last time – well, she was kind of

99

strange, all excited and tensed up. And scared. I remember, I said I'd go with her, meet her somewhere and we'd go together, but she said no, she'd got to tackle it this time on her own. But there was no mention of where. You get what I mean? She'd got me thinking of somewhere in Buckinghamshire. I don't know how, though I suppose that was some sort of subconscious association –'

'Now hold on.' It was a pity to break into the flow. 'I haven't got the slightest idea what you're talking about. You seem to think I'm psychic or something. What's this all about?'

He stared at me with comical surprise, then he gave a peculiar pout of dismay, and a short laugh of amusement at himself.

'I just assumed. Sorry. What don't you understand?'

'Pretty well everything.' I sighed. 'Can we go back a bit? She was going to tackle it, you said, this time on her own. Tackle what?'

He was helpless at organizing his story, going off at all sorts of angles. I just had to let him get on with it. 'I told you. . . I'm sure I did. She'd written, you see. In the end, she'd got up her nerve to write. I was mad at her, I can tell you.' He crinkled his forehead into a frown. I had difficulty imagining him being mad at anybody, but he didn't give me time to say so. 'But she'd written, and on that last Wednesday she said she'd had a reply, and they were going to meet. She just wouldn't tell me where. I can see it now. She knew I'd be around, in the background, if I knew where.'

'Or when.' I dredged for grains of fact.

'That neither. Some time over the weekend, I assumed.' He lapsed into brooding silence.

'Or even who,' I suggested at last. 'Who was she intending to meet?'

He jolted out of his reverie and stared at me. 'Well, her mother, of course.' His scorn swept over me. He was really very immature.

'Mrs Ruston?'

'Of *course* not. Oh dear, it *is* hard work.'

I agreed silently.

'Her *real* mother,' he said. 'The one who didn't want her.'

100

He said this with a passionate disgust, which was disturbing to watch.

I tapped out the dottle from my pipe into the ashtray, and began to fill it. My hands were steady, and I made the movements slow and smooth, indicating no more than a vague interest, when in fact I'd felt the jolt inside me that I always do when a break comes along. Here, at last, was an emotional background, a possible motivation. Suddenly the bar seemed brighter, as though the power had jumped up, and I was seeing everything about me in more crisp detail.

'So she'd traced her natural mother,' I said softly.

'What the hell d'you think I've been talking about?' he demanded, an insignificant and unassuming young man suddenly bouncing with fury.

'It seems to have annoyed you.'

'Annoyed! If only we'd been married I could've put my foot down.' He nodded, certain he could have done so, or at least tried. 'They brought in this stupid law – any adopted person over the age of eighteen could get to know the names of their real parents. It was like handing round lighted fireworks. They must've been crazy. Nancy was adopted. You know *that* much. . .'

'I know that.'

'From birth. So why the stupid buggers had to tell her I don't know. There was no need. It wouldn't have hurt her *not* to know. Now would it? But she had to be told.'

'You mean the Rustons?'

He gave a snorting sound, leaning forward in confidential emphasis. 'That was her doing, I reckon. Sour-faced bitch. She hated Nancy. Oh yes. No good denying it. It was part of it, like as if her nasty-minded dislike had to have an excuse. I never heard her say it, but it sort of hovered behind everything she ever said to Nancy. "You mustn't forget you're adopted, Nancy." Not for a blasted minute! It was one of the reasons Nancy wanted to get away from there.'

'Was it?'

'She actually *liked* Birmingham.'

That was proof if I needed it. And a reason she would want to locate her real mother – the one who'd given her away, as a possible substitution for the one who now rejected her. But as

101

Larry had said, it might not have been a good idea. The psychologists who had decided it was a sensible thing to take the child directly from the mother, might also have been thinking of the emotional effect on the mother. They might reasonably be supposed to have omitted even the mention of the child's sex. The possibilities for upset were enormous.

'So,' I said, 'she did what was necessary to trace her real mother. When was this?'

'Oh. . .ages ago. Fifteen months or so. Just after she was eighteen.'

That long ago? I asked: 'Did you help her in that?'

He shook his head. 'Wouldn't let me. Mark helped her.'

'And the parents were traced?'

'Parent, is all I know. There was no name for the father.'

'So why did she wait all that time before contacting her mother?'

'She'd moved. There was an address given in Buckinghamshire.'

'Which was where you got the subconscious idea.'

'I suppose.' He shook his head. It was an irrelevance. 'She'd got married and moved to. . . somewhere.'

'So you don't know where.'

'She wouldn't tell me.' He flicked the rim of his glass with his nail, provoking a ting. 'They got a detective on that.'

His enthusiasm was failing him. I had to prompt. 'And then what?'

There was no response. He was staring through me as though I was no longer there, his face sad and long.

'What happened when they traced her mother?' I asked. It couldn't have taken more than a month to trace her. 'Larry – you with me?'

His lips twisted sourly. 'She didn't want her, that's what. Didn't want Nancy.'

That anybody could not want Nancy was beyond his comprehension, though he knew one example in Angie Ruston. That Nancy had faced a rejection from her other and real mother infuriated him. He moved uneasily, and one fist clenched.

'You'd better tell me,' I said quietly.

102

9

It was too much to expect that he would continue straight-forwardly. He was lost in memories, and I knew I would have to sit through them. But I didn't need to do much, simply sit there and listen, watching his animation as he spoke of her, and dwell on my own thoughts. There was already an obvious pattern visible. I was mildly surprised that Inspector Poole hadn't uncovered it, but I had to remember that she would have been constrained by the inquest verdict, and wouldn't have been able to expend official time on a death when there was no evidence of violence.

'May,' he said dreamily. 'That time I'd have been getting ready for the summer. I've got a sailing dinghy, and she'd have been back for her long vacation before the month was out. We searched every corner of the Broads in that dinghy. There're private waters the public never see, but the owners knew us, and never said anything. We did no harm. Me taking pictures. . . you know, birds mostly. And Nancy. I've got this marvellous camera with a smashing lens with adjustable focal length. I'll have to show you, sometime.'

'You say you've got pictures of Nancy?' I asked, he having mentioned it.

He smiled. 'Hundreds.'

'I'd like to see one, when you can spare the time.'

'Sure. I'll let you have one. Outdoor stuff, they are. We used to spend the summer out there on the water, all weathers. When I could get the time off.'

He suddenly grinned, a wide, flowing stretch of sheer devilment. 'And sometimes when I couldn't. Mark was mad at me.

Not his dad. Mr Ruston's easy-going, and most of the work's in the winter anyway. We were going to write a book, Nancy and me. The pictures mine, the words hers. It's a secret. Mr Ruston'd got all these fancy ideas, her degree and the yard and designing. She went along with it, not arguing. A degree's a degree, she used to say. Looks good, and nobody cares what you got it for. I said writers – intending writers – ought to study English, but she wouldn't have it. Said you only learn to write correct English, not interesting English. I never understood that.'

He had stopped, his mind miles away. I prompted: 'So you had a secret.'

'We were going to get married and go away together. Work our way round the world, she writing, me photographing.'

'And live on what?'

He shrugged. 'Nancy would've worked it out. Commissions, she said. But that's what sparked off all that business of trying to trace her mother. She said she couldn't go until she knew what she was going from. Can you make sense of that?'

I contemplated the ceiling beams. I wasn't used to handling all this psychological stuff, and could only go by my old-fashioned logic. 'Maybe. It's a matter of identity. Belonging. You need to know where you originated, so that you've got somebody and somewhere to come back to. Nancy would have to meet her natural mother – if no more than that – so that she could sort of relax. It's a question of fixing your place in the scheme of things.'

'I still don't get it.' He shook his head stubbornly. 'Anyway, that was what she wanted. And as I said, she and Mark managed to get a name and address. Why she wouldn't let *me* help her I don't understand.' He stared at me in misery.

I pointed my pipe stem at him. 'You were what she was heading towards. She wanted to keep you separate from what she was leaving behind.'

His eyes brightened. 'You really think so?'

It had been a bit specious, but if it helped him, what did that matter? 'It's how women think,' I assured him, all confidence, as though I knew.

'Well. . .that's what she did. Mark drove there, and she told

104

me afterwards she was absolutely rigid with nerves and fear. I can understand that, right enough. She'd been building up to it for months, not knowing who or what to expect. And I suppose I didn't help her much. There I was, not knowing what to advise her, when she might've met somebody who fell all over her and couldn't make enough of her, and wanted her back – and that'd be a grand thing to offer to Nancy, who'd got nothing to stay with the Rustons for. . .'

I saw what was worrying him. 'And you thought you might lose her?'

'Yes.' His misery mouth was there again, comical if I'd been in the mood. 'Sheer bloody selfish, that's what I was. Not thinking of her and *her* happiness.'

'Which was with you?'

'I liked to think so. Why're you distracting me?'

'Sorry. Go on.'

'She told me, later, that in the end her nerve went. She couldn't go on with it. They parked in the lane, half a mile short of the house, and Mark argued with her, shouted at her, she said. Well. . .I suppose he'd spent a lot of time and money on it. . .' Always ready to find excuses for other people, was Larry. 'In the end he lost patience with her, and said he'd go to the house himself and feel out the situation, then come back for her if it was optimistic. He was gone an hour. She said she nearly went insane. Then he came back all furious and said the damned woman was impossible and she'd almost gone into hysteria, saying she never wanted to set eyes on Nancy. And that,' he said with finality, 'was that.'

But he offered no excuse for this woman. Perhaps it had hurt Nancy too much for even Larry's forgiveness.

'Nancy,' I said gently, 'had been thinking about it for a long while, but it was dropped on her mother without any warning.'

'I blame them in Parliament,' he burst out with a force I wouldn't have expected. 'Them and their stupid laws. Causing nothing but trouble. They want their laws rolled up and stuffed right up.'

'But Nancy gave it time, and then she wrote to her mother. Then what?'

He'd exhausted himself with emotion and now seemed sullen.

'She phoned me, the Wednesday before that. . .that collection Saturday, and said she'd had a reply. She was all excitement, though it didn't sound encouraging to me. Just: "I am willing to meet you and discuss matters." Not very nice, I thought.'

'Nancy didn't mention when or where?'

'I've *told* you she didn't. She knew I'd be there if I knew. Couldn't have kept away, could I?' His eyes brightened. 'But if she had a yellow sticker on her anorak, it must've been Saturday.'

If my theory was correct, and the sticker had been affixed when the photographer found her body, then Nancy could have died any time between the Friday, say, and the Tuesday. I didn't mention that. But we had a clue, or he could at least give me one, on where she'd possibly gone into the water.

'But you'd know,' I suggested, 'about currents. You know where she was found?'

He looked haunted, not wanting to discuss it. 'I know.'

'Say four or five days in the water – Where could she have started from?'

I made this casual, as though she'd been a bit of flotsam. But it didn't work. He saw me as callous.

'I don't want to talk about it.' His image of her was still very much alive, and he wanted to keep it like that.

'It might help. I wouldn't imagine there's much current in the Broads themselves.'

'Only where the river enters or leaves.' His eyes hated me. 'So it must've been in the Thurne or the Bure. Even they're slow-moving. It'd have to be somewhere below Horning Ferry on the Bure, or Heigham Bridge on the Thurne.'

'Horning Ferry, I suppose, is not very far from the Rustons' place?'

'That doesn't mean a thing,' he shot back heatedly.

'I only meant to imply that she wouldn't make an appointment to meet anybody so close to her home. She could've met you there, by chance.'

He relaxed. 'I suppose.'

'Then possibly – Heigham bridge?'

'Yes. Why can't you leave it alone! What's it matter now?'

'I don't know.' But a bridge sounded like somewhere useful for throwing someone from.

'I'd better be going,' he said, uncomfortable now, having unloaded pretty well all he was carrying, and realizing he still had it.

'Give you a lift home?'

He scrambled to his feet awkward with nerves. 'No thanks. I've got a Yamaha. You'll let me. . . well. . . if you find out anything. . .'

'I'll keep in touch.'

It was a solemn promise. I didn't keep it.

I sat and watched him walk away, shambling and as unbalanced emotionally as when we'd met. But he still possessed sufficient grace to pause at the far table and say good-night to Tony and Amelia.

The door closed behind him. Tony got to his feet and looked across to me. As I now had an empty table, I gestured to them to come and share it. This gave me about two minutes in which to decide where I stood with Tony. It would be a flat snub to refuse to discuss what Larry had told me, and yet. . . Tony had come here in response to call from Inspector Poole.

I got to my feet and held a chair for Amelia, who is not really up with things and didn't reject the gesture. They sat. I said I'd get more drinks. Tony said, no it's my turn, but Amelia settled it by standing again and saying she'd do it. 'We've got our equality now, you know.'

'A useful chat? Tony asked, after she'd gone.

'Very. And yours?'

'Amelia's brought me up-to-date.'

'With,' I asked, 'what?'

He grinned. 'You're a suspicious devil, Richard. Your life, your home, your dreams. It was what interested her most.'

'And this damned business?'

'That too.'

He was watching me, challenging me to produce just one confidence. We had originally started our acquaintance on difficult territory, and only more recently had reached anything worth holding on to. Now he waited for me to betray that.

I sighed. 'I suppose Amelia's told you *all* about it?'

'She has. You knew she would.'

'I'll be honest with you, Tony, and tell you I wish she hadn't.'

'No you don't. You're far too crafty for that.'

'You came here, Tony, in response to a phone call from your friend Melanie Poole. She's obviously suspicious of what I'm doing, and she thinks I've tricked her somehow. If Amelia's told you about the yellow sticker – '

'She has.'

'And if Inspector Poole's told you about the photograph – '

'She did.'

' Then you *know* how I tricked her.'

'She didn't actually say you'd tricked her.'

He was smiling, not giving me much help. I could see that Amelia had collected the drinks on a tray. I had little time.

'I rather gather,' I told him, 'that you fancy this Melanie.' He nodded, solemn at my formality. 'So I'm warning you that what I'm about to tell Amelia could compromise your position with Melanie.'

Amelia arrived. I helped her with the drinks, and she sat down. I went on: 'But I suspect you've simply seized the chance to see a bit more of her.'

'Co. . .rrect,' said Tony.

'If you tell her what I've been up to, she'll order me off her patch.'

'Then I won't tell her.' He grinned. 'Don't you think we've got better things to talk about than crime!'

Amelia explained to him. 'Richard hasn't got a romantic soul.' And she pouted at me.

So, having settled our mutual relationships, I felt free to tell them what Larry had revealed. Amelia became more and more silent as I went on, until she was white and angry.

'That poor child! Whoever did this. . .' She stopped, dabbing her lips with a handkerchief, which she'd got out in case her eyes needed it.

Tony said: 'That surely can't be a motive for murder. She can't have been killed for no other reason than that she wanted to meet her natural mother!'

Amelia and I looked at each other. She shook her head violently.

'I can't believe that,' she said.

I looked at my fist on the table. 'I think the time's come for going out and thumping somebody.'

'You think so?' Tony asked hopefully.

I shook my head. Nancy had possessed two mothers, each with no apparent feelings, and I hadn't yet come to the point of thumping women.

'That chap Mark seems a likely subject,' Tony suggested.

'I don't know. He doesn't seem to have done Nancy any harm.' I twisted my glass between two palms. 'Larry had the story from Nancy. She'd have told him the truth.'

'I think we ought to speak to Philip,' Amelia said cautiously. 'It was from their house the photos were stolen.'

Tony lifted his head. 'You didn't tell me that.'

She smiled at him. 'Richard's your friend, Tony. I thought it would be better if it was I who didn't tell you.'

He stared at her for a moment, then he laughed with delight. 'Oh. . . lovely. And Melanie doesn't know?'

I grunted, not at all sure any more about what Melanie did and didn't know. 'She put me in touch with her favourite burglar. I didn't want her to know where he'd been operating.'

'I'm sorry, Tony,' Amelia apologized. 'Now we've put you in an awkward spot.'

'Only if Melanie wants to talk about it. I can assure you I don't.'

'You're doing so,' I pointed out.

'But you're not Melanie.'

This was getting us nowhere. 'We'll just have to get hold of Philip,' I said to Amelia. 'Something went on at that house, and he must know. He's the sort who stands on the sidelines and watches.'

'D'you think he'll tell us?' She sounded tentative.

'We can try.' But even to myself my voice sounded full of doubt. Our joint lack of confidence hung heavily between us.

Shortly after that we broke up, Tony saying he hadn't unpacked. He'd glanced at his watch first, so I guessed he was meeting someone.

We went out to the lobby to collect our key. As usual, there was no one at the desk, so I went round to help myself. The key wasn't in its little cubicle.

'Surely I handed it in.'

'You did,' she confirmed. 'I remember.'

'Oh hell!'

I went ahead of her to the stairs and raced up, a mistake perhaps because I made too much noise. When I reached the room the key was in the lock, the tab still moving from the movements as the door was closed. I looked round to the far shadows beyond. There would be a back staircase somewhere, but it was too late to search for it.

The room light was on inside. We stood in the doorway, with me restraining Amelia from habit. Survey the scene before disturbing it.

The search had been made without any attempt at concealment. Whoever it had been had found themselves in a hurry. We hadn't brought much with us, but most of it was strewn on the floor. I glanced at Amelia. She was staring round with her lower lip between her teeth. There is something personally defiling about the thought of a stranger's fingers exploring your belongings.

Savagely, I said: 'Let's check.'

We did so, tidying as we went. There was nothing missing. We'd left nothing of value to tempt a petty thief.

I straightened. 'Somebody was looking for these.' I patted my breast pocket.

'Yes.' She was still being very quiet and restrained.

'The car!' I remembered. I'd locked it, but doors can be broken open and windows smashed. She made a vague gesture, there being nothing personal and intimate about a car.

So I went down myself. By this time the courtyard was full of cars. If I'd wanted to back out I'd have had to fetch a dozen drivers. The Granada was intact. I checked the locks, and turned away.

Through the courtyard entrance I caught a glimpse of a parked car outside on the road. If my reactions had not been sticking out all over the place I might not have given it a second thought. But I knew the shape, even if the colour was not discernible. It looked like Inspector Poole's Metro.

110

I walked out and across to it. The wind whipped me at once, reminding me I wasn't wearing a coat. Seeing my approach she wound down her window.

'Mr Patton. Good evening.'

'I wish to report that our room has been searched.'

'Very well. Report noted. Anything taken?'

'No. We almost caught him at it.'

'But possibly it wasn't there anyway. You would surely carry it with you.'

'What?'

'Now come along, Mr Patton. Don't be coy with me. That yellow envelope you bought from Harvey Cole. It's obviously valuable to somebody.'

'To me,' I agreed. 'And I'm keeping it safe.' I patted my breast pocket once more.

'Now, isn't that a foolish thing to do,' she chided me solemnly. 'You're indicating where you have it, and publicly, and if what you say is correct, and you interrupted your petty thief, then he can't be far away. You're inviting personal attack. Think about that.'

'So I am.' And in the mood I was in, I would welcome it. Physical action would be a welcome change from futile mental effort.

We had no chance to continue with this back-chat. I heard slow footsteps behind me, and Tony's lazy, easy voice. 'Hello there. Making friends?'

Which meant he'd deduced from Melanie's previous attitude that she didn't consider me a friend.

'Somebody's got into his room,' she told him. 'He refuses to make a formal complaint.'

'Do I? I didn't realize that.'

Tony looked from one to the other of us. 'Anything taken?'

'He's still got the envelope safe,' she informed him, a touch of acid in her voice. Then she excused her mood. 'I've been waiting ages, Tony. The car's freezing.'

'We've been having a session.' He walked round to the other side. 'There was so much to discuss.'

'Then get inside, for heaven's sake. You can tell me all.'

He grinned across at me. I recalled a similar encounter

across the roof of a car, though then it had been raining hard.

'We'll see,' he said. 'We'll see.'

I wasn't sure which one of us he was teasing. But certainly he'd set himself a very tricky balancing act.

His door slammed. The engine started. Melanie called: 'See you again. Always at your service.'

Then they were away, leaving me wondering how dry a sense of humour can get before going sour.

I turned back to the courtyard. Way along the road I heard a motorcycle bark into life, then settle down to a diminishing thrum. Slowly I mounted the stairs, with a good idea of what I was heading for.

She was standing by the window with her back to me. She didn't turn.

'That was Inspector Poole you were talking to, wasn't it?'she asked, her voice empty.

I was non-committal. 'It was. She was waiting for Tony.'

'I'm beginning to think it would be the best idea if we handed over all we've discovered – make a statement, or whatever's necessary – to Melanie. And have done with it.'

'It's tempting.'

She turned quickly. Her voice sharpened. Tempting wasn't enough. 'I'm coming to hate this district, the wind, the weather. . .oh, everything. This room. I don't think I can stand it much longer.'

This was strong language from her. She'd shown she could stand a lot more, and still fight back.

'Another day,' I suggested quietly. 'We've already got most of the truth. There're things we can guess at. You know what I mean, my dear. But surely we ought to try to find the last bit of truth.'

She tried to look me in the eyes, but didn't like what she saw. Her voice sharpened as she glanced away. 'And if we don't like that particular truth, do we go on looking, hoping to find a better one?'

'You know what I mean. She's your friend, my dear. Yours. Not mine.'

'I know, I know. But now. . . oh, I can't explain. But I'm

terribly afraid for Olivia. For Philip, too, of course. I want to *help* them, but I'm so scared of what. . . it's like opening a door that's been shut for twenty years – you don't know what you're going to find.'

She put a hand to her lips briefly, then removed it. 'Richard, please try to understand.'

I reached forward, attempting to put my hands to her shoulders, but she turned away. 'I do understand. One more day. I promise. No more.'

She said nothing.

'If my reasoning's at all valid – '

She came straight back at me. 'Your reasoning! Your logic! You and your puzzles! It's all a cold and empty game to you, fit this to that and see if it matches the other. That young girl. . . oh, what's the use of talking!'

I looked at her sadly. She knew me better than that. But how could I explain my attitude? It had always been the same, in every case I'd ever handled that involved a sudden death. At first there had been the choking feeling of anger, that a life had been lost – taken. But at that stage it had always remained impersonal. And then the first stages had been put into motion. To understand anything it had been necessary to know the victim. Intimately. That was when the agony began, when the pity was no longer impersonal, and I felt the growing, uncontrollable internal demand that I had to uncover the truth. And that had competed with my official experience and knowledge, which told me that I would get nowhere unless I approached the problem coldly and without emotion. It was the internal struggle that had always been so exhausting, so debilitating.

And now I was getting to know Nancy. The sickness was there in my stomach. Amelia had felt it herself, but for her it was a natural compassion, an emotion that could be controlled.

I was not so certain of my own control. I needed help with it.

'I would find a lot of use for talking,' I said quietly, reaching for her understanding.

She grimaced, half conceding. 'To talk, to argue, to discuss theories?'

I thought I'd eased a crack into the situation. We were close to discussion and amicability.

'If you'll tell me in what aspect – '

'Oh, what's the point!' She waved, dismissing my ambitions to distract her. 'All right. All right, then. One more day. But. . .if we could only move from here!'

I hated to look into those hopeful eyes, especially after the concession, and then say; 'But we can't do that. It's known we're here. People come and talk – '

'And search our room!'

Then, as these things go, it was left there, neither of us able to think of a way through it, and nothing was settled. We were silent, reaching futilely across the cold, unfriendly room for a lead, an opening, even an encouraging glance.

We went to bed. Still silent. She lay stiffly, well away from me, and it may have been that my bulk created a depression into which it was difficult not to slide, or she moved in her sleep unknowingly into my arms, but there she was in the morning, and somehow the room held less repression in the daylight, with the sun rising over the sea, but whatever had been between us was gone, and my right arm was numb.

'What now?' she asked over breakfast.

'I thought we should have a word with Philip.'

'D'you want me along?' There was just a hint of the previous evening that intruded there.

'Of course. It could be interesting.'

'You want to see him alone, don't you? I mean – not with Olivia there.'

I nodded solemnly. 'At this stage, I think it'd be best.'

'Then you'd better phone him. Let him suggest what to do about it. He'll know all about her habits and movements.'

'Good idea.'

I went at once to do that from the pay phone in the lobby. She had disliked the thought of keeping secrets from Olivia.

10

At this time, I knew, Olivia should be in her morning dictating session, though I'd gathered the impression that Philip was expected to be in the vicinity in case she had any demands to hand out. It was Philip who answered.

'It's Richard, Philip,' I said.

'Yes.' There was caution in that single word. 'What can I do for you?'

'I think we ought to meet.'

'Come along here – '

'No. Alone. Just you.'

'I don't see how I can help you.' He was still coldly distant.

Help me? That was a strange way to put it, considering it was I, in the first place, who'd been asked there in order to help them.

'I've got some more information about the break-in you had. I thought I'd better discuss it with you before Olivia gets involved.'

There was plenty of hidden meaning in that. I waited while it stirred his interest. At last he answered, his voice now quite normal.

'Olivia's decided to have one of her days out. She suddenly decides she can't stand my face any more, and says she'll take her car and eat somewhere else. She gets these fits. The writing seems to be too much all of a sudden, and she has to soak herself in reality. Off she goes to Norwich or somewhere. So she'll be out of the house from about eleven to. . . say. . . five or six. If you'd like to come here, that could be all right.'

It was one of those offers made with a shade of doubt. He would prefer otherwise, and may not have realized that he gave the impression nothing and nobody was welcome at Mansfield Park. He guarded it jealously.

'We'll buy you lunch somewhere,' I offered. 'That'll get you out of the house yourself.'

'Well yes. Thank you.'

'Where do you suggest? You're the one who knows the district best.'

'How about Potter Heigham?'

I had already decided I would like to see the place where Nancy had possibly died. That he should choose it, so conveniently, caused me to hesitate for a second. 'Well . . . certainly,' I agreed.

'That would be ideal, then.' Now he sounded as though he'd suggested a pleasurable excursion for us. 'I know a good place to eat, there. Shall we say midday, outside. . .' He paused. 'Do you know Potter Heigham? It's a favourite spot of mine.'

'No. I've never been there.'

'Then aim for the bridge. I'll meet you at the Bridge Hotel. You can't miss it.'

'Outside or inside?'

He gave a small snigger of laughter, implying that ex-policemen always headed for inside. 'Oh, outside I think. We'll walk up to the town proper and I'll show you the church. It's very fine. Is that all right?'

'Yes. Of course. Midday then.'

We hung up. He'd abruptly taken complete charge. It was perhaps habit. He ran the house, the affairs of the business, and probably his wife, in a financial sense if not a physical one. He had not seemed unduly interested in the reason for our meeting.

'We're meeting him at Potter Heigham. Twelve o'clock.'

'Where is it?' she asked.

'We'll have to look at the map again.'

This we did. It was best reached by heading down the coast road past Happisburgh, then turning inland through Stalham and Catfield. Potter Heigham was marked as being a little off the A149, but just beyond it the road crossed the river Thurne, and this, clearly, would be the bridge referred to. Heigham Bridge, Larry had called it.

There seemed no point in hanging around uselessly, so we got our coats, because he'd spoken of walking. The wind was already working up to a fury, and the weak sun didn't seem to promise much warmth. It was, I thought, a good idea to look round the location of Nancy's death. So far, we had nothing but Larry's suggestion to indicate this could be so, but it was somewhere to investigate.

There was no difficulty with the trip. I was now used to the landscape, which could change so abruptly from woodland to sedge, from farmland to fen. We spotted the signpost for Potter Heigham indicating a side road to the left, ignored it, and inside a mile found ourselves at the three-arch bridge over the river Thurne.

There was no difficulty in parking at this time of the year. The Bridge Hotel was where you would expect it to be, and there were, in fact, two bridges. Both were low. We left the car and investigated, and there was no doubt at all that here was one of the hubs of the water system that constitutes the Broads. There were notices at the two bridges warning boaters of low clearance at both bridges, there were indicators to tell you the varying clearance caused by changes in water level, there were injunctions as to speed, and advice on where to seek pilot assistance.

The boating facilities had given rise to a whole new village, completely devoted to pleasure craft.

It would, I thought, be chaos in the holiday season. Hickling Broad lay to the north, from which the Thurne ran as a natural waterway connection to a junction with the Bure, with access up the Bure to Hoveton and Wroxham, and down the Bure either to Ormesby Broad or along to the coast at Great Yarmouth. Craft would be edging beneath those two bridges stem to stern, in both directions.

It was quite clear that even in May, before the activity really built up, the area round these two bridges would be too concentrated for any violence to go unnoticed. My vague hopes of finding an obvious place from which Nancy could have been pushed or thrown were therefore dashed. And had she not been a good swimmer? Perhaps I'd imagined that. Yet nobody can display their swimming abilities when encumbered by an anorak, jeans and boots. It was just a thought.

'Isn't it strange?' said Amelia.

'What's that?'

'That Larry suggested this place as the. . . you know. And Philip's asked us to meet him here. And Mark was selling charity stickers here on that Saturday. I mean. . .' She shrugged.

We were leaning over the parapet of the larger bridge, looking at the water. 'Coincidence.' I suggested. 'In any event, Philip mentioned the town proper, as he called it, which is about a mile away, and it was probably there that Mark was selling his stickers.'

'Hmm!' She leaned further forward. 'It seems to me there'd be more people around here than at the town proper.'

'It's a point that could be checked,' I said without enthusiasm. 'Look, there's a tow-path along the river bank. Care for a stroll?'

So we descended to water level and walked a little way downriver. Here, the territory was completely open. There was rough ground or marsh on both sides of the river, with clear views. The wind raced in from our left. After about a mile there was a waterway leading in from our right. The footpath turned up alongside it.

'Have we got time to look along here?' I asked.

She glanced at her watch. 'It's well after eleven. A short way, then.'

We didn't expect to find much, but within a quarter of a mile there was one of those basins, wind-bobbing with laid-up craft, and with the deserted offices of a boat hire firm. The flag at the pole whipped raggedly. They'd need to hoist a new one for next season, I decided.

'This'd be all activity in the season,' I said.

And I wondered when the season normally started for this comparatively small and remote centre. Would it, for instance, be as deserted in May? The vessels lay low in the basin, high in the water. The best swimmer in the world would have difficulty getting out of there, hemmed in by hulls and with nothing to grasp at but tow ropes well out of reach.

We turned back and returned at a rather more brisk pace,

both of us having felt a chill at the same thought. We emerged from the path on to firm surface to find Philip waiting for us. He seemed a little surprised to see where we'd come from.

'I noticed your car,' he said. 'I knew you couldn't be far away.'

'Just been to look along the river,' I explained.

'Ah! But you should come here in July and August. You just wouldn't believe your eyes. Now. . .shall we walk up to Potter Heigham?'

'Well. . .' I said, having stretched my legs a bit further than they cared to go. I glanced at Amelia. She pursed her lips and nodded.

'I really must show you St Nicholas's Church. Come along. It's quicker along the main road, then we cut across from the Folgate.'

There is one thing you can say about the Broads, there aren't many hills. Potter Heigham itself turned out to be the best part of a mile from the bridge, and Philip marched towards it with the gait of an animal recently freed. He talked without a break, and we, conserving our energies, listened.

'The bridge is thirteenth century, you know. They're quite proud of it, but I expect there'll come a time when the traffic needs something wider and stronger, and seven centuries of heritage will be tossed away. They'll have to divert the road. Have to. The whole ecology of the Broads is breaking down, destroyed by the holiday industry. Waterways polluted, land being exploited. It's a crying shame.'

And so on. There was, it seemed, no curiosity about the possible reason for this meeting. He was a proud local, demonstrating the beauties and disasters to his visitors. Proud and personally involved. He shrank from the persecution represented by the incursion of an outside world. He should have got together with Nancy, I thought.

Potter Heigham was more a large village than a town. We walked between rows of picturesque and virtually untarnished houses, and, I saw hungrily, past a café that was open and waiting for us. But no – Philip marched on. He was relaxed here.

'The church is at the far end,' he told us, but by this time we could see it, distinctive with its octagonal top to a round tower.

We stood and looked at it. We walked all round it, he enthusing over an octagonal font which, he assured us, was quite unique.

'We've got to talk, Philip,' I said.

'You really must see the font.'

'I'd rather talk about Mark.'

That stopped him in his stride. His ebullience was quenched, and for a moment his comic face, for exaggerated distress, which he used when wishing to mock Olivia, was on show. Then he controlled it and was serious and concerned.

'You're talking about Mark Ruston?' Thus calmly he confirmed what had been a guess up to that moment.

'Yes. I'd like to know more about him, and his visit to Mansfield Park.'

'The damned young fool,' he grumbled. 'Still causing trouble.'

He turned about, and we began to walk back to the café. I would have preferred to talk facing each other, so that I could examine his expression, but I had to accept what was available.

'Was it trouble he brought with him?' I asked, as though only mildly interested.

'I thought this had all blown over,' he complained. 'It was a long while ago. Oh, eighteen months, I'd guess. I can't remember exactly. All I know is that Olivia was in the middle of a book, and the last thing she wanted was disturbance.'

'She does seem to work hard,' Amelia commented, walking at his other shoulder.

'Oh, she does. She does,' he said loyally. 'Then along comes this idiot, this clown, this stupid and impossible young man. . . oh, I can't find words strong enough to describe him. Overbearing and persistent. I told him to leave. I mean, I get enough stupidity to handle through the post, without having it knocking on the door. And how he got her real name and address I can't guess. Her publishers wouldn't have let him have it. I checked that, and they said no. I mean. . . we'd be wide open to all sorts of abuse if every – '

'Can we back-track a bit? I cut in. 'Start again. . .'

I don't think he even heard. He was involved with one of his burdens, and had to boast about how well he handled these things.

'You'd never guess what comes in every post. Forwarded from the publishers, of course. I wouldn't dare to let Olivia see most of it, so I intercept. You'd think she was one of these magazine aunts, available for advice on their love lives. Those're the reasonable ones. But some are abusive. You wouldn't believe it. "You bitch, you used me in such-and-such a book, and I'm saying nightly prayers that you'll shrivel up and die." That's pretty well a straight quote. Can you imagine such a thing? They try to get at her. And harm her. Oh yes, they do. And the common one: "You used my name and you ought to pay me something." They resent her success, you see,' he said blandly, suddenly explaining as to a dull child. 'Isn't it as well the address is a secret! I dread to think how it'd be. . .'

He stopped abruptly, perhaps realizing his complaints had gone on long enough. He was the sole defender of the battlements, and he saw the invaders creeping in through all its cracks. But we'd reached the café, and he was calmly reading the menu displayed in the window.

We entered, found a table, and the rest of the interview was conducted as we ordered and ate. At least, I could now watch his expression.

'So tell me about Mark.'

'He came – this lout – and almost forced his way in. He wanted to speak to Olivia Martin. He'd even got her maiden name correct. It was only because of this that I allowed him inside. Then it all began. There was this fantastic story of Olivia having had a love child she had not acknowledged. As though anybody worries about illegitimacy these days,' he said, completely missing the point.

I assumed he'd been influenced by Olivia's writing, that he'd used such an expression as 'love child'. Perhaps, for Philip, there hadn't been all that much love. There was, apparently, no child of theirs.

'Of course,' he went on, 'I told him to leave. He wouldn't. He said he would go when he'd spoken to her, personally. I couldn't allow that of course. It's part of my job to shield her from unpleasantness. But you can imagine, voices were raised, and there was an undignified scuffle in the hall when I tried to force him out.' He stared at his hands with disgust. 'He was stronger than me. More angry, too. If that could be possible. And as I say, voices were certainly raised, and unfortunately the inevitable happened. Olivia opened her door and called out to know what was happening, and what the shouting was about, just when the young fool was shouting his head off about illegitimate children. Then,' he grumbled, 'the fat really got thrown in the fire.'

He paused, staring at his ice cream and meringue. Amelia had abandoned all pretence at eating, and was staring at him with wide eyes.

'How would *you*,' he demanded of her, 'like to be accused of having an illegitimate child?' She said nothing. 'I thought so, you'd be shocked. Appalled. Of course, Olivia handled it well. She was in one of her majestic moods, and tried to get rid of him by staring him down and telling him, over and over, that it was nonsense. He was downright abusive, I can tell you. In the end, she simply tossed her head and walked away, back into her room, and left me to it. Lovely. It took me a good ten minutes more before I got the door shut behind him. I advised him to get legal advice before trying his tricks again. I can tell you, I needed a stiff drink after that, and my hands were shaking so much that I could hardly pour it. I felt absolutely terrible.'

I hadn't said anything all through this. There had been nothing to prove that the house to which Mark had driven Nancy had been the Dean's, only the link of the photographs, so I was counting myself as lucky that I hadn't had to drag it out of him word by word. But now he'd stopped. The story agreed very closely with that Larry had told us. I put in a prompter after the coffee came.

'What did you think was behind it, Philip?'

'Oh, some sort of blackmail, I suppose. In some way he'd managed to get her name and address, and because she writes that sort of fiction – it's all sexual irresponsibility and aberrations – then she wouldn't be able to face a scandal. Or so he might've thought. It was stupid, of course. Such a thing would boost her sales a hundred per cent.'

'There was no mention of a pay-off for a closed mouth?'

'Nothing like that.'

'So that was the end of it?'

He stared at me with his eyebrows climbing. I was a moron, lacking in imagination and understanding. 'The end? The *end*! By heaven, it'd only just started. Olivia had seen him walk away, from her window. She came back in and threw a hysterical fit. You can just see it. It was all my fault. I'd slipped somewhere. And so on. It went on and on. I was instructed to find out how the information about the address got out. Somebody'd got to pay, or she'd know the reason why. It took me an hour to calm her down, and then later we got the reaction. She was really ill for several days, and I got scared of a nervous breakdown. She wouldn't have a doctor in. Not Olivia. But eventually she got back to her dictating. She'd lost ten days. You can tell – read that book, it was published three months ago – and you'll see in the middle where it changed and went flat. I remember her publishers were quite concerned.'

'And *that* was the end of it then?' I didn't think I'd get anywhere with that, but there was no harm in trying.

Philip, though, was in an expansive mood, and in any event he couldn't resist the temptation to display the versatility of his duties and talents, and the pressures to which he was exposed.

He grimaced. Then he leaned forward as though Olivia might be hiding beneath the table.

'No, it wasn't. There was another try, in the spring it would've been. Around April this year. They'd given us a period to relax in, you see, and this time it was a more subtle approach. From a female. A young woman, going by the wording. A letter. Posted in Birmingham. This was more calm and tentative, designed I guessed to attract sympathy. It was addressed to Olivia, but of course I didn't dare allow her to see it. A meeting was suggested – requested, if you like. So I replied, saying I agreed to meet her.'

'And you signed it – '

'"P. Dean p.p. O.D." No more. She could make of it what she liked, as far as I was concerned.'

'You agreed to meet her. . .where?'

'Why, here. Potter Heigham. At the church, as a matter of fact.'

'You thought she might like to see the font?'

'It would,' he said seriously, 'have established a certain rapport.'

'Can you remember when this meeting was to have been?'

He raised his head and gazed above mine in thought. 'The beginning of May, some time. A Saturday, as I recall it.'

'And Olivia knew nothing of this?'

'She was supposed to be meeting her publisher for lunch in London that day. Agent in the afternoon.'

'Can you recall whether it was a flag day?' He looked at me blankly. 'A charity collection day,' I amplified.

He snapped his fingers. 'Why yes. I remember now. A cause I could happily support. The conservation people.'

'And what happened when you met her?'

He shook his head. His opinion had to be that I wasn't very bright. 'That's the point. I didn't. I hung around the church for nearly an hour – she should have arrived at three – and she never turned up. Lost her nerve, I suppose, and couldn't go through with it. I had a long chat with the verger, who's a friend of mine.'

This version was a lot more detailed than the story told to me by Larry, as related to him by Nancy. It held more detail, which of course Nancy could not have known. What surprised me was that Philip, who had given the impression of being the protector of Mansfield Park, should have agreed to leave it for an appointment with somebody he thought of as no more than a pest. He need only have refused to meet Nancy. But perhaps he was trying to keep her well away from the house, and further disturbance. I could not dig at him to clarify this. In the circumstances, he having been so forthcoming, it would have been ungracious. Nor could I go to Olivia herself to confirm the details of the visit. It was Mark himself I'd have to tackle over that.

'And *that* was the end of it, then?'

He turned up his palms. 'Never heard another word from her.'

'But surely. . .' Amelia began. Then she glanced at me. I

124

smiled her onwards. 'But surely she signed her name. To this letter of hers, I mean.'

'Oh yes indeed. She used the same surname as that offensive young man. Ruston.'

'Nancy?' she asked.

'Yes. That was it. But how do you – '

'But Philip – dear man – you must have heard. It would've been in the local papers. She died. That same day – or so it seems – that she was to have met you.'

'I don't really have time to read the local news.' He cocked his head at her. 'Where did this happen?'

'Somewhere around here, Philip. She was drowned.'

'Ah! Poor girl. That explains why she didn't turn up.' He seemed relieved to have the explanation, as though it'd been worrying him. 'Whatever game she was playing, I can't help but feel sorry for her. She sounded so young. Well, I suppose she would have to be, to claim Olivia as her mother. But all the same, it's saddening.' He looked searchingly from Amelia's face to mine, then back again. 'We get so many drownings in the holiday season. It's not to be wondered at, Midlanders not used to the water. A girl from Birmingham might easily venture where it isn't safe.'

'She might,' I agreed. 'She could very well have done that.'

I paid the bill, and we walked back to the bridge to pick up his car. I thought that he'd completely forgotten our original reason for being in Norfolk, but I didn't prompt him. He actually had his key in the door lock before it came to his mind. Though it might have been carefully timed. He turned.

'But Richard, you said over the phone that this related to our break-in. And all we've spoken about is this unpleasant episode. . .' He left it hanging.

'It seems they could be linked,' I told him gravely.

'Linked? Surely not. In what way?'

'By the robbery itself.' My choice of words was careful. The word 'robbery' suggests something taken.

He didn't miss it. 'But nothing relative to what I've been saying was stolen.'

'Can you be so sure of that?'

'Since you came, I've checked again. I'm certain there's

125

nothing missing, other than those two Meissen figurines I mentioned. If you have any news of those. . .'

I smiled at him, trying to be enigmatic. 'If there's really nothing else, then *that* could be the important point. Probably even vital.'

'I don't know what you mean.' He was uneasy, his bafflement overdone.

'I'm not sure myself. When I know, I'll be in touch.'

This, as I'd intended, he took as a dismissal. For having given so much, he'd obtained very little. He got into his car, started the engine, and drove away with a casual wave.

We walked over the bridge to where we'd left the Granada. We belted ourselves in, but I did not at once start the engine. At last Amelia broke the silence.

'Did you believe him, Richard?'

'Not entirely, though I'm not certain in what respect. We know from Larry that Nancy made an appointment, but I got the impression she thought she was going to meet her mother.'

'That could well be true,' she put in. 'It's just that p.p. isn't always understood. It's short for *per pro*, and it's then often confused. It can mean "By the agency of" or "on behalf of". You can read it either way.'

'There you are, then. She could have thought she was going to meet Olivia.' I would, too, I thought. Oh, the advantages of a decent education! 'Whether Nancy turned up or not is another matter entirely. Philip's a clever man. What he does in the background of Olivia's work must require extensive knowledge, a financial ability, and I'd guess at quite extraordinary patience and tact. He *would* shield Olivia from the normal trials of life. Their livelihood depends on her. *His* livelihood. He knows that. He would lie for Olivia as smoothly as he'd lie for himself.'

'Yes,' she agreed. 'Total commitment to her. Devotion, even. Did I tell you, he rather fancied me, all those years ago?'

'You did tell me.'

'Well. . . there's no hint of that now. . . and a woman can tell. I'm just not there, with Olivia in his life. I wonder,' she said thoughtfully, 'whether she knows what she's got. Or maybe she's too involved with her spurious love.'

It surprised me that she'd allow herself even a suggestion of criticism of her friend, but it'd been there. 'D'you think he'd kill for her?' I asked quietly.

She turned to face me. I couldn't understand the look in her eyes. Were they close to tears for the long-lost love, or for the dead Nancy, who could well have been threatening his present one?

'You're painting him as a villain, Richard.'

'He was evasive. I got the impression his story was prepared. But if he was evading the truth, it could be nothing more serious than the fact that he did meet her, and isn't proud of what happened then.'

Her face was pinched, her eyes dark. 'You've got something in mind, I take it?'

'Suppose he met her, and dismissed her so curtly and coldly that he shocked her. Suppose he *does* read the local papers, and has been afraid that he's the cause of her suicide. That would explain his attitude.'

'You don't think it's suicide, though!'

'As you said, it would be self-destruction. No. I don't think that, my dear. But he might. And he was certain he'd caused it.'

'Yes.' She thought about that. 'But somehow, even if he was, I don't think Philip would blame himself. No. He'd simply be glad it was over and done with.' She nodded, her lips a very thin line.

'Do you think he'd kill for his Olivia?' I repeated gently.

She surprised me. 'He could do it efficiently and unemotionally.'

'And lie for her?'

'I don't know what you mean. You've been saying. . .'

'Suggesting. Now let's consider Olivia. If she had killed Nancy, would he lie for her?'

'Most certainly. He'd believe implicitly in his own lies. What particular lie had you in mind?'

I shook my head, wondering how to put it. 'He's saying he knows nothing about what was stolen. One of them must know. If he's not lying about that, then he's as good as accusing Olivia.'

'Are you suggesting we ought to see her next?' she asked flatly.

'Would you fancy that? Anyway, she's in Norwich.'

127

Her lips twitched. 'If that wasn't one of his lies.'

'We could test that out by driving to the house right now.'

'No,' she said sharply.

I looked out of the side window. There it was again. Any mention of the possible involvement of Olivia, and Amelia became cool and unresponsive. Her support for her must have rested on a nostalgic memory of the Oxford days, as I'd seen nothing in Olivia, so far, to justify any strong support.

'I'd rather tackle Mark first,' I admitted.

'All right. Mark it is. But I warn you, I'm not going to stand for any fisticuffs.'

I laughed, reaching forward for the starter switch. She'd been reading Christobel Barnes on the sly.

11

We had to cross the bridge in order to reach the road to the Ruston's yard. I took it slowly, my eyes on the old dear who was leaning over the downriver parapet and staring at the water, and who seemed as though she might step back under my wheels. She turned. The bulky imitation fur coat, the baggy combat khakis, the yachting cap, all these had misled me. It was Inspector Melanie Poole.

I stopped. Amelia wound down her window. Melanie bent, and spoke past her. 'You can't stop here.'

'I didn't wish to. You on duty, Inspector?'

'No. I was waiting for a word with you.'

'Get in the back, then,' I offered, and Amelia reached behind her for the locking button.

'The slot he drove out of is still free. Why don't you use that and walk back?'

It was a polite invitation, but she'd made it clear that I had no alternative. She had seen us talking to Philip. There was now no need for her even to enquire his name; she would've recorded his car's registration number in her copious brain. She was almost telling me she had had us under observation. Not on duty! Didn't she ever relax?

We nipped into the slot under the nose of a Ford Fiesta driver, who remonstrated with his horn. I was not in a mood to respond. We got out and we walked back.

She was still staring at the river, her forearms resting on the parapet. We were granted no more than a glance as we lined ourselves up each side of her.

'Look,' she said, pointing. 'That piece of branch. I threw that in. . .' She glanced at her watch. '. . . a full half hour ago, and it's moved no more than ten yards.'

A half hour ago, I thought. If that were true, she had not followed us to Potter Heigham. 'And so?'

'The fall of the river,' she went on, 'is no more than four inches to the mile. Did you know that, Mr Patton?'

'I didn't know that. What're you trying to work out?' As though I didn't understand.

'I'm conducting an experiment. My conclusions are that Nancy's body could not have found its way from here to where it eventually fetched up in the time involved. Any thoughts on that?'

'It's not a likely place for a drowning – for one that went unnoticed, anyway.'

'Hmm!' She thrust up the peak of her yachting cap. 'There's a boatyard further down. Just along a spur leading to Womack Water. What did you make of it?'

So she'd observed us going there. The woman was every-where. 'An ideal place for a drowning. I can't advise you on the current flow along there, I'm afraid.'

'I don't expect too much from you, Mr Patton.' In that tone of voice it meant she expected nothing.

I had to remind myself that she had no official inquiry to pursue, no official manpower she could deploy. She had an accidental death, and a possible burglary, which had not been reported. She had no right to expect anything from me, except a courtesy exchange of ideas, in response to having put me in touch with Harvey Cole. But now, shortly, she would have Philip and Olivia's address – could have it even now if she'd used her car radio. Would she dare to intrude there? I felt reasonably confident that she would not. Then what could she expect from me? I didn't offer anything.

'Where's Tony?' I asked.

She shrugged and grimaced. 'Sulking in the car. I had to be rather severe with him. Was he always like this – these ridicu-lous scruples?'

From her other side, Amelia touched her arm to attract attention. 'You shouldn't underrate him, Melanie. Tony means what he says, so he's careful how far he commits himself.'

'Hmff!' She was scornful. 'If anything, I've overrated him. I'm

130

talking about scruples. He refused to go along with me.'

'This would be when you followed us?' I asked.

'Followed? Indeed I did not. It's open ground. You can see, if you lift your eyes. With a good pair of binoculars it's possible to see the junction with Womack Water. I watched you from here.'

'If we'd known, we would have waved,' I told her, aware that Tony would consider this to be spying, when a friend was involved. 'And where are these binoculars now?'

'Tony has them in the car.' She said this while looking away. Quietly.

I tried to keep any smile out of my voice. 'He took them from you?'

She turned on me quickly, just in time to catch the grin I'd been unable to control. It annoyed her.

'He did it sneakily. Took them out of my hands. He said he wanted a look. Then he walked away with them.'

'So he's not really sulking.'

'What?'

'Smiling, perhaps.'

I was trying to smooth this over, but my flippant tone did nothing to help. There was a dangerous light in her eye.

'For your information,' I went on, 'our walk along the river was quite innocent. We found the yacht basin by chance. We came back. All we were doing was filling in time before lunching with a friend. He showed us the church. Fascinating.'

'I'm sure it was.'

'We didn't get to see the font.'

She raised her chin. I was still being facetious. 'You lied to me, Mr Patton. I don't fancy that, not after the help I've given you. And you made me a promise.'

'To do what?'

'To show me what you got from Harvey Cole.' She was now speaking with a definite crispness in her voice. 'You didn't do that.'

'I showed it to you.'

'But not all of it,' she snapped.

Had she got this from Tony? Or deduced it, or guessed it?

'I didn't promise to show you all.'

'You're playing with words. You're not being sincere with me. I don't like that. We could co-operate – '

'On what?' I demanded, getting a little heated myself. 'You haven't got an official case. And nothing I've come across indicates one. Tony knows what I've got, and he'll have told you – '

'Has he? Has he really?'

'Ask him. Here he is now.'

Sure enough, he was ambling across the bridge, his smile tentative, a pair of binoculars hanging from one shoulder. I was aware that I'd been pressured into that remark, and prayed desperately that I hadn't landed him in an impossible situation.

'Have you?' she demanded, facing him.

He lifted his eyebrows, shrugging at me. I plunged in, trying to rescue something. 'She means – have you told her what I've dug up, so far?'

She darted me an angry glance, then swung back to Tony. 'Have you?' she insisted.

He hesitated, I thought in order to control his voice. He was not used to such a peremptory tone from anybody below the rank of Superintendent. His voice, when he'd decided on it, emerged bland and unemotional.

'Seeing that our talk on this has been on an unofficial basis – a friendly one I thought, Melanie – I've told you all I thought you'd need to know. Like a story, to whet your appetite, sort of. You know damn well that if it ceased to be an appetite and became a meal you'd got to swallow – became official, in other words – then it wouldn't be friendly any more. And I wouldn't like that. All right?' He raised his eyebrows again at me. He knows it gives him an appearance of innocence. 'All right, Richard?'

I thought so. He'd placed his standing in this with great precision. For a moment it seemed she would turn from him and walk away. Then she said: 'Give me those damned binoculars. There's a couple walking off along the towpath, and it'll be dark soon, the young fools.'

Tony handed her the binoculars. He didn't say that it was perhaps the darkness they were looking for. He looked past her and winked at me. I nodded. All was not lost.

132

'We don't want another drowning,' I agreed, and we walked away, leaving them to it.

Amelia didn't say anything until we were well clear. Then she took my arm possessively, as though to make sure that my anger, which she knew had been stronger than I'd revealed, had not spilled over on to her.

'You were sailing a bit close to the wind, Richard.'

'I was.'

'You landed him in trouble once before, you know.'

'I did. But that was for you, my dear.'

'But this time there was no excuse.'

'Tony's now got all his self-confidence on tap. He can handle it. But she irritated me. She never lets go. Always on duty, twenty-four hours a day. There're police officers like that, you know. They get just a sniff of something, and can't leave it alone. Like a dog sitting outside a butcher's shop.'

She laughed, tugging at my arm. 'You've just described yourself. Exactly.'

'Was I like that?'

'You know very well you were.'

'Then I forgive her.'

'But will she forgive you?'

I didn't reply. I was uncomfortably aware of a growing respect for Inspector Poole, and suddenly it mattered whether or not she forgave me.

We got in the car and headed out of the yachting area, north, intending to turn left at the Folgate Inn. I was now, having studied the map so often, becoming more knowledgeable about the district.

A calm, green twilight now lay over the land. The sky was clear and the wind had dropped. The temperature was falling rapidly, and there was a distinct possibility of frosty road surfaces before long. Already, I thought I could just detect a sparkle of our own reflected headlights in the trees, and as we progressed further inland, where the marshes and fens were open and the trees scarce, the stretches of water lay still and waiting, already feeling the approaching touch of ice.

I wondered whether they would still be working at the boatyard. It was only a little after four, and they'd surely carry on with their artificial light in the sheds. Did it matter to me? I decided it might. I would rather talk to Mark in one of the sheds than with his parents present. There was an uneasy feeling that he would not wish them to hear what I expected he would have to say. Or rather, what I intended he should say. This time I was after the truth, and I was recalling that I'd promised Amelia it would finish that night. Promised myself, too.

I took the road from Hickling as Ruston had advised, negotiated the tricky side roads, and eventually spotted the sign for Ruston and Sons. But I didn't want the house, and drove past, locating the muddy yard entrance. The tyres crackled crisply on the hardening surface. Well short of the gate, I left the car. If necessary I would back all the way out. I cut the lights and opened the door.

'Are you going to wait here?' Which would be thoroughly miserable for her.

'I'm staying with you,' she said firmly.

The gates were nearly closed, but had sagged so much on their weary posts that they wouldn't shut entirely. There was a gap of two feet. I stood and listened. The water to our left seemed to sigh and rustle with movement. I wondered whether the wildfowl had to keep moving in order to maintain an ice-free surface, then decided they probably came ashore. Or did they migrate south, looking for food? Nancy would have known.

I became aware of the faint sound of pop music. It seemed to come from one of the sheds further along. We approached it, until we could see the bar of light around the edges of the wicket door.

We went inside. The door creaked. Larry Carter didn't hear it. He had his portable radio on the deck of a motor cruiser, which looked to me to be worth a few thousand. It had a wooden hull, and whatever had happened to it had required the replacement of wooden staves, and eventually a few coats of marine paint. This was what Larry was doing. Painting. He was doing it with a brush and a fine and tender regard for detail, producing a beautiful surface that was destined for heedless scratching and bumping in the summer.

For this he needed full light, and the overhead floods up in the steel rafters were on. I could see now how they got the boats in.

134

The crane lifted them from the water and carried them to the doors, from where they were winched inside on a cradle. A hook in the towing ring, attached to blue nylon rope, stretched tautly to a winch at the far end of the shed. I walked round to the rope and twanged it to attract his attention. It thrummed. He looked up.

'You've got something to tell me?' he asked eagerly.

I shook my head. 'Nothing of interest. Is Mark around?'

His eyes indicated interest. 'You're gonna grill him?'

'Talk to him, that's all.' Larry was too eager. The idea had his approval, but he'd lost interest now.

'He's up at the house. You want to watch your step, there's a grand old row going on there.'

'With his father?'

'Never.' Nobody argued with Malcolm Ruston. 'He's away at Lowestoft, ordering supplies.'

'His mother, then,' I decided, there being no one else.

'I could hear it from here. That's why I put the tranny on.'

Then he returned to his painting. Nothing done here seemed to permit interruption. But he said over his shoulder, 'I left you that picture.'

I nodded my thanks, and we went out into the darkness. After the bright light, this was positively dangerous, with so much cast-off ironware littering the place and the water not all that distant. We stood and waited for our eyes to adjust.

'There's a torch in the car,' she reminded me.

'I'm not sure I could find the car.'

Then I could detect the reflected purple of the sunset on the water, and there was just enough moon to assist our progress along the yard.

We heard them before we reached the steps. Mark and his mother. With a hand on Amelia's arm, I paused.

'We can't intrude,' she whispered.

We didn't need to. Mark's voice rang out, and light appeared at the top of the steps as he opened the kitchen door.

'You always hated the sight of her!' he shouted back.

'What could you expect?' she screamed.

'You signed the bloody papers. You signed for her, damn it.

135

Like a soddin' load of coal. And that's all she ever meant to you. You drove her to it!' he bellowed, and cut off all possible response by slamming the door behind him.

Then, before I could decide if he had now decided Nancy's death had been suicide, and was blaming his mother for it, he was bounding down the steps as though he could see them. This he obviously couldn't, because he was completely unaware of our presence, and would've crashed through between us if I hadn't spoken up quickly.

'Mark! It's Richard Patton.'

He came to a dead halt, breath hissing between his teeth.

'For God's sake! D'you want to give me a heart attack?'

'Sorry. We were coming to see you.'

'Then why not come the proper way, and ring the front door bell?'

'I thought you'd be somewhere in the yard.' Now I could see him dimly. He looked dishevelled and unorganized. 'I wanted a few words with you.'

'Not now.'

He tried to thrust his way through but I caught his arm and held him. 'It's got to be now.'

I felt his weight tense against me, and for a moment it seemed he was going to use violence. In the dark, and with no stance to go by or expression to interpret, I had no way of guessing from which direction it might come. Then he relaxed, and shrugged himself free.

'Keep your blasted hands to yourself.'

'I don't want to have to chase you round the yard, Mark. You're going to have to answer some questions, sometime. Rather me, I'd have thought, than the police Inspector.'

'You're off your bleedin' head, matey. There's nothing to tell you. Now clear off out of these premises. You're on private property.'

Amelia put in: 'We could come again tomorrow, Richard.'

This was a strange concession from her at this time, but she could feel we were very close to violence and she hates the sight of blood.

'And it *is* private property, as he says,' she added.

I realized, then, that she was playing the soft and reasonable

136

part of the duo. In contrast, my persistence would be more effective. I spoke, therefore, angrily.

'It's business property, and he knows it. It's business I've come to discuss with him, and I'm not leaving here until I do.'

Above us the kitchen door opened again. 'Is that you, Mark? Who've you got out there? Answer me.' There was trepidation in her voice. Clearly, Mark was a forceful son to handle.

'Oh Christ!' he said softly. Then he raised his voice. 'It's all right, ma. Visitors.' The door closed with a thump. He turned to me. 'What bloody business?'

'Relating to Nancy and to Olivia Dean.' He has silent. I could feel the silence, the tenseness of it. 'I've been talking to Philip.'

He grunted as though I'd hit him in the belly. Then he growled, 'The office, then. And this'd better be short. Dad'll be back soon.'

This time I allowed him to thrust his way between us. We would need his lead, and follow his bulk against the lighter shadows of the yard.

Fortunately the office was the nearest shed. The smallest, too, though it was constructed, like the worksheds, of steel girders and corrugated iron sheets. The door was wood, and the naked, unvarnished desk surface was wood, but nothing else in there was. Even the two chairs were metal. A single unshaded bulb swung from the roof rafters, apparently set moving by the opening of the door. With an angry gesture, Mark indicated the two chairs, but we declined, Amelia preferring to stand by the door, and I not intending to lose the psychological advantage of my height. I stood in the middle of the floor. Mark sat, almost upright, against the edge of the desk, with an attitude of contemptuous ease.

I looked round. As an office it was a mess. Papers were scattered on the surface of the desk, which was a set of planks roughly nailed to battens and supported on angle-iron legs. A similar but smaller desk against the wall held an unshrouded old Royal typewriter, laden with dust, no letters visible on the keys. There was a metal filing cabinet, a black phone bolted to the metal wall, and a picture facing it of a sea-going motor yacht, which at one time the Rustons might have fitted out. Or even owned.

I returned my attention to Mark. His black and unresponsive expression was no doubt a hangover from his recent dispute with his mother. This put him at a disadvantage. On the reverse side of it, though, was the fact that I would not be able to gauge his response to what I had to say unless I had a clean sheet of expression to start with. He was poised between an attitude of annoyed innocence and wary defence, conscious that he had already committed himself by reacting to my mention of Philip and Olivia. He knew what I intended to talk about. He didn't want it, but he couldn't avoid it.

In an attempt to relax him, I opened quietly.

'You know I'm not a policeman, Mark. I can't give you warnings, and I can't demand answers. All I can do is talk, and you don't have to answer if you don't want to.'

This was as near as dammit to an official warning, but he might not have known that. Because of this, it had emerged in a rather more formal manner than I'd intended. He laughed lightly.

'Then that's all right. We know where we stand. I can tell you to leave. Right?'

'Quite right. Say it calmly and after consideration, and we'll have no choice. We would have to leave.'

Couldn't be fairer than that, I thought. The temptation was there, I could see it fighting away behind his eyes, but already I'd said enough to arouse his curiosity. He waved a hand invitingly.

'Then say what you've got to, and *then* leave.'

I nodded. Amelia leaned back against the door, and sighed.

12

'We met Philip Dean for lunch, Mark,' I began, in the way of introduction. 'I wanted to know more about that time you went to their house, and – '

He interrupted. 'Why?'

'Why. . . what?'

'Why did you want to know more about it?'

'Because I thought it could be related to Nancy's death.'

'Her death was an accident. The coroner said that.'

'All the same – '

'Are you arguing with that – or what?'

He had gone directly on to the attack, and it took me by surprise. It would have taken a long while, and a complex argument, to have explained how I'd come to that conclusion.

'I'm not disputing it, Mark, but there're other things that've happened, and if I put everything together I get the impression she didn't die of any accident.'

'Impression!' He had contempt for such vagaries.

'A reasonable supposition, then.' I took it along with a smile, trying to keep the talk on an amicable basis.

'Didn't die accidentally!' he said, using exactly the same tone as I had. 'What does that mean? If not an accident – what?'

'Not what your remark to your mother suggested.'

'What remark? You've been spying!'

'That your mother had driven her to it.'

'Ha!' He threw back his head, but the bark of mirthless laughter was loaded with contempt. 'Impressions again. It just goes to show how you can get yourself all tied up – '

'Just what was the impression I should have got?' I asked, trying to go on the attack.

'What ma drove her to was that bloody stupid idea of trying to trace her real mother. You knew she was adopted?'

'It's been mentioned.' I inclined my head. His attitude was one of belligerent innocence in what he had in mind. It seemed safe to let him run loose with his ideas, and see what emerged.

'Yes. So it was. So it has been. For as long as I can remember, it was always being mentioned. By ma. Oh. . . she was going to make sure Nancy knew she'd been adopted. No child of my mother – Nancy wasn't – and she'd better get that into her head right from the start. Is it any damned wonder that Nancy got to wondering who her mother really was? I mean – everybody's got a mother. Or so Nancy was always telling me. When she was little, she used to say, "but Mark, you've got a mother, so why haven't I?" I mean, what could anybody say to that?'

He stopped. It had been a genuine question, expecting an answer. But, from Mark as I knew him, it had all been too sentimental, as though he'd scripted it for use when necessary. Now was the necessary time, and his eyes were on me, waiting for my reaction. All I could do was shake my head and offer: 'I can't see any answer to it.'

'Well. . . exactly. I couldn't understand what she was worried about myself. What's the odd mother here and there, anyway?' This was more the real Mark. He looked from one to the other of us, clearly believing this was amusing and would lighten the atmosphere. We stared back stonily, and he shrugged.

'You didn't take her seriously, then?' I asked. 'I mean, young girls are likely to go all sloppy over – '

'Oh, but I did. Don't think. . . oh hell, how can I put it? I'm just fifteen months older that she was. We grew up close. Well, we started our lives at this place, and it's a bit lonely. We were close. Close, see. I didn't understand what was getting at her, but I wasn't going to jeer at her and try to laugh it out of her. If Nancy said it mattered to her, then it did. You get me? I told her she'd got me, so what more did she want? But I didn't measure up, seems to me. I didn't fill her life right up.'

I wondered whether he knew Larry had done that. 'But she

filled yours?' I asked, very quietly, so as not to distract him now that it was coming without any prompting.

His knuckles whitened as he increased his grip on the desk. 'There was dad and the yard, and I grew up with dad's ideas and ambitions, and he taught me all I know. Nancy filled the rest. You could say. Yes, you could say that.'

I heard Amelia stir against the door behind me. I thought she wanted to say something, but she remained silent.

And so did Mark. The impetus seemed to have run from him, perhaps chasing after the truths he could dare to confide. When we'd run out of those, it was going to become more difficult.

'And the time came,' I prompted, 'when she could apply to the authorities to discover the name and address of her mother? I expect that put you to the test.'

'How's that?' he challenged. 'What're you getting at?'

'Your concern for her. She'd always said how much she missed knowing who her real parents were. Now the time had come to find out. What did you think of that?'

'Ah well. . . yes. . . I see. It came as a bit of a shock, I'll tell you that. I thought those things were secret. But there was a new law. It wasn't a secret any longer. What do they care, these high-ups who make the laws? What do they know about people and their lives – and what a thing like that can do! Jesus – there she was, Nancy, nearly dancing with excitement 'cause she'd found out she could do it, and me expected to help her. Me! When I knew it'd all end up in tears. I mean – a complete stranger! You meet her. . . and she's your mother. What can you expect? You've still got your own life to lead. And all that. . . all this upset! It'd be sure to lead to trouble. What else?'

In this, his sentiments closely resembled Larry's, yet whereas Larry had seemed concerned about the effect on Nancy, Mark seemed more concerned about the effect on Mark.

'Yet you *did* help her?'

'Couldn't get out of it.' Now his smile held a shyness I hadn't seen before. 'It was expected of me, if you see what I mean. All her life, old Mark had been there, to help her get anything she wanted. Now she wanted this. I could hardly tell her to do it herself, could I!'

He still had not indicated any understanding of Nancy's

sense of emptiness. Amelia stirred again, but this time she spoke.

'And all this,' she asked, 'was about her mother? Wasn't there any mention of wanting to meet her father?'

'Father?' His eyebrows contracted. 'Well no. Not that I can remember. It was always her mother she missed. You know how it is. It was ma who'd always got at her for being adopted. Dad didn't care a tuppeny cuss about that. So I suppose. . . oh, I ain't much good at this. . . but I suppose Nancy naturally missed her real mother, 'cause dad was as good as any father she'd find.'

'I can understand that,' Amelia murmured.

I wandered over to the picture of the motor launch, casually, deliberately taking my attention from him. At the moment he needed no driving.

'So that when it came to it,' I said easily, 'and Nancy insisted – however much you were against it – that she wanted to do it, you jumped into the breach and helped?'

'Oh, sure. No skin off my nose, I thought. At the time.'

At the tone in that last sentence I turned. 'But later. . . it was?'

'It got tricky.' He rubbed the back of his neck. 'I've got to admit that. But at first it was easy enough. I took her along to see a solicitor, and he got things moving. After a bit, the answer back. The name of her mother. It was Olivia Augusta Martin, at an address in. . . in Buckinghamshire, I think. Yes. That or Wiltshire. Anyway, I took her there in the pick-up, one weekend, and we found the place. It was a doctor's house, and he didn't know a thing about it. Or pretended he didn't. When we told him what it was about, he looked at Nancy and said it might be just as well if she let it drop. She didn't say a word all the way back. It was a miserable day, all round.'

He was frowning at the memory, silent. This account was full of detail, and I thought was true. A practised liar will fill his stories with false detail, aware of the value of background in the creation of verisimilitude. Mark had a rough simplicity and not much imagination, I thought. This had the ring of truth.

'But she didn't let it drop?' I suggested.

'Nor her! Not Nancy. We went to the solicitor again, and I had to lay out a fair amount of money for a private eye. That's what you ought to be, Mr Patton, a private detective. They must make a fortune.'

'Only if they can get results. Go on.'

'He came back with an answer. She was married and called Dean, and lived at a place called Mansfield Park. Not all that far from here. Fancy that – after all those years, and Nancy's mother'd been so close!'

'So of course, you had to take her there.'

'Had to. But by that time. . . it'd all been a bit of a strain, for Nancy, you see. . . by that time she was in a fine mess of nerves. And things weren't so easy for me, I can tell you, shoved into doing things, and then told not to, then pushed again. And in the end finding I was doing the whole thing for her. I hadn't bargained for that. You can bet your life on that.'

'But surely, Mark,' Amelia said, 'you ought to have expected it.'

'How so? How so?'

'There'd been no mention of her father on the papers – I gathered that from what you said. So Nancy already knew she was illegitimate, and there'd be no chance of tracing him. So her mother was her last chance. Of *course* she'd be all nerves. I'd have been myself.'

'Well yeah. Yeah, I suppose.' He swept both hands over his hair. 'If you say so.'

'So this would be *it*,' she went on. 'Her one chance. All or nothing.'

I thought she was piling it on a little, but I didn't say anything.

'I suppose you're right,' Mark agreed. 'Whatever the reason, we found the place and she got me to stop in the lane. We could see the place – and you could tell there was money around. That seemed to put her off even more. "Oh Mark, I can't! Just can't!" You never heard such a stupid lot of fuss. After all the trouble we'd taken – that I'd taken – then she couldn't face it. I nearly lost my temper with her, and that's a fact. Nothing to it, I said, you just go there and ring the bell. And she came straight back at me. "Then you do it, Mark. I can always go later, if it's all right." Did you ever hear such a stupid idea?'

143

He looked round, staring at me in appeal. He meant it as a question, and addressed it to a fellow male, as most likely to understand what he meant.

I obliged. 'You'd brought it on yourself, lad. You'd made yourself indispensable to her. I reckon you like that part of it – well, this was the pay-off. And I suppose you agreed?' I knew he had.

It was at this point that he showed reluctance. Up until now it had flowed freely. What he had had to relate had reflected on him kindly, on the whole. He had done what he could for Nancy. There had been no self-justification to put over. In fact, he had spoken with an underlying pride. Now he didn't want to go on. I had mentioned having spoken to Philip, and it was possible that no pride in his performance in that house was possible for Mark. Here, he would have to work harder to maintain our sympathy.

'I didn't have much chance but to agree,' he said moodily. 'Of course I had to do it. I wasn't going to sit there all day arguing. So I walked up to the house and a man answered the door. Yes, it was Philip. I thought he was insane at first. He seemed to think I was up to something. . . something nasty. Tried to throw me out, he did. I wasn't having that, I can tell you. How was I to know she was a famous author? He didn't say. He just assumed I'd dug up some damned murky secret or other, and was on the make. Anyway, I reckon we made a bit of noise. She'd been in the place where she does her work, and she came out. "How can I do a stroke with all this noise, Philip?" And: "Who *is* this, anyway?" And that was where it all went wrong.'

Mentally, I had to agree with him. Everything went along with what I'd heard of Nancy – by way of Larry – and from Philip. Until Olivia came through that door. Mark wasn't proceeding with his narrative, was standing there, having levered himself away from the table, with his face shadowed deeply by concern and uncertainty.

'And she went into hysteria?' I asked.

He hesitated a long while. But he had to assume, from what I'd just said, that I already knew it, and this was his chance to present his own point of view, unsullied by other tongues.

'You could call it hysteria, I suppose,' he agreed ruefully.

144

'She went into something, but I ain't so good at words. I can remember it in detail, though. I'll never forget it. Every blasted detail.'

I glanced at Amelia. She had felt it too. There had been a change in his voice.

'Every detail,' I prompted.

'The way the light was slanting into that hall, the sun across her feet, and how it kind of walked up to her face as she came towards me. And what she said.Every word. First of all: 'But it can't be. . .' Just that. Kind of sucking her breath in. Then she got a bit closer. The sun was cutting her off at the waist, I remember. Then: 'Oh my God, no. . . it is! Say it is!' It was all nonsense to me, but she was closing in on me fast and I couldn't do anything but stand there like a fool, and she just flung her arms round me and kissed me, and then held me away with her hands on my shoulders, and her face was all kind of crinkled up and swollen at the same time, and even through the tears I could recognize Nancy in her eyes and her mouth, and she said: 'Oh, my dear son, you're the image of your father.' And that. . . that's what happened,' he finished weakly. His story, having flowed like a racing stream, had spent itself in calm and murky shallows.

Amelia took in a great gulp of air, as though she'd been holding her breath. The sound she made was close to a sob. Still trying to absorb it and its implications, I was at a loss as to what to say. Yet Mark could not have invented this, and there was a certain validity to Olivia's reaction, as described. As a professional writer, she would have had to keep in touch with any legal change that might offer her a new twist in her fiction. As such a situation would. So, perhaps subconsciously, she could have been prepared for some such approach. Prepared or not, the outpourings of suppressed emotion would have been more than the stolid Mark could handle. It had undermined him. In the telling, he seemed to have become bashful and uneasy.

'It would,' I suggested, 'have been very difficult to come out with the truth.' I offered this to encourage him.

'I couldn't come out with anything,' he admitted miserably.

'But surely you tried. That was the time – '

145

'What the hell d'you think I am!' he burst out. 'Ain't you got any imagination! How'd you like to stare into that face, and say: "It's not true, I'm not your son." Could you do it?'

'All the same – '

'Richard!' Amelia cut in. 'Be sensible. There was the other thing. Isn't that so, Mark?'

He turned to her, giving her a brief flick of a smile. I looked round from one face to the other, struggling to understand. 'The other. . .'

Mark stabbed at my shoulder with his hard finger. 'Don't you see!' he shouted, his voice nearly breaking. 'In that second she told me my father was also Nancy's father.'

'Of course. I understood that. But you need only have said – '

'Said! Said!' he cried, waving his arms. 'I'd walked in there, just to get things off to some sort of a start, lay things on, then get out quick. And *that* was thrown at me. I was dumb, you stupid clown. Numb. My mind was whirling away. . . it was as though everything had gone flying off in all directions. It'd chopped the legs right from under me.'

I couldn't deny his sincerity. It shone from him, from every line of his earnest and strained expression. But surely he was indulging himself in too violent a stream of emotion to fit the circumstances involved. I turned to Amelia for guidance.

She was shaking her head at me in sorrow for my stupidity.

'Richard, you dear man, it's so obvious. Mark as good as said it. The fact is that Olivia had projected herself straight into the middle of just the sort of emotional conflict that she uses in her books. It'd be amusing if it wasn't so tragic. She spends her working life coldly and practically, creating and exploiting these set-ups, and when one of them enters her own life it completely breaks her up. And poor Mark! She could hardly have understood – any more than you do – what it meant to Mark.'

I stared at poor Mark, and he read me accurately.

'Don't you see! You're too bloody stupid for words. We grew up together. Me an' Nancy. Close. And we both knew she was adopted. I told you how close we were, damn it. And it wasn't simply brother and sister. Of course not, 'cause she wasn't my sister. But I heard the other kids at school, talking about *their*

146

sisters. Nobody could be uglier and less wanted than a chap's sister, and anybody who fancied them must be mad. I didn't understand that. But Nancy was adopted, and that made the difference. It was all right if it wasn't a blood relationship. You know. And I wanted her. Oh, make no mistake, nothing was ever said. I thought it was kind of accepted. We'd getting married. *That* was what I thought – assumed. No word or gesture. I liked it like that. An understanding. Because she was adopted. And then, this woman. . . this Olivia Dean, she was telling me that Nancy was my own father's girl! It meant we *were* blood relations – and everything was snatched away from me. That was what hit me between the eyes. That was what I was struggling to take in and understand, when you say I ought've spoken out. Spoken! When I was near choking, and she thought it was because it was the same feeling as hers, and crying and weeping and saying where have you been hiding yourself and telling me that oh we'd got so much to catch up with. What the bloody hell d'you think I am?'

What I thought was that he was a frightened and disturbed young man, who had seen the chance to reveal his actions in all their long-suffering glory. He was sincere in that he genuinely felt this, that he'd martyred himself to Olivia's sentimental obsessions. We were the outlet for the self-justification he'd been feeding himself for. . . how long? For well over a year. As I was wondering how to go on, because this wasn't an end to what he had to tell by a long way, Amelia again rescued me.

'But Mark,' she said gently, sorrow for him hampering her voice, 'you were wrong in any event.' And because he did no more than stare at her, she continued, 'You couldn't have married your adopted sister, anyway. I know it's not in the religious list, but it's a social thing. It is not allowed.'

'Don't I know it!' he flung at her. 'Don't I know it *now*! I found out. I went and saw a solicitor, and he looked it up. Showed me in a legal book. But I didn't know *then*.' His voice eased from its pitch of intensity. 'Probably Nancy always knew it. Maybe she never gave it a thought, and never thought much of me, in any event. I was just a brother to her.'

He stared at us defiantly. He'd risked a criticism of Nancy.

147

'But you allowed it to go on,' I pointed out. 'And you lied to Nancy.'

He answered as to a mentally retarded child, using heavy precision.

'At *that* time I hadn't found out. I assumed *she* thought we could marry. I thought it'd be as big a shock to her as it'd been to me. I had to have time to *think*, damn it.'

His motivations were clear, but in no way satisfactory. He had continued to deceive Nancy. Didn't he realize what he'd done to her?

'You were at the house for an hour,' I reminded him.

He sagged. The critical point had been passed. 'Yeah. Couldn't get away. You can imagine. All my life to go through, and how we were going to catch up with what we'd missed. I was caught, making promises that were all tying me up in knots.'

'What sort of promises?'

He stared at me as though I was a stranger. So far, it had burst from him like seeds from a dried husk, but his internal drive had now cooled. He spoke with renewed, but forced, anger.

'What's it to you? I ain't sayin' another word.'

'It's all the same to me, Mark. I can work it all out from here.'

'Work what out?'

'How you tricked Nancy –'

'Tricked nothing! I hadn't got any choice.'

'It seems to me you had. But of course. . .' I gestured dismissal, and half turned away, 'if that's the way you want to leave it.'

'If you only knew.'

'I would if you told me.'

He wiped his hand over his craggy face, smoothing out the exasperation. 'There isn't much more. She was all over me, Olivia was. When could she see me again, and all that. Oh – such wonderful plans. There was even – and I could see it coming – even the idea that I'd go and live there.'

'That which was lost and is found,' I said softly.

'What? Oh yeah. That sort of thing,' he agreed.

'And Philip?' I asked. 'What was he doing while all this was going on?'

148

'Oh. . . him. Sitting there. We were in their lounge by that time. He was just sitting, like a ghost at a wedding, saying nothing. Not a damn word. And. . . well, the way it ended was that I had to promise to meet her again, away from there because Philip was giving me the gripes, and I had just two minutes to think what to say to Nancy, on the walk back to the pick-up.'

'So you stalled? Anything so that you wouldn't have to tell Nancy the truth.'

'What else could I do? I told her Olivia had had hysterics, which was as near true as dammit, and didn't want to see her, which *was* true, and I thought that'd give me time to sort something out later.'

'But you never managed to?'

'I tried. You don't know how I tried! My mind got tangled up with all the ways I could do it. Dad thought I'd gone funny. I couldn't concentrate on anything, and made a right balls-up of everything I touched. And Nancy went quiet about it. Didn't say another word. I thought that let me off the hook a bit, and there was only the other end of it to worry about.'

'The other end being Olivia?'

'*That* got worse. She was. . . well, she kind of took over. I had the idea, when I met her – it was in Great Yarmouth that first time – I thought then that she'd have got over it, somehow. You know, might've looked at it all calm-like, and I'd be able to tell her the truth. Lord. . . how wrong I was! It was worse. I was her little boy. Yes. Little boy. You can laugh if you like. She wanted to gobble me up, like one of those sticky cakes we were eating. Looking at her, leaning forward over that café table, I remember thinking: how was I going to get her home if I told her the truth. She'd fall apart. It's a fact. She was all sentiment, and couldn't stop touching me. Enough to make you sick.'

'You were certainly in a fix,' I agreed.

'And it went on and on from there. . .' He was wearied of it, of the remembrance and the telling. His mouth sagged.

'When was all this? I mean, fifteen, sixteen months ago?'

'Sure to be. I remember we met – every damn week and maybe more often – met all through the summer. The summer before the one we've just had.'

I nodded. It would have to have been. 'And Nancy? Nothing more about it from her?'

'She'd decided to go to college. Somewhere different, she said.'

'Birmingham is different.'

'It took a bit of a load off me.'

'Her going?'

'She started in the September. More'n a year ago. Then it got worse for me. I mean. . .' He waved his hand around to encompass the tatty office. 'All this. Nancy'd done it all, and I had to take over. It's been bloody hell. I'm no clerk.'

'I can see that.' I waited, but he seemed to think he'd finished. 'And the other business – Olivia – that progressed?'

He was sullen. I'd made it sound as though any progression might have had his assistance.

'I think you'd better leave,' he told me, no force in it.

'Now?'

'I don't want to talk any more about Olivia.'

I glanced at Amelia for guidance. She took it up, seeming to understand him better than I did. 'But Mark, Olivia is my friend. All three of us, four counting Philip – your father, Olivia, me – we were friends. How can I meet her and talk to her, if I don't know what to say? What not to say, really. You must help me in this.'

'I haven't seen her for ages. Since. . . well, since Nancy died.'

'You make it sound as though it was a great relief,' Amelia said, smiling him on.

'Yeah. Well, it was. Sort of. Though I was getting used to the idea by that time.'

'What idea?' I asked, feeling he was about to dry up.

'You've only got to use your head. Nancy'd gone quiet, as I said, but she didn't drop it altogether. Not Nancy. So I was all poised, waiting for the top to blow off. Every time I met Olivia, I didn't know what to expect. But it was always more of the same, only getting worse.'

'Don't you mean better?'

He moved closer to me. I could see the sweat on his upper lip, and his brows were drawn together. 'I mean worse. For me.

I was her little boy – didn't I tell you that! There was nothing she wouldn't do. Presents all the time, that I had to hide. And from wanting me to go and live there she switched to another tack. I nearly went mad, trying to stall that off.'

'Something interesting?'

'She'd heard from me all about the yard, and all about dad's wild dreams of expanding. She offered to finance it. Now how the hell could I cover up a thing like that? She said she'd give me the money. I didn't want the damned money. That really worried me. She seemed to think dad knew all about it – about us. I mean, where were we going to get it? She said she'd give me this money in bits, if that was how I wanted it. Wanted it! I didn't bloody want it. She said I could fake the accounts, pretending it was profits.'

I laughed easily, dismissing it as farcical. 'Like an inverted fraud?' But the laugh didn't take my eyes from his face.

'Like that. But how *could* I, when Nancy was doing the accounts at that time? This was *her* office. So I had to tell Olivia I'd got a sister, and that really got the hair prickling on my neck, but she didn't react. I was weeks persuading her it wouldn't work. She was almost in tears, because she couldn't do more for me. And gradually she was taking me over. Beginning to be a bit bossy. Momma's little boy, for Chrissake! I don't think she was right in the head.'

He stared blindly at the picture of the motor cruiser.

'But in the end,' I told him, in a tone indicating I didn't think he knew, 'Nancy *did* contact her. By letter.' I thought he hardly needed to know how Philip had intercepted the letter. 'Did she tell you about that?'

He didn't turn to face me, and answered in a jumbled mutter.

'Pardon. I didn't hear that.'

He raised his voice. 'She phoned me. From her college. Yes, she said she'd done that. I knew it was all over, then.'

'She phoned, and she said she'd got an appointment?'

At last he turned. 'Yes.'

'Did she say where and when?'

'Not exactly. It was kind of a hint. She told me she might see me at Potter Heigham, on the Saturday.'

'Which Saturday?'

'The Wildlife collection Saturday. She knew I was doing that pitch, round the bridge area. And I guessed she'd fixed this appointment somewhere in the area.' He stared from one to the other of us. 'To see me,' he explained impatiently. 'When it was over.'

But if she'd kept the appointment, would she still have wanted to meet Mark? 'Of course,' I agreed equably. 'She'd see you around, collecting.'

His face was crumpled, his eyes blurred. 'It was the day she died.'

'Was it? The police don't seem so accurate.'

'Well, it must've been.' He was impatient. 'It was the day she went there.'

'Do you know for certain she went there on that Saturday? Did you see her?'

He shook his head violently, his hair falling all over his face. 'I don't know anything. I didn't see her. She wouldn't tell me anything. She said I'd tried it once, and now it was her turn. I didn't see her. I wanted to get to her first, if I could, to kind of prepare her. Oh Lord. . . I don't know. Maybe I'd have told her the lot, if I'd had the chance. But *she* had to turn up.'

'Which she?'

'Olivia! Olivia, damn you. Who the hell d'you think I mean? She insisted on having lunch, and then she gave me a tenner and bought most of the stickers I'd got, so that I wouldn't lose from the loss of time.' He groaned. It was forced out of him, from way down inside. 'And so I didn't see Nancy at all.'

'And she, Olivia, didn't mention an appointment?'

'She just said she had something to attend to.'

I glanced at Amelia who was looking pale and drawn. She reached for the door, but I shook my head. She made a gesture of despair. I turned back to Mark. He spoke as I turned, as though he'd been waiting for the chance to add something.

'It was the last time I saw her.' His voice was hollow.

'Olivia didn't arrange another meeting? Didn't contact you?'

He stared, looking desperate. 'No. No, she didn't. I assumed she was leaving it to me.'

'Didn't even send you something like this?' I asked.

I reached inside my jacket and produced the yellow photo packet. I held it out. He stared at it.

'Go on,' I said. 'Take it. Look inside.'

His eyes lifted from it to my face, down again, then he wiped a hand down his trousers and reached for it warily. He opened it, and drew out the two photographs. I noticed they were shaking in his fingers.

For a long while he stared at them, then suddenly he thrust them back at me. 'I don't. . .'

'You know what these are?'

'It's Nancy, isn't it? I don't want to look at them. Nancy dead.'

'But you've seen them before. Or copies of them.'

'No,' he whispered. He lifted his head. 'No!' he shouted.

'Then why did you pay a man called Harvey Cole to steal these for you?'

'It's a lie. I don't know him.'

'He lives near Happisburgh.'

'I've never heard of him. Where is he? I'll stuff these down his bleedin' throat.'

'He's gone abroad.'

'Y' see. Where he's safe. I don't know what you're talking about. Now get out of this office. I've had enough. Sod off. Both of you.'

I heard Amelia make a choking protest, and I flashed her a look of restraint. She had felt it safer to sit down. She was now staring at me appealingly, but I couldn't leave it now. In a second I was facing Mark again, and was trying to take advantage of his anger.

'You're lying, and you know you're lying. When I go to the police, they'll know you're lying.'

'No. Please.' The anger sagged from him.

'Somebody sent you the copies of these. It was some sort of a threat.'

'Oh, Jesus, no. It. . . it was a promise. A promise that was a threat, as well, if you want. But it was all crazy. She'd got it all wrong.'

'Who had? In what way?'

He put a hand over his mouth for a moment, restraining his

153

anxious tongue, then he went on quietly. 'Nancy died. We didn't know she'd died, not till a week later. The police said about a week. I didn't know where I was or what to think. Then. . . *those*. . .' He pointed. 'Copies of 'em, anyway, they arrived. No note, no anything. But I knew. It was her. Olivia. Just like her. I didn't know what it meant. Really I didn't, Mr Patton. Then I saw the difference between the two.'

'The yellow charity sticker?'

'That's it. Yes. Then I knew. She'd found the body, come across it – oh hell, for all I know she might've guessed Nancy was dead, if she didn't turn up for that appointment. But however she did it, she'd found Nancy's body, and she believed – thought – God, what fantasies that woman used to fling around! She must've thought I'd done it, though where she got that idea I can't imagine. And those pictures, they were saying to me that she knew, and forgave me! *Forgave*, for all that's holy! They were meant to tell me I was a naughty boy, and I mustn't do it again, and mommy knows, but look what I did for you, you little terror! I've given you an alibi with the yellow sticker. I've made it look as though she died on the Saturday. And who can give you an alibi for that Saturday, you darling boy? Who but your adoring mommy? That was what she was telling me, for pity's sake, and if I wasn't a good boy. . . Haven't I said enough yet? She'd got me. Trapped. She'd gone clean bonkers. I was going to have to behave, and that meant going along with her stupid fantasy that I was a little boy who'd got to be. . .' He thrust his fingers through his hair and turned away. Then he whirled on me, furious with me because I'd listened to him.

'And if you so much as smile, Mr Clever Patton, I'll wipe it right off your face.'

I didn't feel like smiling. I gave it a few seconds, then I spoke evenly, so as not to disturb too much. 'And you thought all that, just from the sight of two pictures?'

'You don't know her, mate!' He glared at me with flat contempt.

'And since then?' I asked wearily.

'I'd had enough. I couldn't even face her again. It went. . . oh, months went by. She was waiting for me to make a move. But I was nervous, and I reckoned. . . if she had copies and I

154

could get hold of 'em, then she couldn't touch me. I had to have a bit of peace. It was pounding through my head every minute of the day. Somebody in a pub put me on to Harvey Cole.' He gestured to the envelope still in my hand. 'The rotten bastard cheated me, letting you have 'em. So help me, I'll kill him if he ever comes back.'

For a long while I stared at him. He looked as though he'd kill me if I didn't go away. I turned to Amelia.

'Let's get out of here, shall we?'

She had a handkerchief to her lips. She nodded. I opened the door for her and we went out into the cold, crisp night. The moon was well up now. We could see our way. We didn't pause to say goodbye to Larry.

13

The windows misted up as soon as we got inside the car. I started the engine and put on the blower and the rear de-mister, and too impatient to get away from there I backed up the lane, more by instinct than ability, and out on to the road. Then I headed for our hotel.

It was a long while before Amelia ventured a word. Then it was tentatively.

'Did you believe him, Richard?'

I wondered how to put it. It could have extended itself into a lecture: liars I have known.

'I think it was mostly true. It's a basic principle – tell the exact truth when it doesn't hurt, then slip in the odd bit that's a lie. But I think he stuck pretty rigidly to the truth, because he had complete control of himself and his emotions. The fact that Harvey had tricked him by selling me the pictures, that tripped him up. He'd have strangled Harvey there and then. But for the rest. . .'

I shrugged.

'Then what *do* you think?' she asked quietly.

'That bit about thinking he might marry Nancy, and being so shocked when he heard his own father was also Nancy's – that was nonsense. They'd been brought up as brother and sister, and that's how he'd think of her. No, that was a cover-up, to make sense of why he didn't explain the situation of as soon as he realized Olivia's mistake.'

'Hmm!' she said doubtfully.

'You don't accept that?

'We can't speculate about Mark's feelings for Nancy.'

'No. Perhaps not. But you can see the truth in Malcolm

156

Ruston being Nancy's father. He arranged the adoption before the birth, knowing he was the father. Olivia, career woman even then I'd guess, didn't want to be lumbered with a child, and poor Angie, who's probably known Malcolm since they were toddlers, and in love with him, had to live with the fact that he'd fathered an illegitimate child, and thought she might lose him if she refused to adopt the baby.'

'The terrible things people do to each other!' She thumped my knee. 'Yes, that could be true.'

'And that would explain Angie's attitude to Nancy.'

'Nancy didn't stand a chance, poor child.'

'Oh yes she did. It might have made her nervous of facing people and angering them, but it toughened her up. She'd have gone far.'

'Why must you keep talking about her like that?'

'Not to upset you, my dear. But Nancy's in the centre of it. I think that Mark, once he'd got over the shock of being welcomed as Olivia's son, did some quick thinking and realized he was on to a good thing. There, he could see a lot of money around, and what he needed, craved for, was money. He's got his father's ambitions. He decided to carry on with the deception, and see what happened. All he'd have to do was keep Nancy well clear of Olivia. And he knew how to convince her, and what to tell her that would do the trick.'

'Tell her she wasn't wanted?'

'As simple as that.'

'But that would be vicious,' she said disgustedly.

'Wouldn't it! But it left him clear to carry on with the deception of Olivia, and I'm quite convinced it went just as he's described it. Olivia has always been emotional. You said that. And she writes books packed with strong emotions. That could have been a natural choice. But it would've broken her up if she'd let herself become too involved, and she'd soon realize that. So I'd say she set out to control her emotions when she was writing. Got a firm grip on them, and made it all a technique. But you can't just change personalities by walking from one room to the other, and the one invaded the other, and Philip couldn't help her there, from what I've seen of him.'

'He's a dear, sweet man, but he wouldn't even realize there

157

was any help required. I can see what you're getting at, Richard. It's my thinking entirely. Olivia got so that she didn't know any more who she was, Olivia or Christobel or Lovella. And all the genuine emotion was locked away, just waiting for a chance to break out and flood all over somebody. It'd be typical of her. Then into that situation sailed Mark. Oh, he was quite correct there. She'd flow all over him like a tide.'

'I don't know who to be most sorry for,' I admitted.

'Don't waste any on Mark. I agree with you. He pounced on it and couldn't do enough to encourage her. He didn't mind playing the part of mother's darling boy, and I don't care what he says. He's so transparent. He said she gave him presents – oh, I can believe that. It's just what she'd do. But I'd certainly like to see some of those. He hid them away, he said. I bet he had a job persuading himself not to accept a nice car or a racing yacht he could drool over. She can probably afford that sort of thing. But he'd accept something like a Rolex chronometer. Water resistant. I can imagine what pleasure that'd give her. She's very generous. A diamond tie-pin or a gold-plated shaving set. You name it. But I'm sure he played up to her, and all the while it was leading up to some method he could use to feed money into the boatyard in an acceptable way to his father.' She nodded to herself. That was it in a nutshell.

I grunted, picking it up. 'Then Nancy went to college, and that left Mark in charge of the office, and even when she got her degree he knew very well Nancy wouldn't be coming back to it. It'd leave everything wide open for a neat bit of exploitation.'

'And isn't that a fine thing to contemplate!' She turned in her seat, anger in her voice. 'You can just imagine him agreeing – reluctantly, mind you – to allow Olivia to give him money. Perhaps that was started. But then, after nearly a year, when Mark must've thought he was in the clear, Nancy tossed a spanner in the whole scheme. She told him she'd written to Olivia.' And, satisfied with this version of it, she twisted back and stared bleakly through the windscreen.

I wasn't so certain he was as black as she'd painted him, but I didn't say so. I could feel the patches of the ice under the tyres, the abrupt changes in the feel through the steering wheel. But I was in a hurry, and pushed the car to the limits of its adhesion.

'And we know Philip intercepted that,' she reminded me, because I hadn't answered.

'But Mark didn't know that.' I corrected a slide. 'At that stage, Nancy had become a distinct menace. If she met Olivia and the truth came out, not only would his scheme fail but there'd be all hell breaking out around him. So he reckoned he had to do something. He stationed himself with his collecting box at the bridge at Potter Heigham – and who turned up but Olivia! From her attitude he'd know she hadn't yet met Nancy, and after lunch she said she had something to attend to. Maybe she had, but it wasn't the business Mark thought it was. All the same, his last chance was to stay at the bridge and hope to intercept Nancy.'

I was saying this to myself, really, to persuade me of its validity. But I was worried about Mark's attitude at our recent meeting. I would have expected him to resist my questions, to wriggle and fight and oppose me all the way through. But he'd told us his story without too much pressure. It could have been that he realized I already knew too much, and only his eager self-justification could rescue him from doubt. If so, he'd been much subtle than I'd have expected. He'd handed it to me on a plate.

We were nearing the coast now. Ahead, I could see the wink of the Cromer lighthouse, once every fifteen seconds.

'So you think he managed to intercept her?' she asked.

'It seems certain. If he did, she'd be completely unsuspecting, and if he asked her to walk along the river path and talk it over, she wouldn't raise any objection, always supposing she was early for her appointment with Philip. And if he got her to that boat-hire basin, and if it was deserted at that time. . . he'd only need to push her in and walk away.'

'How you can say that!' she burst out. 'As though Nancy was a block of wood.'

I'd been trying to get across the enormity of what had been done, and equate it with what we knew of Mark. 'Policemen are like Olivia with her writing, my dear. We just couldn't do the job unless we looked at it with detachment.'

'You're not a policeman now.'

'It's beginning to wear off. You're a better tonic than Philip.'

'Even *that* you say without feeling.'

'I need both hands on the wheel. Bring it up again later.'

'I will,' she promised. Or threatened.

Then there seemed no way to get back to the subject of Nancy, until I forced my mind into behaving.

'What happened next has to be a wild guess,' I said, breaking the silence. 'We don't know how Olivia came to find the body. In fact, we don't know why she looked for it. And when she found it, I can see no reason why she would suspect Mark – '

'No, no, Richard,' she cut in positively. 'It couldn't possibly have been Olivia. You're forgetting, she didn't know Nancy was going to be there that Saturday. Heavens, Mark only ever made one mention of her to Olivia. As far as she was concerned, Nancy didn't exist.'

I lost it in a wild skid on an icy corner, spun twice, and ended up facing the wrong way. Amelia exclaimed violently, but I had my own cursing to do. She had, in those few words, destroyed my whole chain of reasoning, and my stab at the brake pedal had been a reaction of self-annoyance.

I edged the car round and started again, more slowly.

'It was Philip who knew Nancy was going to be there,' she said, after she'd recovered her composure.

'Yes.' Philip?

'It was Philip who was the photographer in their partnership, after all. Look at it now, and it seems obvious that Philip must've been the one who took the photos.'

'Obvious?' I risked a glance at her. 'Let's not do too much assuming.'

'You're always doing it.'

I nodded. That was only too true. 'Look at it like this – '

'It was *my* idea, Richard,'

'Then you look at it.'

I concentrated on the road as she did her bit of looking, and then she admitted: 'All right. Be fair. It might still have been Olivia who took the photos. Philip's the photographer – he said that – but I bet he's got more than one camera, and she could easily have borrowed one. . .'

'And borrowed the boat? Philip's little boat with the outboard motor, Amelia.'

'I didn't know he had one.'

'I must've forgotten to tell you. Sorry. But Olivia would be able to handle it as well as Philip, I've no doubt. She used to get away from her concerns for hours at a time. Why not on the waterways? What better way of easing the tension?'

'You make a good case, I'll say that for you, Richard.'

'Thank you.'

'The difficulty's in deciding what case it is. Are you now saying that Olivia or Philip took the photos?'

'Either. It doesn't really matter, as it's turned out.'

I drew to a halt on the road outside the hotel, and edged my door open a couple of inches to put on the interior light. I wanted to watch her face.

'Doesn't matter?'

'Mark assumed the two photos had been sent to him by Olivia, as a warning and as a kind of trap. A lure, say. But if Philip sent them, they were intended as a definite threat. Mark's assumption might have been wrong, but the same result has been achieved. It's kept Mark away from Olivia. Olivia wouldn't have wanted that, which seems to me to show that the meetings were more at Mark's initiative than hers, which is not what he implied. But Philip most definitely did want it. He couldn't face any more. Mark was invading their lives.'

'That's true enough. Why have you stopped out here?'

'For a quick getaway.' I smiled at her, a little bleakly I must admit. 'You did say you couldn't stand the idea of staying another night.'

'But we can't leave it now. We're so close.'

'Close to what? Think about it. Where are we heading? Huh?'

Still arguing, we entered the lobby. The clock over the desk indicated it was close to the time for the bar to close. There was, as usual, nobody on the desk.

'And Richard. . . have you thought of this – we don't *know* Nancy looked like her mother.'

'Umm?' I was looking round for the manager.

She tugged at my sleeve. 'We've assumed Mark went really desperate when he thought Nancy was shortly going to meet

161

her mother. He didn't dare to allow it. Why not? Because Olivia would take one look, and at once recognize her own daughter! That's what we believe. Is it not?'

'It is.' I tinged the bell, with no result. 'Nancy wouldn't have had to prove anything.'

'But we don't know what she looked like. If she looked like – well, a female Mark, then Olivia would've just assumed she was Mark's sister, and probably sent her packing, whatever Nancy said.'

I stared at her. She said: 'You didn't leave the room key, if that's what you're after. It's in your pocket.'

My mind was jumping about. We didn't know what Nancy looked like! How many other people hadn't known that?

'Yes, here it is. There's something in our cubby-hole, though.'

'Then go round and get it.'

I did that. It was a manila envelope, unsealed. Written on the outside was: 'Mr & Mrs Patton.' I recalled that Larry had said he'd left us a photo. I returned to her side and slid out the contents.

We were looking at a 6×4 colour print of a young woman seated in the stern of a sailing dinghy. It was heeling in the wind, and she had flung herself back against the angle, the wind streaming her hair in the sunlight, laughing with white, perfect teeth, her eyes dancing, and with all the joy of living shining from every line and every element of her existence. It was a perfect photograph for a magazine. This must surely have been Larry's finest achievement.

Amelia had been holding her breath. She released it on a sigh.

'Richard. . . it's her. To the life. Olivia as she was, twenty years ago, with her whole life before her, and every bit exciting. Oh. . . Nancy, Nancy. . .'

'There's your answer,' I said quietly.

We went up to our room. I threw our empty suitcases on to the bed.

'You're determined on leaving, then?' she asked quietly.

'Call it running away, if you like. Will you start the packing, while I go and dig the manager out and settle our account?'

'Running away from what? It's not like you, Richard.'

I sat down on the edge of the bed and ran my fingers through my hair. 'Amelia. . . my dear. . . it's not as though I'm still in the police. In that case I'd have to carry it through. I'd have to get statements and make a charge. And I'd have a backing of legal experts I could send it all to, in a great thick file, and they would say if there was a case they could put before a court. I was just a cog in the machine. The rest was the law and the judge and the jury. But what have we got now? We've talked to people, and we've put two and two together, and that could make four or twenty-two. But we know Mark killed Nancy. So what can we do about it? There's absolutely nothing but conjecture, nothing we can hold up and say: because of this, no one else could've done it, and because of that, only Mark could've done it.'

'Let Melanie have it all.'

'Have what? My statement? Your statement? They'd mean nothing. Would Larry or Mark, or Philip or Olivia repeat to the police what they've told us? No. They would've had time to think about it. The only thing physical I can produce is the photographs. And Melanie's already indicated they mean nothing. Even what they mean to us we've differed about. And you've got to agree, the photos mean nothing tight, not definite, not positive.'

She was staring at me with a frown, searching my face. 'But we can't just *go*,' she protested. 'There's this terrible thing hanging over Olivia. We can't leave without an explanation. I'm her friend, Richard. You can't get round that. I ought to stand by that. I *want* to be with her. She couldn't stand the truth, not alone, and Philip would be useless. We've got to stay, Richard. Oh yes, I know I said I wanted to leave. I can change my mind, can't I!' And she attempted a weak little smile.

I could barely force myself to look into her eyes, afraid of what my own would reveal. Every element of my dormant police officer's instinct demanded that I should go on. I'd spoken of the lack of proof. Very well then. That only meant I had to search until I had it. Otherwise Mark would go free. She offered me the chance to do this, but I couldn't hurt her by accepting.

'And what explanation would you like me to give Olivia?' I asked. 'Would you care to stand by her, supporting her, while

I tell her that the young man she thought was her son was in fact not, and that she'd made a complete fool of herself? She'd need your support then, sure enough. And I'd have to go on and explain how Nancy became a threat to the relationship between herself and Mark, so that he had to kill her. Oh yes, she'd need your support. And I'd have to tell Olivia exactly why Nancy was a threat, because Nancy was her daughter, her real child. By heaven, you'd have your work cut out for you by then, my love. And to prove it, I'd have to produce the picture of Nancy alive. Very much alive. Damn it all, it'd break her up completely.'

'Oh dear Lord – it wouldn't come to that!'

'It's how it would be. And all through this I'd be her attacker, you the defender. That's how it would seem to her. Would you want that? Huh?'

She looked away, drawing in her lower lip. Then she turned back.

'You're stopping me from going to her. . .'

I shook my head. 'No. I'm stopping myself from going to her. Our hands are tied.'

'So we simply go away and let Mark get away with it!'

I sighed. 'What do I do? Go and beat it out of him? Force him into putting it in writing? If *anything* I did resulted in his arrest, it couldn't help but add suffering to what's already happened. How could Olivia be kept out of it? Ask yourself.'

She looked round the room miserably. 'But he should pay for it. He should!'

'Judge, jury, prosecutor. And hangman, too? That's me.'

'You exaggerate everything out of all proportion, Richard.'

'I'm trying to be realistic.'

Trying, too, to speak in a calm and reasonable voice, when inside I was raging to do all that Amelia asked: to see that Mark paid for it. But at what cost? I had to keep asking myself that. At what cost, too, to us?

She was looking at me as though I was a stranger. 'Of course, you're right. I can see that. Only. . . oh, very well, I'll start the packing. You go and settle things. Everything's sure to look worse in the morning.'

I left her to her tears of frustration, which I saw were close. The bar was closed, so I found the manager in the lobby. He

164

clearly thought it was a strange time to leave, but we settled matters, and I told him I'd leave a letter on the desk when we left, along with our key.

When I got back to our room Amelia had recovered her composure, and said she would share the driving. It was something she'd be able to put her mind to. I didn't argue. Take it as it came. It was going to be an exhausting journey, certainly. Then I sat down and wrote a note to Tony.

Tony,

Amelia and I have come to a point where I'm convinced there's nothing more to be gained. All I can see is distress and unhappiness. Please feel free to reveal anything of our conversations to Melanie. I'll leave it to your discretion. If she comes to the same conclusion as I have, I'm sure she still wouldn't be able to make an arrest, certainly not a valid case.

Best wishes to yourself and to Melanie, and love from Amelia.

Richard

I sealed this in one of the hotel's envelopes, addressed it to Mr Tony Brason, left envelope and keys on the desk on the way out, and we loaded luggage and ourselves into the car.

Then I drove away from it.

14

Christmas came, and slid past almost unnoticed. Mary had gone to stay with her sister for a week, so we were quiet, Amelia and I and our Boxer, Sheba. We had not gone visiting, and it had seemed too much effort to send out invitations. We had nothing to celebrate; the Norfolk affair still hung heavily between us.

Every morning I had expected some sort of communication from Olivia, who must surely have been wondering about our sudden disappearance, but there was nothing, not even a Christmas card, though we had dutifully sent one, after much careful consideration. This consideration was the only time our conversation even touched on the events in November. At other times we spoke together casually on day-to-day matters, and behind it all was the haunting knowledge of failure. Or perhaps even worse. The matter had not been resolved. We were tense, waiting. We couldn't have said for what.

I had an uneasy feeling that Amelia was searching her mind for some obscure way in which she could have helped her friends. Beneath her composure I could detect that there was a certain coldness towards me. I had not handled the matter conclusively; I had not tried hard enough.

January came in, damp and dreary. The river was running high, and when I took Sheba for her run along its bank, I reckoned we needed only another foot of rise in the water level, and we'd not be able to take our walks. These were becoming precious to me as I could allow my thoughts full rein, without Amelia observing, and deducing the subject of them.

On the third of January Mary came back, full of news and chatter to which we tried to respond cheerfully. But she soon detected the atmosphere, and became more silent. I guessed she thought we'd had a disagreement. I couldn't explain that it was an agreement that was troubling us.

On the following day the spell, as I was now beginning to think of it, was broken. At ten in the morning, when I returned from Sheba's walk, the water having gone down, I found that Tony had come to visit us.

Amelia said 'Here's Tony.' She meant, here's Tony with trouble.

'Just timed it right for a pot of tea,' I said, trying to sound welcoming.

Tony smiled awkwardly. 'If you don't mind, I don't think there's time.'

'You're in a hurry?'

'If you're going to get back tonight.'

I looked round at Amelia, trying to lighten the implication with a laugh. 'He's very mysterious.'

But she was frowning, her eyes on his face. 'Tony, what is it?'

'Melanie wants to see Richard.'

'Oh?' I asked. 'She issues her orders and I go running?'

'Richard . . .' Tony sighed. 'I'm not trying to be officious, but it *is* official. She phoned me, because she didn't know how to contact you. I wasn't going to tell her and leave it at that, not knowing. So I had a word with the Super, and he phoned her back, and . . . well, it's now official. I'm to escort you to Melanie's office.'

'But you can't expect . . . What's happened?'

'I can't tell you.'

'Can't or won't?'

'My instructions are to say nothing. She'll do the talking.'

'So you know what it is, Tony?'

He nodded solemnly.

'Then it's serious. I'll have to go, Amelia,' I told her, making it sound as though I was decidedly reluctant, when I couldn't wait to get there and find out.

'I'll come with you.'

'She didn't say . . .' Tony bit off the sentence. 'Oh, what the hell! As though I'm going to stop you, Amelia.'

167

'I'll throw some things together, then,' she said, 'just in case.' And she hurried away, no doubt to mystify Mary even more, leaving Tony and me staring at each other and wondering what to say.

'We could use my car,' he suggested.

'I'd rather take ours. That'll leave us both independent.'

'Please yourself. To tell you the truth, I'd prefer it that way.'

'Oh, why?'

'With you in the same car all the way there, I can't see how I'd hold out against your everlasting questions.' He grinned. 'Safer like this.'

'And I'm in trouble?'

He cocked his head. 'To put it mildly, yes.'

We left it there, and though round for other topics. Tony told me Ken Latchett had sent his best regards. Then Amelia was back, thumping two cases down the stairs. I threw them on the back seat of the Granada, and we drove after Tony out on to the road.

Tony, I noticed, was using an official car, not his own. We therefore proceeded at a steady and fast pace, he using his blue winker and siren sparingly, and only when any traffic seemed to be holding us back. The visibility was poor, and I had to keep too close to his tail for my liking. But Amelia was fascinated at the way the obstructions seemed to melt away, as though a preceding shock-wave was parting them, though at the same time the urgency disquieted her.

Melanie Poole had an office in a new building, square and purposeful and seemingly innocent of activity. There was even a lift. She was on the third floor, with her window overlooking the car park. I wondered whether she'd watched us arrive, from that window, and had posed herself at her desk accordingly. She looked up from its surface and said, 'Here you are then. Good. That was very quick, Tony.'

'There was no trouble.' I hoped he meant with the traffic.

'And Amelia. I'm glad to see you again.'

She didn't say she was glad to see me, simply pointed a pencil to the chair facing her. There were two other chairs, set back against the rear wall. I could no longer glance at Amelia for guidance. I sat. Melanie gestured.

'I have a tape recorder, and as you can see it's switched off. No one's taking notes. That's just so you'll know how we stand.'

I nodded. So we were just going to talk. But when she began her voice was too crisp, more positive than for mere talk.

'Mr Patton, when we spoke together last time, my hands were tied because I had no case. A young woman had died – Nancy Ruston – but her death had all the elements of an accident. I could do nothing. Now the situation has changed. I have a case. At the moment I'm in charge of it, but as you know that can't go on for long before the big boys from HQ come charging in.'

I nodded again. She was telling me it was an important case. To her. I wasn't going to interrupt.

'Naturally,' she went on, 'I intend to clear this up before that can happen. I know you can help me. I know that I can demand that you should help me, but I don't think it will come to that.'

I cleared my throat. She waited. I said nothing. Undeterred, she went on:

'I know that you were very active during the few days you were here. From that, I suspect you saw and interviewed a number of people I had no official access to, and I can deduce, from the fact that you left so hurriedly, that you discovered something you didn't like the sound or the smell of, and wanted to keep it to yourself. Well, now is the time to reveal it.'

This was all very formal. She might even have had it written down on her blotting pad, and was reading it. There was nothing else on her desk.

'Why is this the time?' I asked.

'Mark Ruston is dead, Mr Patton.'

Amelia made a sound in her throat. No more. Then silence.

'And this . . . Are you saying it was suicide?'

She didn't answer directly. 'He was found, late last night, hanging by a noose from one of the rafters in a shed.'

'And you believe I can – '

'Can explain it? Possibly.'

She leaned back in her chair, rolling the pencil in her fingers. Now she could not have been reading her lines. I saw that her eyes were shadowed, her hair not as tidy as it might have been.

169

She would have had no sleep, and could expect none for a great number of hours.

'All right,' she said. 'You're showing no enthusiasm. I gather you're a cautious man. But I'm going to remind you, Richard, that you owe me something. You were careful not to tell me one direct lie – oh, don't worry, I noticed that – but you were devious with me. Is it only your own discretion you think you can trust? No – don't trouble to answer that. I'm coming to my point. You owe me, and I now want to call in the debt. Tell me to go to hell if you like, and you can walk out of here. Then you'll owe me even more, because you know damn well I could charge you with obstructing the course of justice. Yes. I think I could make that stick. And I might do it, just out of sheer cussedness. You haven't co-operated in any way. Now I'm giving you that chance. Yes or no?'

This was a different Melanie Poole from the one I'd met before. She was in her own office. She was confident, proud, official. She knew what she was doing, and in no way was she conceding one iota of her pride.

'Perhaps justice *has* been done, and I didn't obstruct it very much,' I suggested.

'Don't try your word play with me, Richard, please. Not now. I'm asking for your co-operation, because I believe you can cut straight through weeks of official enquiries for me. And my enquiries, which aren't going to last very long, wouldn't get anywhere in the time I've got.'

'I can show you why it is unarguable that Mark Ruston killed his sister, Nancy. Circumstantial evidence, but nevertheless valid.'

'Can you indeed? The why haven't you told me before this?'

I hesitated. 'Oh, come on, Richard,' she said, a touch of impatience in her voice. 'Stop playing around. This is a murder enquiry I'm talking about.'

I allowed the air to sag from me inaudibly. But it was a huge sigh. Of relief? I didn't know. But a murder, and official one, forced my hand.

'So it wasn't suicide?'

'I'll tell you. There was a blue nylon rope tossed over one of the crossed rafters in the roof. One end went to a winch, the other had a hook on it. The rope had been placed around Mark's neck, and the hook looped on to it. You can see, it formed a noose. Then he was hauled up with the winch. There was a bruise on the back of his head, so no doubt he was knocked out first. It's early days yet. But from the look on his face he was allowed to become at least aware of what was happening to him before his feet were hauled from the floor and the ratchet locked in place on the winch. Anyone would have been capable of doing this. Do I make myself clear?'

I said she had. I'd heard Amelia make a choking, sobbing protest. I agreed that Melanie had a murder on her hands. In view of the fact she'd been using my Christian name, I said:

'I don't know what you want from me, Melanie. I said I can prove Mark killed his sister. How does that help you?'

I was still trying to protect Amelia's friend, Olivia, from the lurking horrors, but at that moment I was having difficulty understanding why I should. It had all gone beyond hurt feelings and trampled emotions.

'That,' she said fiercely, 'tells me you know a damn sight more about it than just Mark and Nancy. His motivations. Her involvement. Don't, for Christ's sake, go on looking at me like that! I didn't ask you to come here just so that I could practise my interrogation.'

For the first time Tony spoke. One word. 'Richard!'

I raised a finger to him, not looking round. 'Have you got any further with this?' I asked her. 'Clues? Statements?'

'I have Laurence Carter in custody.'

'Have you, by God? Has a charge been made?'

'Pending further enquiries.'

'That's nonsense. Not Larry.' I stopped. Had she done that in order to force my hand?

'His fingerprints were on the winch.'

'As they would be.'

She inclined her head. 'Naturally. He has admitted to having listened outside the wall of that office, the night you got Mark to tell you his story.'

I tried to keep my voice level. 'Did he tell you the gist of that?'

'No. He refused. It's his legal right.' She smiled, a thoroughly relaxed and benignant smile. '*You* can tell me.'

'Can I see him?'

'Larry? Yes, of course. Later.'

'Then I'll co-operate.'

'Thank you. It's like drawing teeth.'

'I have loyalties I'd like to preserve.'

'You and your loyalties! There's only one person you owe loyalty to.'

'You?'

'No, you fool. To your wife.'

I realized, then, that Melanie was even more subtle than I'd guessed. She'd understood the form and manner of my reluctance. I glanced round. Amelia sat, knees touching, her hands wrapped together upon them, her face set and white. Quietly, she nodded. I turned back.

'What do you want to know?'

'All of it, of course,' said Melanie.

So I told her all of it, from the original phone message until the moment we'd driven away from the hotel. Every detail I could remember. Nothing added, nothing taken away, like the bread you can't get now. She listened quietly, and when I'd finished she sat a few moments longer, considering the situation.

'I think I can understand why you left it all and went home,' she said at last.

'Yes.'

'It might have been better if you'd stayed.'

'Let's not hold inquests, Melanie. Can we go home, now?'

She raised her eyebrows. 'Where's your curiosity gone, Richard? Never mind. Of course you may go. After you've seen Larry. But I'd hoped . . .' She got up from her chair and came round to the front of her desk, leaning back against its edge just as Mark had done. 'Perhaps you can't appreciate how that leaves me. Oh yes, I can go to all these people, the two Rustons and the two Deans, and I'd know the questions I'd need to ask. But if *you* did it, if we went together, then it would give you some authority. Then any questions you asked them they could hardly wriggle round, because you've already spoken to them and they'll recall what they said at that time.' Her hair was back-lit, her eyes deep and dark. She raised her chin. 'And I would have it all officially then.'

172

'No doubt. I wouldn't argue about that. But look at my position. I'd hardly care – '

'Care?' she demanded. 'Haven't we gone past the point of dodging awkwardnesses – yours and theirs!'

'I suppose that's true.' But I hadn't yet had time to assimilate all the implications. The loyalties, the responsibilities. What was hammering inside my head was the fact that Mark would have been alive at that moment if I'd not walked out on it.

'Must I remind you,' she was saying crisply, 'that you didn't consider my feelings when you showed me that photograph of Nancy, with the sticker on her anorak. Did you take me for a fool? Were you pleased with your little deception?'

'I don't know – '

She cut me short, swinging round and leaning back over her desk, which entailed quite a stretch, the kicking up of her skirt with one leg, and an angry yank at one of the top drawers. She turned round, waving an envelope.

'Official photographs,' she said. 'Nancy, as we found her.'

'We're back with Nancy?'

'Of course. That's where it's all sprung from. Nancy's death. Look at them.'

I slid them out of the envelope. There must have been fifty, but I had no intention of sorting through all of them. One was enough. Two, perhaps, too much. Nancy, on the bank after they'd brought her out, lying on her back with her face swollen and distorted, a travesty of her real beauty and vivacity. There was no yellow sticker on her anorak. And one as she'd been found, lying in the water with her face hidden. There was no sticker on that one, either.

Silently, I handed them back. I reached inside my pocket an brought out the two pictures I'd had from Harvey Cole, and the one I'd had from Larry with Nancy in the sailing dinghy.

This last, Melanie examined first. I watched her lips tighten. Then she handed it back and spoke quietly.

'Larry had the means, the opportunity, and the motive for killing Mark. This photo only confirms his motive. The person who took this picture would surely have reason to kill her murderer.'

'I agree with that. He said he'd got hundreds of them. You're now satisfied she was murdered? I mean, my evidence against Mark would never have got as far as a court.'

'It doesn't need to. And I'm convinced. Now . . . these other two you had from Harvey . . . you showed me the one with the sticker on, when I knew there hadn't been one when we found her. It was because of this that I knew you were being tricky with me. And too clever, Richard, because you'd worked out, by some complex reasoning of your own, that the photo showing the sticker had to be the way she'd been left for us to find. No . . . please let me finish this. I knew this wasn't so, and I was sure the sticker hadn't been on when she was found by the photographer.'

'Why?'

She sighed. 'Because I conducted experiments. I went to the length of contacting the charity organizers and getting a few left-over stickers. I experimented, this way and that. One: a sticker wouldn't stay on for long when it was stuck to a damp surface, and her anorak *was* damp. Two: a sticker stuck to dry material, even left for a few hours, fell off as soon as the surface was wetted. So I knew it was impossible that she'd been found originally with a sticker already there, and I knew there wasn't one when we got there. D'you see what that means, Richard? It means the photographer deliberately put a sticker there for one of the two photographs. It would only need to stay there for a minute. Then the body was left as it was found by us.'

'Ah!' This was no more than a dismal comment. I saw then how my reasoning had been faulty from the beginning.

'Is that all you can say?'

'I'd assumed the fiddling with the sticker had been intended to fool you – the police. I see now I was wrong. The intention was purely and simply to take a photograph that'd fool the person who was to receive the pictures.'

She positively grinned at me. A row of small, white teeth displayed themselves. 'And so . . .' She plunged her hand into the envelope of official photographs, and produced a yellow envelope, very like the one I already had. She offered it to me.

From its right-hand pocket I drew out a pair of photographs. They were duplicates of the ones Harvey Cole had sold to me.

174

But of course, the sender would have sent one pair, and kept the other pair for himself.

'You found this lot in Mark's room, I suppose?'

'Yes. Turn them over, Richard.'

I did so. On the back of the one showing Nancy without a sticker on her anorak there was printed: D/D? I assumed this to mean: date of death – any time. On the back of the other one, with the sticker, was printed: D/D 7/5. This meant: date of death – 7th May.

I stared at them a long time. 'The top left-hand corners,' Melanie prompted.

The one without the ticker was numbered 1. The one with the sticker was numbered 2.

I looked up. She nodded, and said: 'The pictures were meant to say – '

'I know. Intended to tell Mark – not you – that the body had been left with a sticker on, and that this indicated she'd died on the collection Saturday, and Mark had therefore been given an alibi for that day. Always providing he *did* have an alibi for that day . . .'

She took over, calmly overriding me. 'We've enquired, as well as we could in the time available. It seems much of that day is covered. He collected his tin and his stickers in the morning, and he was stationed at the bridge. There was a natural gap at lunch time, but now you've covered that, as he had lunch with Olivia Dean.'

'You can't have checked that!'

'Not yet. But afterwards . . . Richard, he naturally had friends around there amongst the water people. Between them – those we knocked up in the night – he was noticed at various times in the morning and afternoon. Then he took his takings in to the collection centre, and spent some of the evening in the pub with his friends, probably spending more money than he'd collected all day, and went home. He's well covered for the Saturday.'

'When in fact it'd be no use whatsoever to him as an alibi.'

'And why is that, Richard?' There was a glint in her eyes.

'Because you've said there wasn't a yellow sticker on her anorak when she was found, and you claim there couldn't possibly have been one after so long in the water.'

She showed me her teeth again. I couldn't understand what she was getting at. 'Now look in the other pocket.'

I put my fingers in the other pocket of the envelope, and withdrew a strip of four 35 mm negatives. The outer two were blank. The inner two were clearly those relating to the prints. I stared at them a long while, breathing deeply, controlling my anger at Harvey Cole, and my fury at myself. Of *course* Harvey had not sold me the full record of his robbery. He'd already sold the negatives to Mark. No wonder they'd been worth £1,000 to him.

'Negatives!' I said. 'Not once . . . not *once* did I give a thought to negatives. The rotten, treacherous sneak. Your precious Harvey. It was the negatives he was asked to get for Mark. Not the damned prints. Harvey kept the prints back for whichever fool should come along. And that was me.'

She said, 'We have no time to waste on self-castigation, Richard.' But she was smiling openly now, dead pleased with herself and her choice of words. I had to assume she was just as pleased with the performance of her favourite burglar.

'If you look at the negatives with a magnifier . . . here . . .' She once more did her athletic reach back and her yank at a drawer, and came up with a hand magnifier. 'Use this. The colours are reversed in relation to the spectrum, so the little yellow sticker shows up as a dark purple spot.'

Holding them up to the light I checked this with her magnifier. As these were on 35 mm film, the frames were numbered. 12 and 13. The outer two had been deliberately blanked out. The one numbered 12 was the one that showed the purple dot. The other one, the second in the exposure sequence, did not.

'That's strange,' I said.

'What is?'

'The negative showing the sticker was exposed first, but the prints sent to Mark are numbered the other way round, with the sticker one second.'

She made an impatient gesture. 'He – or she of course – could number them in whatever way was required.'

I handed the magnifier and the envelope back to her. 'But all the same . . . just imagine it, Melanie, that scene as it was when the photographer came along. According to you, Nancy could

176

not have been wearing a sticker at that time. So . . . assume that. But the photographer needed one showing a sticker, in order to send it to Mark. Now . . . surely it would've been logical for one picture to be taken as she was found, without any sticker. Then stick one on for the second shot. Then the negatives would've been in the same order as the prints were numbered. One: stickerless. Two: with sticker. But in fact . . .' I hesitated, feeling a brisk and warm surge of quickening interest.

She didn't seem to see what I was getting at. 'Yes?'

'In fact, he – the photographer – ignored the fact that Nancy's body was in an ideal position and condition for his first picture, which he wanted stickerless, and put a sticker on the anorak for the first shot. Then he took it off and exposed the second one. That's illogical behaviour, Malanie. Damn it all, are we going to accept that he then stuck on another sticker, in order to leave her showing one? It's all too complex. This was May, and daylight. These photos aren't flashlight. Daylight, and May, and although he wasn't spotted doing it, the area couldn't have been all that deserted. It'd be too big a risk, wasting time, when the quick and simple thing would've been to take one as she was found, then one with the sticker . . . and simply get as far away as possible as quickly as possible.' I shrugged, not having apparently received much response.

Then slowly she smiled. 'Very good,' she said quietly. 'That was quick. It was ages before I saw all that.' The smile became a grin of conspiracy. 'I wanted your unprompted opinion. Now you can understand why I need you. The way those photos was taken is illogical, as you say. It's got a special reason we can't see, and it was done like that deliberately. When I can see why, by whom, and how it came about, then, Richard, I think I'll have a lead to Mark's killer. It all links up. I can feel it. Make sense of the actions . . .'

I was hearing her words, hearing them in my consciousness like a distant chant, while at the same time my mind was running wild, embracing all the details of our last visit to Norfolk and analysing them. Because I knew, with a sick and certain despair, exactly why the pictures had been taken in that way, why the prints had been numbered as they had been, the intentions and the motivations. All this I saw with a bleak clarity. I sat and stared at Melanie, watching her lips moving, feeling the blood run from my face and hoping she wouldn't notice, feeling my fingers tingling. I wanted to leap from that chair and march out and walk and walk and walk, until my brain settled and relaxed. And until I knew what to do – what I had to do. Though I hated the thought, I was certain I knew who had done it, and equally certain I'd been the cause of Mark's death. So I was trapped.

I was aware that Melanie was gesturing the end to her little speech, raising her arms and allowing the gesture to round it off. She appeared not to notice my distress. If I missed the last few words it didn't matter. She wanted me to go with her to Mansfield Park.

I marvelled that she, who'd had the evidence so much longer than I, had not seen the answer at once.

Then at last Amelia, aroused by the nature of the forthcoming expedition, spoke out. She had sat there quietly, apart from the sundry exclamations that had escaped her.

'He deserved to die,' she said flatly. 'It's not right to . . . to persecute. . .'

Melanie looked at her with sympathy. Her voice was quiet and persuasive when she spoke. 'You ought to know, Amelia, that officially a death is a death. A murder is a murder. If we'd been after Nancy's killer, you would've approved. Mark's, no. I can understand that. But it's got to stop some time. I've got Larry in detention. Am I going to sit back and let it take its course, all the way to court? There'd *be* a case, you know. And if I released him now, who would be the next one to look for revenge? It's got to stop. You must see that.'

Amelia tightened her lips stubbornly, but she said, 'I suppose you're right.'

I cleared my throat, not certain my voice would work. 'She is right, my dear. We've got to go on with it now.'

'Must I come with you?'

'No. No real need. The decision's yours.'

'I ought to be with Olivia.' She stubbornly clung to that.

'If you think so.' But I couldn't get any enthusiasm into it.

She shook her head. It would be agony for her. 'I'd better come along then.'

And Tony beamed at her with pride, blast him.

Melanie straightened to her full height and slapped her thighs. 'Now . . . I suppose you haven't had lunch, and neither have I. So I'll introduce you to our canteen. Perhaps you'd like to see Larry first, Richard . . .' She left it hanging, raising her eyebrows. I nodded. 'Very well. Amelia and I will go along to the canteen, and Tony can take you down to see Larry. He knows the way. Coming, Amelia? You'll be fascinated by our canteen, I'm sure.'

Damn it all, she was pleased as hell at the anticipation of the forthcoming visit.

Together they preceded us from the office. I looked at Tony, and he smiled.

'Knows how to get her way, doesn't she!' I commented sourly.

'You're dead right. She adapts the technique to the circumstances. Come on. Brand new cells. You'll like 'em.'

'Do they know you?'

'I've been introduced.'

We went down to see Larry.

15

Brand new cells, yes, as clean and soulless as they could possibly be, and equally depressing as the battered boxes I'd been used to. The officer on duty let us to it. He didn't trouble to shut the door.

Larry got to his feet. He'd had a choice – stretch out on the unwelcoming plastic-covered mattress, or sit upright on a plain hardwood chair. He'd been sitting, reading a thick book. For a person accused of murder, he seemed strangely undisturbed. He was still at a stage where he could tell himself that it didn't happen to people like him, and wouldn't continue to do so for long. He put his book face down on the bed, and wiped his palms on his jeans.

'Shut the door, will you. There's a hell of a draught.'

Tony eased the door shut with his hip. I said: 'You're in a bit of a fix here, aren't you.' Not a question. He was.

'Have you come to dig me out, Mr Patton?' He eased himself down on to the bed. I sat on the low chair with my knees high.

'There's some work to do on it yet, Larry. You could save us all a lot of trouble if you'd just admit you did it.'

'Oh sure. I reckon so. The snag is that I didn't.'

'Have they got a solicitor for you?'

'Ma was round. I told her I didn't want one. It's guilty people who need solicitors.'

'Hmm!' I said. 'Well see. But you must agree, you're the one with the best motive. You'd *want* to kill Mark.'

He was eager, pouncing in. 'That's just it. I did want to kill him. Oh Lord, how much I wanted that! I've nearly driven myself crazy, trying to work out a way of doing it. But I didn't like the idea of *seeing* him die. I can't understand that, but it's how it was. The *idea* of it, bringing it about, sort of, that was great. I thought of poison. But that wasn't a very good idea, quite apart from the fact that I don't know where to get any. But poison, anyway – I mean – it might've got the wrong person. And that would've been awful. Can you think of a more terrible thing than killing the wrong person! It'd be even worse than letting the right one go on living. Don't you think?'

I said I quite agreed. He was expounding basic law. 'But you were still thinking about ways and means?'

'Oh yes.' Seriously, that was. 'My best idea was dropping something on him from a good height. But there'd be all that blood, see.'

'Yes, there'd be a lot of blood,' I agreed. 'And where were you last night?' I looked up at Tony. 'It *was* last night?'

'Yes. The ME reckoned about eight. It'd be dark. No moon.'

'Larry?' I prompted. 'At eight.'

'I was out.'

'Out? Out where?'

'On the water. In my dinghy.'

'In the dark?'

'There wasn't any moon, but I had the stars.'

It sounded a bit thin to me. 'Sailing? At night?'

'I can see her clearer then, on the water, in the dark.'

I got to my feet abruptly. 'We'll get moving, I think. You all right, Larry? Plenty to read?'

He gestured to the book beside him. 'Ma brought me that. It's by somebody called Lovella Treat. A bit sloppy for me, but it's got a lot of words.'

'Fine. See you later. Okay?'

He smiled thinly. We left. The officer came along and put his head in the door, then locked up.

'Well?' said Tony.

'She must be mad, charging Larry. You heard what he said.'

'I heard.' He was non-committal.

'I reckon she's using him, to force me into this.'

'Do you, Richard? She has her ways.'

We went back up to the ground floor, and to the canteen, which, like the cell, was new and modern and utilitarian, and just about as cheerless. We sat and we ate. I can't remember what it was. Not one word was said about our proposed visit. Not many words were said at all, as I recall it. None at all by me. Eventually, we left.

Before we reached the front office the sound of raised voices and thumping noises became clear. Melanie marched ahead, into trouble.

Malcolm Ruston was standing at the desk, demanding something, anything. Still a big man, still with his strength slumbering unleashed, he was nevertheless stricken and shattered. Seeing us, he was silent. His face was collapsing into something older and greyer. His eyes were wild.

'Inspector . . .' appealed the young constable at the desk.

She plunged straight in. 'Mr Ruston . . . you really can't do much good – '

'What's going on?' he demanded, his voice coarse and rough. 'What're you doing . . .' His lips continued to move, but nothing emerged.

'We're still making enquiries. It takes time, Mr Ruston. Time.'

'What am I going to *do*?' he asked, his eyes roving. 'My wife . . . oh dear God!'

He had lost a daughter and a son in eight months. His life was falling apart.

'I'm sorry,' she said.

'And Larry? What about Larry?'

'We're holding him for now.'

'Y' must be crazy. Not Larry. I want to see him.'

He made a movement to thrust past her. He'd been angry and frustrated for a long while and his mind was exhausted with it, but the fury wasn't far beneath the surface.

'I can't allow that,' she told him firmly. 'You ought to know you can't. Why don't you . . . Constable, will you get someone to take Mr Ruston for a cup of tea – '

'No!' he shouted, his face red now, resenting the suggestion that his wounds could be so easily healed. 'I want to see . . . to see . . .'

Baffled at the complete lack of progress he'd made, he stared blindly about him, then he swung around and stumped out into the open air.

Melanie ran her fingers across her eyebrows. 'Sometimes I hate . . . oh, hell, let's get on with it.'

When we got out to the parking area she said we'd use her car. She meant her official one, a plain Ford Cortina but fitted with radio link-up. She threw her briefcase inside, some of her frustration in the gesture. 'If you'll just sit with me, Richard, please.'

I sat in the front with her, Tony and Amelia behind. Amelia was silent, and very pale. Melanie had no need for directions to Mansfield Park.

'I want to discuss strategy, Richard.'

I din't want to discuss anything. I listened. It was going to be difficult, she explained, because I had no official standing, and it would be necessary to make that clear. We would get further, she thought, by maintaining an informal atmosphere. Yet the official aspect had to be there. She decided that she would go in first, establishing her position, and then allow me to continue, on the grounds that I'd come along purely for the purpose of keeping things on a friendly basis.

I noticed that there was no suggestion that we might have to issue official warnings that anything they might say . . . etc. Yes, it was going to be very unofficial.

'And if,' she said, 'I think at any time you're lapsing from the theme, I'll interrupt. You understand, I'm not going to have you put leading questions, prodding them in a direction that's in their favour.'

'I can't see, from what we've got so far, that I'll be able to discover much in anybody's favour,' I said without enthusiasm.

'But you'll try?' She glanced at her rear-view mirror.

'Maybe. It depends. What's the time? Just after three. Then I'll tell you that Olivia will be in the middle of one of her afternoon dictating sessions. It could well be difficult to dig her out.'

'We'll tackle that when we come to it.' She was being very brisk and dismissive.

Once more she glanced at the mirror. 'Damn,' she said. 'There's a pick-up following us.'

'That'll be Malcolm Ruston.'

'We can't have that.'

She reached for her microphone and gave brisk instructions

183

for a two-man patrol car to proceed to Mansfield Park. I was wondering what hell might be let loose if Ruston interfered there. But she seemed satisfied that she had it under control, only slowing a little, I guessed to give time for the patrol car to meet us there.

It was a fifteen mile run. The pick-up hung on our tail all the way.

'It's along this side turning, I believe,' she said at last.

'It is.'

The pick-up was still behind, following us along the causeway, staying back a little when we parked on the same spot the Granada had occupied. Melanie didn't get out, simply waited until a patrol car drifted in behind the pick-up and stopped. Then she got out, me with her, and we walked back to them.

Malcolm jumped to the ground. 'What *is* this place? Why've you come here?'

'Mr Ruston,' said Melanie calmly, 'I'm doing what's described as pursuing enquiries. Into Mark's death. I will not have you causing any trouble. Do you understand?' She cocked her eyes at the two uniformed men, who'd come up behind Malcolm. 'You heard? He may remain here, or go home if he wishes . . .'

'Home!' Malcolm groaned.

'He's not under arrest. But if he tries to interfere, you're to restrain him. Right?'

They nodded. Two young, slim constables, who, together, wouldn't have made one Malcolm Ruston. He now stared bleakly, baffled, at us, and ran his damp palms down the rump of his jeans. He sought my attention, fastening his eyes on me. A possible friend. 'Richard? And Amelia's with you. What's going on?'

I shook my head in apology. 'Behave, and you might find out.'

He slapped his thighs, anger rumbling deep inside him.

We walked back to the car, where Amelia was standing with Tony. I explained that this was really the rear of the house, but Melanie didn't seem interested in that, just collected her brief-case and headed directly for the door.

We had not been seen arriving, and she had to use the bell-push. Philip appeared, blinking, in the hall, the Great Dane peering past his shoulder and the Spaniels past his knees.

He was still losing weight, I thought. Now he was positively gaunt, and the pipe clasped in his hand was quivering. But he managed a look of astonished query, which turned to blank surprise when he saw Melanie and Tony.

'Richard? And . . . why yes, Amelia's with you. Do come in. And who are your friends?'

He carried this off very well, and had completely destroyed Melanie's planned approach. She tried to recover the initiative.

'I am Inspector Poole, and this is Sergeant Brason. From the police,' she added, in case he might be thinking in terms of drains.

He stood back, gesturing with the pipe. 'Come in, anyway.' He said something to the dogs, who wandered off forlornly, deprived of a good bout of ear-pulling.

'The lounge, Richard. You know the way. This *is* a surprise. I'm afraid Olivia – '

'We'd like to speak to her, Philip. Both of you together, if that can be arranged.' I tried not to allow any sarcasm to enter this phrase.

'Oh dear,' he said helplessly.

'Think you can dig her out?'

'Well . . . go on through. I'll see what I can do.'

Amelia led the way through into the lounge. Melanie's eyes were all about her at once, not admiring the furniture and fittings the pictures and the porcelain, I was sure. She was deciding where was the best place for us all to sit, when it came to sitting, and how to place all six of us to the best advantage, if any choice arose.

Amelia clutched at my arm. 'I feel terrible,' she said miserably.

'I know you do. I'm not happy with it myself. Why don't you sit over. . .'

We were interrupted. Olivia swept in on a surge of annoyance, and cast her eyes around.

'Amelia! Darling!' But this time there was no warmth in it,

185

real or assumed. 'And Richard.' She had not advanced to kiss Amelia's cheek. She had been told who our companions were, so that Amelia and I were included in the lack of welcome. She nodded, first to Melanie, then to Tony.

'Philip tells me you're from the police. How very extraordinary.'

Again Melanie introduced herself and Tony, and smiled as she did it, in a way she clearly believed to be encouraging.

'It's a police matter, Mrs Dean.' She had automatically assumed that Olivia was the one to address. Philip had slipped to one side quietly. 'As it's a complicated business, and as Richard, here, knows more of the background than I do . . .' She laughed self-deprecatingly. '. . . which is next to nothing, he's very kindly agreed to come along and explain things to you. If that's all right. I wonder if we can sit down – I think this could take a little time.'

Olivia looked round distractedly. Melanie had so placed herself that it would seem only natural for her to sit back into the wing chair behind her, which just happened to be to one side of the french window. She waited. Olivia now had the choice of a single chair, upright and possibly uncomfortable, a little in front of the window but nevertheless to the side of Melanie, from where it would be difficult to keep a wary eye on her, or she could take one of a couple of fat, upholstered chairs facing the window. She chose one of the latter, the one furthest from Melanie. Amelia at once went to the other one, sliding it along to be beside Olivia, thus offering proximity as comfort for her friend. This left the upright chair for me, and for Philip an embroidered stool, which he picked up and plumped down, ostentatiously facing the window, from where danger might be expected to come. But he carefully situated it further back and a little to one side of Olivia. Possibly so that she could not observe his reactions? Or simply to demonstrate his inferior status when his wife was around?

Tony, with no seat, stood negligently against the back wall, where neither Philip nor Olivia could see him. He stood with one hand clasping his other elbow, and supporting a hand over his chin and mouth.

I took the upright chair and placed it down facing the Deans.

It was padded, but hard. I started to fill my pipe, then looked up.

'You've made this seem all very stiff and formal, Olivia. I didn't want it like that.'

'Philip can get drinks,' she said, as though her lips were stiff. 'If that would help.'

'No, no. No need for that. Look, I don't like this. You asked me here – us, rather, Amelia and me – to help you with a little business regarding a burglary that wasn't. That's all it involved, and I couldn't do much to help. Sorry about that, but when you both insisted that nothing had been taken from the house, then there really wasn't anything left to do. But the thought did occur to me – you'll understand this, Olivia – I thought that if what had been taken was quite small and insignificant, then one of you might not have known it was there. And the other one would . . . might, I should say . . . might not have wanted to admit it'd been there. Oh Lord, Olivia, don't stare at me like that. You're putting me off.'

'Why should I want to do anything else?' One hand lifted for a moment impatiently from her knee.

'Well . . . that's what I don't know,' I admitted. 'That's what I'd like to find out. As I said, one of you might've known what was taken, and not wish to admit it'd been there, and now wasn't.'

'Not me,' she said with finality. She half turned her head and jerked out, 'Philip?'

'What? I didn't . . .'

'You're not listening. Did you know of anything hidden here secretly, and not want *me* to know about it?

He smiled, and glanced at me, sharing the thought: Women! 'Is there ever anything I can keep from you, my love?'

She gave a tiny snort of disgust, probably at 'my love', and said to me, 'There you are, then. There's your answer, Richard, and I can't see, I'll have you know, why you're making such a fuss about it. If that's all, I'll just get back to my work. I might possibly salvage something . . .'

She had her hands on the arms of her chair, about to lever herself to her feet. I got in quickly.

'It isn't all, Olivia, I'm sorry to say. You see, the burglar left his personal marks. They all do this – it's related to how they do the job. It's called an MO in the force. *Modus operandi.* And this one had left a very personal MO, his care and tidiness, the way he got in – '

'That roof's going to cost a fortune to put right,' Philip put in brightly. 'It's a matter of matching the tiles. You'd never believe.'

'But I would, Philip.' I decided he was trying to lighten the mood, that he felt Olivia's attitude wasn't helping. 'Blame your burglar. Sue him for damages.'

'You know who he is?' he asked, as though he might put that in hand at once.

'I did manage to find out, with the help of Inspector Poole over there.' I gestured towards Melanie. She was a blurred shape on the outer edge of my peripheral vision. I couldn't detect how she took that. 'She was good enough to take me to him, because of course she recognized the MO, and introduce us – '

'Introduce!' cut in Olivia. 'Dear heaven, is this a madhouse! Introduce – to a burglar – I've never heard anything like it.'

'The police,' I assured her, 'have to keep on friendly terms with all their crooks. Otherwise they might leave the district in a huff, and where would the work be then? There'd be queues of out-of-work coppers – '

'Can we keep to the point?' Olivia demanded acidly.

Philip was darting his gaze from one to the other of us, quietly enjoying the exchange.

'He lives,' I said, 'quite close to Happisburgh, in a cottage he calls Honesty.'

Philip let our a yip of laughter, then clamped his hand over his mouth, with his eyes dancing above it. His reaction appeared forced.

I knew that I was treading on the edge of farce, here, having deliberately ventured into facetiousness. But I wasn't going to get anywhere if I couldn't break away from our formality, which was leading me much too close for my liking to conducting an interrogation. I was very near to antagonizing both of them.

'It's true,' I said. 'Honestly. Anyway, I didn't want to make a case of it with this burglar. His name's Harvey Cole, by the way. All I wanted was to discover what he'd stolen from this house.'

188

Olivia raised her chin. 'Nothing was – '

'Something was, Olivia. He admitted it. He even sold me what he'd got.'

'I do not believe you, Richard.'

'Sold it to you?' asked Philip blankly.

'Well yes.' I put my hand inside my jacket and produced my yellow envelope. I was getting used to this, and could now whip it out like a cross-handed pistol draw. 'I paid two hundred pounds for this envelope, with two photographs in it. Like to see?'

'No thank you,' said Olivia, lips pursed in disapproval.

'I was asking Philip,' I said gently.

'Let's have a look, then,' he conceded, just to keep me happy, and he reached forward. His attitude was one of a person humouring someone slightly insane.

I had to stand up in order to take the envelope to him. I stood at his shoulder, head tilted, and handed them over.

'What's this?' he asked, suddenly serious, drawing them out.

'Two photographs of someone lying drowned in the reeds of a river.'

'And you paid a hundred each for them? Richard . . . really!' He thrust them back into my hands.

'Strictly speaking, I bought them for you, Philip. You did say, out-of-pocket expenses.'

Olivia twisted in her seat. 'Is this true, Philip? You asked Richard to buy back . . . Let me see.' She reached for the pictures and he leaned forward to hand them to her. Some of the authority had gone from her. It was a snatch she used, and I saw that there was a flush on her cheeks. Her fingers fumbled them. She peered with a creased forehead, turning them to catch whatever light there was. I realized she was lost without her reading glasses.

'What is it? What?' But it was closer to a plea than a demand.

'These are two photographs,' I explained, 'of a body lying in shallow water. I did say that. If you look closer – '

'How can I *see*!' she cried. She waved a hand towards Philip, who at once went to search drawers for her spare reading glasses.

'I'll describe them,' I offered. 'They are identical except for

189

one tiny detail. They're of a young woman who was drowned. At the beginning of May, it was.'

'Let me see them again,' Philip put in, reaching across to hand her her glasses, and at the same time taking back the photos. 'A tiny detail? I don't see . . . oh yes I can. Olivia, he means that one of the photographs shows a round yellow sticker stuck to her anorak, or whatever it is. How very strange.'

'Isn't it!' I agreed.

'Do you know this person's identity?' she asked, making an effort to keep her lips moving correctly.

'Well yes.' I took the prints back from Philip, who'd been glancing at their backs. Then I returned to my seat. Now it was Philip who was bright and attentive, Olivia who was uncertain, her hands moving in her lap. 'Her name was Nancy Ruston.'

'Nancy . . .' Then she clamped her lips shut.

'Yes. You know, Mark Ruston's sister. He must have mentioned her, some time or other.'

She flapped her hands and looked around wildly, 'I'm not going to listen to any more of this nonsense. Burglars and photographs, and a young woman dead in the water. Oh, this is too much!'

Philip reached forward and placed a hand on her arm. 'You will please let me handle this, Olivia.' This was her business manager speaking, the man whose job it was to protect her from the unpleasant aspects of life, such as me. For a second she seemed about to fling his hand away, but he whispered, 'Please,' and slowly she subsided. But still he watched her. Her head was jerking, as though attempting to shake free from unwelcome thoughts, and her cheeks were moving with a chewing action. He removed his hand and looked across at me, quite calm, but his eyes were deeply sunken and dark. I sensed an inward retreat.

'Richard, I'm counting this as an insufferable intrusion. Will you kindly explain why you've brought this strange and even fantastic story here, and what it's got to do with us.' He smiled in the general direction of Melanie. 'And with the police. Then afterwards, you will please leave, and I think I'm safe in saying you will not be welcome here again.'

190

'I had to risk that, Philip. But the chain of evidence is quite complete. Can I explain?'

'That's what I'm asking.'

'Very well. This house was entered illegally, in such a way that it pointed to a specific burglar. When I saw him, he admitted it quite openly, and produced these photos as the items he'd stolen. He sold them to me – on your behalf, Philip – but in fact he cheated me. This man, you see, has always operated on contract. That's to say, he was paid by someone to take one or more specific items. But in this case, as I've now found out, he was paid to obtain the negatives, and not particularly these photos, which were printed from them. Once in control of the negatives, you see, his client could start calling bluffs. Or at least, to evade the danger they represented. Harvey Cole cheated me, Philip, because he sold me the prints. He'd already disposed of the negatives to his client.'

Philip spread his palms. 'This is all very interesting, but I don't see how we can help you. In what way does this concern us?'

'Philip – for heaven's sake – the stuff was stolen from here! You or Olivia must therefore have been the photographer who took these pictures.'

He smiled, this time hideously exposing his teeth in a predatory manner. 'But Richard, you've said he cheated you. So why can't you see – he also lied to you? Those photographs mean nothing to either of us.'

'I hadn't really finished telling you how far the link extends, Philip. Do give me the chance.'

'Quite frankly, like Olivia here, I'm convinced you've gone quite far enough already.'

'For an extra hundred pounds, Philip, he told me the name and address of his client.'

He was leaning forward, knees apart, hands swinging between them. For a moment he stared blankly at me, the tip of his tongue just visible between his lips.

'Who was?' he asked softly.

'Mark Ruston.' I turned my gaze to Olivia. 'The same Mark I've already mentioned. Who might have mentioned his sister to you.'

191

She moved her head. The sound she made might have been one of disgust. Philip took it on.

'Mark Ruston paid a burglar to steal photographs . . .'

'To steal the negatives,' I corrected.

'To steal the negatives, then, from this house! Really, Richard, you're taking this too far.' He cocked his head, now once again in full control of himself. 'I suggest you take your questions to Mark himself. He'll have your explanation – or whatever it is you want.'

'I can't do that, I'm afraid. Mark is dead.'

I said that to Philip, but my eyes had been on Olivia. She gave a gasp, then plunged her face forward, her hands coming up to clasp and contain the anguish, and from between her fingers came the protest: 'Mark! He's dead. Oh dear Lord!' It was almost as though she'd written it in purple prose, I thought miserably.

Amelia was at once on her feet, whispering to her, glancing back at me in disapproval and blame.

It seemed a good time to pause, and look round to Melanie. I was appealing for help. It was another woman's reactions I'd found myself baffled by. But she inclined her head with a wry smile. You're doing fine, Richard, her eyes told me. Fine, hell!

I had my eyes back on him by the time Philip spoke again.

'My wife thought a lot of Mark.' Not himself, I noted. No sympathy for Mark there. 'When was this?'

'He died last night. I'm sorry, you couldn't have known. I didn't realize that.' You damned liar, Richard!

'How?' he asked flatly. 'How did he die?'

'He was found hanging by a rope from one of the rafters inside a shed.'

'I didn't like him,' he said blandly. 'I'll admit that. But . . . such a death! There is something pitiable about suicide.'

I didn't correct his assumption. 'I've always thought so. All that internal suffering.'

'And remorse.'

'That too,' I agreed.

We were carrying this on, giving Olivia time to recover her composure. Remorse, he'd said!

Olivia whispered: 'I don't believe this.' She raised her head, and one hand thrust Amelia aside.

'I'm sorry,' I said to her. 'But it's true.'

She shook her head, put two fingers to her lips, then again stared at her lap, and at her hands as they moved down and wrestled there together.

Philip continued in his uninvolved, even disinterested, voice. 'Very well, Richard, you've told us Mark is dead, and those photos are of his sister, Nancy, also dead. Will you please tell us why you've come here with your eternal questions.'

'You speak as though you've never met her.'

'Of course I haven't.'

'But you told me you'd made an appointment to see her, at Potter Heigham, possibly on the very same day she died.'

'She didn't turn up. I also told you that. Perhaps because she was already dead. Do you think?'

'Perhaps.' I clamped my teeth on my pipe stem at a sudden thought. Then I firmly docketed it away.

'Then I repeat, Richard: why're you pestering us with your questions? We know nothing of these things.'

I sighed. 'Please don't pretend to be stupid, Philip, because I know you're not. It should be obvious, now. There's evidence that Mark killed his sister. Mark is now dead. The facts have got to be assembled in their correct order for the coroner, and it's obvious from the photos, which were stolen from *this* house, Philip, that something was known by the photographer about the time and manner of Nancy's death. For pity's sake – it must be obvious! We have to know when and why and how those photographs were taken. Do I make myself clear?'

'Quite clear, Richard. You don't have to be so pedantic about it. What is not clear is how you've come to the conclusion that your photographer is here.' His eyes were wide open with innocent enquiry. He might even have been laughing at me.

I stared at him. Was he mad? His attitude certainly bordered on the paranoid. How much longer could he continue to deny it?

'Very well, Philip, I will tell you.' And I felt like hell.

16

I stood up to ease the stiffness the chair was causing, and managed to catch Melanie's eye once again. Couldn't she now take over, before I went beyond the point of no retreat? She stared back at me blankly, sitting firm and straight with her briefcase between her feet. My pipe wasn't drawing properly. Nothing seemed to be going right. I returned to my chair and took up the thread of my theme. Amelia had slid her seat closer to Olivia's, and was now sitting with a supportive hand on her arm. It was difficult to continue when I could detect no apparent sympathy from any direction.

'Look, Philip,' I said. 'You're the photographer around here. Those shots are good. Sharp and crisp and correctly exposed. I know very well that anybody with a modern camera can get good results, but all the same, this photography indicates a fair bit of experience. The negatives were recently recovered from the man who paid Harvey Cole to steal them from here. . .' I signed. 'And if you think I'm repeating myself and stating the obvious, that's because you refuse to budge an inch.'

He pointed a finger at me. 'Then tell me, Richard – why should I go to all this trouble you've mentioned. . . all this photographing and sending pictures to Mark? I don't see this. Please explain.'

'Is that what you really want? Think about it, Philip.' It was his wife I was considering.

He nodded rapidly. There was no time to waste on thought. 'Let's hear it, by all means.'

Amelia made a gasping sound and seemed about to speak,

but I glanced at her, and something in my eyes silenced her. I turned back to Philip.

'You'd been looking for some way of getting Mark Ruston out of your life and out of Olivia's. He was becoming a pest. I know how it all began. Mark came to this house. There's a law about adopted children; they can now trace their real parents. Or parent. In this case, only one was recorded – the mother. That was Olivia.'

I saw Amelia whisper something in Olivia's ear, and prayed it might not have been the wrong thing. At that time, Olivia was looking neither distressed not guilty. Now she suddenly spoke up, reaching way down for her composure.

'There's no need to be portentous, Richard. Yes, I had a child. It was Malcolm Ruston's. There was no chance that we could marry. Later, I married Philip. It's all very straightforward, and your attitude is frankly quite ancient. Mark came here. . .'

'And you welcomed him?'

'Of course. Would you expect me not to?'

'Perhaps. Having discarded a child –'

'How dare you!' she flared at me, and now Amelia clutched at her arm, her eyes snapping at me, and saying, 'That was inexcusable, Richard!'

'All right,' I said. 'All right, Olivia, I apologize. Attitudes change.' I meant hers, not mine. 'I was saying to Philip that he had no reason to like Mark, himself. You may not have thought about that, Olivia. Mark was welcomed too heartily for Philip's comfort, and over the next few months he took over far too much of your interest and concentration and time – well, Philip saw Mark only as a thick, black cloud in his life. Am I correct, there, Philip?'

'I didn't have any impulse to cheer at the sight of him,' he agreed sourly. He seemed not to be aware – or blithely ignored the fact – that I had just proved his previous story to Amelia and myself to be a complete lie.

'So when you had reason to believe he'd killed his sister – '

'Killed his sister?' demanded Olivia, her voice strained, her eyes wild. 'Whatever's this? Why on earth would Mark. . . he'd never harm a soul. . .' she darted a glance at Philip, who looked away quickly.

195

'There was a very good reason, Olivia,' I said. 'In fact, it came to the point where Nancy became a positive menace to Mark. But I'd rather leave that for now, if you don't mind.'

'I *do* mind!' Olivia declared. She nodded sideways to Amelia. 'Really, Mellie, your husband must be impossible to live with.' She was recovering fast.

'In a minute,' I promised. 'It would interrupt what I was saying to Philip.'

He waved a hand. 'Oh, don't mind me.'

I took him at his word. 'Philip, you see,' I explained to Olivia, 'knew exactly why Mark would want Nancy dead.'

She swivelled in her seat, staring at him. 'Is this true?'

'Yes, I knew.'

'And you didn't tell *me*?'

'The things I keep from you, Livie, run into the thousands. I treated this as one more annoyance to be kept from you.' He made that sound deliberately offensive.

Her eyes and mine were both on him when I said: 'So you knew about Mark's motive for killing her. Was that the reason you took those photos?'

'I haven't said I did that.' Again I got the bland denial.

Olivia's attention shot back to me. 'And neither did I. So there's your answer. Isn't that enough? I'm tired of this, and I'd like to rest. . .'

'I'm sorry, it is not enough. Whoever took those pictures rigged them so that when they were sent to Mark they represented a threat. Keep away from here or I will send these pictures to the police, something like that.'

Olivia shot to her feet, leaving Amelia's hand suspended in the air. 'Are you implying *I* would send threats to Mark? You must be quite out of your mind.'

'Mark believed it was you sent them. He told me that. He assumed it was you.'

'As a threat! Never!'

'From you, he didn't take it as a threat.'

'Then what?'

'I'd rather not say.'

Amelia breathed out. She tried to smile, but her eyes, on me, were bleak.

'I demand –' began Olivia, but I had to interrupt that. I'd led myself into a tricky situation.

'The fact remains, Olivia, that Mark thought that. It's clearly untrue. They originated from this house, and if it was not you. . .'

I was talking to her back. She had whirled around, and now stood over Philip. He was still sitting there, hands dangling free between his legs. He looked up at her calmly, waiting.

'Philip!'

He managed a smile. Heaven knows how he did it, against the imperious boom of her voice. Yet it was a smile of defeat.

'All right, Richard,' he said past her. 'You can see I've got no alternative. You did that cleverly, I'll say that much.'

I had not. It had been forced on me. I didn't contradict him.

'Sit down, Livie,' he said coolly. 'What I did, everything, it was in your best interests.'

For a few moments she stood there, then she turned from him, and though her face was now expressionless she fell heavily into the chair. 'Livia!' said Amelia. She offered her hand. I saw Olivia's fingers clutch at the hand, urgently, fiercely.

'It's taken a long while, Philip,' I said. 'But now we've got to it. You admit, then, that it was you who took the photographs?'

'I admit that.' He smiled. It might have been that he thought he had gained something.

'Why?' I asked, embarking on the next stage.

'Why what? You've already said. I sent them to Mark.'

'I didn't really mean that. I meant, why did you spend some days. . . and she'd been in the water quite a while when she reached the place she was found. . . why go to all that trouble to find the body?'

'To photograph it. Damn it, I've said I did that.'

'But that wasn't all of it, was it? You did a bit of jiggery-pokery with a yellow charity sticker, which you must have kept for several days just for that purpose.'

'Oh. . . that!'

'Yes, that.' I paused. He didn't seem about to add anything. Then he straightened, realized he was on a stool and couldn't lean back negligently, so compromised by sitting straight up, arms folded across his chest, looking defensive although he

197

intended to imply confidence. He said nothing. I had to go on.

'Will you tell me what day you found the body?'

He seemed to feel there was no danger in admitting that. 'On the Thursday.'

'You mean the Thursday following the charity collection?'

'That Thursday, yes. The police found her two days later, so how could it've been any other Thursday?' He raised his eyebrows mockingly, having gained a point.

'I'm sorry – of course – I wasn't thinking. So you found her, on the Thursday, wearing a sticker. . .' I used my eyebrows, equally expressively.

'Of course. Yes.'

'But Philip. Ask yourself. How could she possibly still have had on a sticker, after all that time? It would've soaked off long before – '

'Pure conjecture. In fact, it was still there.'

'Very well. So you took a picture of her, still wearing that sticker, and then took the sticker off in order to take another one. For Mark's benefit.'

'Yes, yes. Now you're understanding. I needed one to show him she hadn't been wearing one when I found her, and one to show I'd left her wearing one. I switched the prints around, you see. To show him that I'd given him an alibi, and could easily withdraw it. If necessary.'

He was smiling as he said it, complacently. Clever me!

'And this was because you knew he'd killed her on that Saturday?'

'Of course.'

'You're saying that you knew what he'd done – killed his sister – but all the time you were willing to give him a faked alibi?' I waited. He waited. I went on: 'But you're said you wanted to get him out of your lives – your own life. Wouldn't it have been easier to have him arrested, tried and sentenced? That would've done the trick.'

'Richard! Richard!' he chided. 'Don't be so foolish. That would have hurt Livie terribly, to discover such a thing about her darling Mark. No – it was a warning, no more. And you must admit, it did work.'

198

'But you were taking a big risk, yourself. Withholding information, falsifying evidence. . .'

'In what way?' he demanded.

'You're said you found her wearing a sticker, and took if off for your second shot. That's what the negatives prove.'

'I put one on again before I left her.'

'They found her without one.'

He shrugged. 'Not my fault. As you say, it probably didn't stick properly, to a damp anorak.'

I sighed. He made everything fit exactly with the evidence. In matters involving self-protection, Philip had a razor-sharp mind.

'And all this was to show him that you'd rigged him an alibi for the Saturday. No. . . let me finish. This, I suppose, was because you knew he was pretty well covered for that Saturday?'

He nodded, his mouth twisted sardonically. 'Apart from one short period.'

I didn't want to be side-tracked just then. Olivia was moaning softly and beginning to rock herself backwards and forwards. Reality was intruding too forcefully. Amelia had no time to glance at me, even in disapproval. My forehead felt clammy and my eyes gritty.

'I don't understand, damn it. Would you really have gone to the police and admitted this – said it – when you'd given him a faked alibi? They'd clap you inside. . .'

He shook his head. 'Richard, Richard, it's only that you're a bit slow. If things got too difficult, *then* I'd have gone to them. Don't you realize, this was a *false* alibi for Mark. To the police it wouldn't be. I told you, I could destroy it. It was a threat to Mark, to keep away from this house, from me, from Livie. In emergency I could always have fallen back on the truth, and he'd have been arrested, with all the pain and suffering –'

Olivia whispered: 'I'll kill you for this, Philip! So help me. . .'

Neither of us took any notice of her. There might have been nobody but us two in the room.

'Which you would have done, if things became desperate?' I asked him.

'Things,' he said distinctly, his voice still steady, 'were already pretty desperate, anyway.'

199

'Why doesn't he stop!' moaned Olivia. 'Make him stop, Amelia.'

I felt cold at the empty tonelessness with which she said this. She had entered a second stage of shock, in which she had to retreat from it to a recognized and familiar formula. She gave instructions, and they were expected to be carried out. She meant me, of course. I was to be made to stop.

Amelia stared at me with dull eyes. It was clear that I couldn't carry on much further without revealing details that could send Olivia way over the edge.

In desperation, I tried another approach. 'The police are under the impression that Mark did have an alibi for the whole of Saturday, Philip.' He inclined his head. I went on: 'But you said something about – apart from one short period. I've got to assume it was something that would destroy Mark's apparent alibi. Can you explain that?'

'Well, if you wish, Richard. Certainly. Isn't that pipe drawing? Here, I'll get you. . .' He went across the room and fetched me a large ashtray. 'There, my dear chap, scrape it out into that. All right now? Fine.'

He went back to his stool, fetched out his own pipe, looked at it, then lit it. Blew out a stream of smoke, and smiled.

All this was to give himself time to marshal his thoughts, I knew. Olivia had followed his movements as though he'd gone insane. My throat was dry. I coughed, and he went on.

'This short period, eh? Well, of course, this was why I knew he'd been the one to kill her. I was at Potter Heigham myself, that day.'

'At the church, yes. For an hour around three o'clock. So?'

'I was at Heigham Bridge very much earlier. I had an appointment to meet Nancy Ruston, as you know. But I was down by the bridge earlier. In fact, I saw Olivia and Mark meet, and go away together. I suppose they had lunch. So did I. Then I was back again. It was still only two o'clock. I saw Mark walking away along the path beside the river. . .' He paused and licked this dry lips. He was wondering how to go on.

'Walking away?' I prompted quietly.

'With a young woman. They disappeared.'

200

'This would be in the direction of Womack Water?'

'Yes.' Again he paused, hesitated, then continued. 'I waited, and half an hour later Mark came back. And he was alone.'

'I see. You're saying this was Nancy he'd been with?'

He tapped his fingers on his knee. 'I didn't realize then, of course. But I had to get off to St Nicholas's, to wait for her, and when she didn't turn up I began to think –'

'What did you think?'

'That the girl Mark had been with had to be Nancy.'

'And that he'd done away with her?' I asked flatly.

'Yes, yes.' He was impatient.

'But surely, that was a rather far-fetched assumption, Philip. From where I'm sitting here, I can't see the logic. You saw her walking away. . .'

'And not coming back.'

'Perhaps she was *going* back.'

'I don't understand.'

'There's a yacht and boat basin there. You ought to know that. Where people hire boats. There'd be parking space.' I turned to Melanie. 'Inspector, you'll know. . .' I hoped she would lie, even if she didn't know.

'There's parking space there, yes.'

I returned my attention to Philip, who'd had to lean forward to ease his back. 'You see? Perhaps she'd parked there. Perhaps she'd walked *from* there, and Mark was simply escorting her back. Perhaps it wasn't Nancy at all.'

'If it was,' he shot back, 'she wouldn't have left her car there. It'd be a long walk from there to the church.'

I rubbed my face with both palms, peering at him between my fingers. 'Look, Philip, I'm trying to understand. Really I am. But from what you've said, I can't see why you'd assume that girl was Nancy.'

'She didn't turn up at the church,' he said simply.

'That could've meant she was delayed –'

'She was desperate to see me. I knew that – the way she wrote.'

'In fact, she believed she was going to meet Olivia.'

'What?' Olivia said. 'What's this, Philip?' She stared at him dazedly.

He ignored her, his attention on me. 'How d'you know she thought she was meeting Livie?'

'She said that. To a friend.'

'And she might have said the same to Mark,' he claimed in triumph. 'And then *he'd* have been in a desperate position.'

'And on those two points, her failure to be at the church, and Mark's motive, you based the decision that he'd killed her! And from that you searched for her body, and did all that trickery with the photographs! For heaven's sake, Philip, don't you understand why I'm here? Don't you see? It's not enough, just supposition and motive.' I flapped my palms on my knees. 'It's no damned explanation at all.'

Then I twisted from the chair and thrust myself to my feet in annoyance, and from behind me Olivia threw in, coldly and bitterly:

'Motive, Philip? Will you kindly explain that.' Yet she didn't seem as though she would understand if he did.

When I turned back to him I saw that he was trapped. A cold and bitter Olivia was more than he could handle. Some time he would be forced to tell her, and it was clear to him that I already knew. He slumped for a moment, then straightened.

'Very well, Livie,' he said, then he raised his shoulders at me, as though we'd been engaged in no more than a conspiracy to protect her from the facts.

'Mark came to this house,' he went on, trying to keep his voice neutral. 'You'll remember, my dear. He came, talking about you having had a child. I'd never heard about that, but I suppose I had no right! That's beside the point. You recognized him as the son of his father. You remembered him, it seemed. One assumed he was the father in question.' Now his voice was far from neutral. This was a bitter man.

'This isn't quite what you told me,' I put in.

He turned on me, momentarily furious. 'All right. I lied. Make something out of *that*.' Then, calmer, he turned back to his wife, who sat as though the words were washing over her and leaving her cold with shock.

'I sat – in here, it was – sat and listened to what was said, Livie. I remained on the sidelines, as is my place, and watched you mooning all over him, just like one of your empty and vacuous heroines, for Christ's sake! All *right*. I'll keep to the point. The fact is that from that moment on he became the centre of your life. And this, it seems, was a child you'd never even seen. You'd had him adopted, and I've come to understand you didn't even ask the sex of the wretched little sod. No, for God's sake don't try to interfere. I'm going to say this. You let him take over. Your writing went to pot. Yes it did. God, that's a laugh! Coldly and calculatingly, you've been able for years to write emotional scenes that break people down in tears. Then along came some real emotion to occupy your personal feelings, and your writing went flat. It did. Ask your publisher.'

If it did anything, his sudden and fierce attack on her jolted Olivia towards normality. Not all the way, but enough for her to be able to organize a response.

'Very well, Philip,' she said acidly. 'I appreciate your opinion. Now bloody well get on with it.'

'Ha!' he said. 'And that's about the sum total of the emotion *I've* received for a hell of a long time.'

'Will you get on with it!'

He stared into her eyes. 'With pleasure, my love. So be it. You can't deny you went crackers over Mark, buying him this and that. Don't trouble to deny it – I'm the one who does the accounts. Promising him the world, I expect. All very well. What could I do about it? You were happy.'

'For over a year I've had happiness,' she said softly, her mind searching the past for comfort. 'And now he's dead.' A flat, empty statement.

'Yes. . . well. . . it was going to end some day or other. I found out the truth. A young woman wrote to you, Livie. Of course, I intercepted her letter. She claimed to be your daughter. Nancy Ruston. Mark's sister. Claimed to be your daughter,' he repeated in emphasis. 'What a pity you didn't even ask about its sex, before you gave your child away! But this one was telling the truth. She enclosed a copy of her birth certificate, and the legal documents relating to her mother. It was conclusive. *She* was your daughter – Mark was not your son. Now d'you see why I kept it from you?' He smiled, as though he'd done her a great favour, and because he'd enjoyed every moment of the telling.

Olivia remained every still. Her hand, which still clutched

Amelia's, must have been giving her pain. Now the fingers relaxed and her hand went over to her lap. She stared down at it. When she raised her face it was set and cold, with tiny flares of red on sallow cheeks, as though someone had slapped her. Slowly she came to her feet. That much she managed with apparent ease, but when she turned to face the door and began to walk towards it her movements were the stumped and stiff march of someone who cannot control her legs. Somehow, Tony was now standing in front of the door, casually, smiling at her. For some moments she stared at him, then she turned about and marched awkwardly back to her chair. There, she sat heavily, put one elbow on its arm, and rested her forehead on her hand. I could see her shoulders shaking.

If Philip noticed, it did not distract him. He stared at me, eager to have me understand.

'So you see, Richard, with that sort of motive. . . perhaps Nancy had even confided in Mark. They seemed friendly enough, walking away along the river path.'

I was impatient to have done with it, anxious to confront the pitfalls ahead before I faltered. I tried to speak slowly and distinctly. 'Yes, I can see he'd simply have to stop her reaching you, or Olivia, whichever one it was. I understand his motive even better than you do, because he told me himself. But Philip. . .' I rubbed my hair into a mess in exasperation. 'Philip, we didn't come here to discuss what we already knew. The important thing is what might have driven him to suicide. In other words, what did those photos mean – which I can't see – but which *he* might've seen. Hell, Philip, we've been on this for hours already. It all comes down to your reason for taking the blasted photographs. You must've had a damn good reason, to go to all the trouble of hunting around until you found the body.'

He looked puzzled. 'But I've explained. I'd seen him and Nancy walking –'

'That's another thing. I still can't see how you knew it was Nancy.'

'That was obvious.'

'Was it? How was it obvious?'

'Nancy didn't turn up at the church, Mark would've wanted to stop that. He *did* stop it. I saw him walking along the river –'

'With a young woman. *A* young woman.'

'Clearly it had to be her.'

'It need not have been even a *young* woman.'

'Of course –'

'You saw no more than her back.'

'*Will* you listen!' he bleated, then abruptly he was calm again. 'The way she walked. A free kind of young walk. I put two and two together, Richard. People do. I'm not stupid, you know.'

'But from that you assumed it was Nancy, and later that he'd killed her?'

'It took a little time. Of course. A day or so later. I don't understand you. Don't you ever use ordinary common sense?'

'I'm trying to, Philip. Trying to. Very well, I'll go along with that. You thought he'd killed somebody. You thought it was important to find a body, if only to confirm a death.'

'Exactly.' He bit on the word.

'And at the same time, because you'd had time to think about it, you'd worked out how you could use one of the stickers to scare the daylights out of Mark.'

'It worked, didn't it.'

'It did. But only because he thought those pictures had come from Olivia. Not from you, Philip. From Olivia, they meant something very different to him.'

She lifted her head. The tears had been real. Her face was streaked and blotched. 'What?' she demanded. 'What d'you mean by that?'

'Mark entirely misconstrued the meaning of those photos,' I told her, hoping she would leave it at that.

'I don't understand,' she appealed in a dull voice.

I admit I was tired. The concentration was giving me a headache, and sweat was running down my nose. I said: 'Olivia, Mark thought you were using them to tie him and you together even closer than you'd been before. And it was stifling him, Olivia. I'm sorry, but there it is.' I was trying to gloss over it.

Her lips fluttered and she drew in a breath. She gave in a tiny moan. Amelia said: 'Richard!' I knew that tone. I'd have some explaining to do. I dragged my mind from it.

'Yes, Philip, it worked,' I agreed. 'By the way, where did you get the sticker? It was days later –'

'Livie threw away a whole bunch of 'em.'

'Yes. I guessed so. All right. Where were we?'

'You were blundering on,' he said helpfully, 'trying to make something out of nothing. Getting at me. You're as bad as the rest.'

'Yes,' I agreed. As bad as the rest? 'So you searched for a body. How?'

'My little boat. It was the simplest.'

'Of course. All the same, when you did find a woman's body, how did you know she was Nancy? I mean, even though you'd put your two and your other two together. . . that could've been any girl's body. How did you know it was Nancy? And don't tell me you guessed. Your actions prove you knew it was Nancy.'

I'd gradually eased my way to this point. I knew exactly what he'd done, and why. But it had to be prised from him.

'Well of course,' he said, spreading his hands. 'When I found her, I knew. She had to look either like Livie or her father – in other words like Mark.'

'That's a bit of a sweeping statement, but never mind. You hadn't previously seen her face, so I suppose. . .'

'Oh, you *are* clever.'

'Philip,' I said, my voice failing, 'you not only searched for her body, but you did it with your camera and the stickers, all ready for when you found her. You must have been absolutely certain before you even set out.'

He licked his lips. 'Certain enough to take them with me – yes.'

'And which face was it, Olivia's or Mark's. . .' I was trying to keep the shake out of my voice, because he simply stared. I grated out: 'When you found the body, that confirmed it?'

'It's all so simple when –'

'For God's sake, whose face?'

'Well of course, there was some difficulty,' he admitted warily.

'I should imagine there was.' I cleared my harsh throat. What I wanted to do was shout it out loud, in a sudden overload of anger, but it came out quietly enough, if a little rough. 'But in the end, you were certain – huh? So who did she look like – Mark or Olivia?' It was the third time of asking.

206

He nodded. Now he really got my point. 'Oh. . . like Livie.'

I sat for a moment. My legs felt stiff and painful, but I levered myself to my feet, turned, and moved towards Melanie. She'd anticipated me, and had her briefcase open. I stood over her as she sorted through her envelope and produced the picture of Nancy, lying face upwards on the river bank.

'For Christ's sake!' I whispered. 'It's for you now.'

'We can't switch at this stage.'

'I didn't anticipate this,' I pleaded. It was a weakness. 'I can see where we're heading. It's yours, Melanie. The truth's obvious. I don't want to go on with it.'

Her voice was quiet but fierce. 'If I take over now, it becomes official. He'll dry up. You must see –'

I snatched the picture from her fingers. 'I know, damn you! I owe you something.'

I got back to my chair. Philip was watching me ironically.

'If I'd known you wanted time for a conference, I'd have fetched drinks.'

'There'll be time for that later.' And possibly necessity, all round.

I was uncomfortable in that Amelia had now moved from her own chair and was perched with one thigh on the arm of Olivia's, clutching one of her hands and with the free arm round her shoulders. There was no doubt where her sympathies lay, and I couldn't watch Olivia's face without observing Amelia's. My wife was set in her intention, her thin lips told me that. Olivia, who had looked up, was holding on to her control with blind determination.

For a few moments I stared at the picture of the dead Nancy, trying to keep the disgust from my expression. Then I forced myself to my feet again and walked over Philip. I put the picture in his hands.

'That was how she looked when she was found. Can you see Olivia's face in *that*?'

He seemed to be staring at it, head down, but I realized he'd simply been unable to look at it. I knew that, because when he looked up his eyes were just opening. I took it from him. He cleared his throat. I waved it wildly under his nose.

'Can you, Philip?'

'No,' he croaked.

'Let me see,' Olivia put in.

'No!' I snapped, and I took it back to my chair. 'So we've got nowhere,' I said to Philip. 'You still haven't justified all the trouble of hunting her out and taking the photos. You hadn't seen her face before, and when you found her you couldn't have recognized her as *anybody*.'

He stared at his palms.

'Perhaps you did see her face,' I offered to him. 'If you'd met. . .'

'Then she'd still be alive,' he said sharply, fighting back.

'Of course. That's true. The moment she met you she'd be safe. Safe from Mark. Then when did you see her, when she was still recognizable?' I was wary of it, not wishing to approach too clumsily in case I scared it away. My heart was beating heavily, and I wasn't sure my voice was under control. 'Perhaps that's it. Still recognizable.'

From my inside pocket I drew out Larry's masterpiece and grimaced at it. No, not like this, I thought, not laughing like this.

'Did she look like this, Philip?'

And this time I didn't get to my feet. I wasn't sure I could, but I knew he'd have to see what I held. He was looking towards me, but I wasn't sure he could see me. Nevertheless, he got himself to his feet and headed in my direction. He took the picture in his fingers and held it up, but seemed unable to focus on it. He walked to the french window, twisting and turning it to the light. For a moment I wondered if he was going to plead poor eyesight, but when he turned I saw that it'd been temporary. For one short second he'd been blinded by tears.

But of course he didn't need to see it – he knew.

'Philip?' I demanded.

Two yards to one side of him Melanie sat, still with the briefcase between her feet, her face drawn and pinched. She watched him. She made no move.

'Philip!' I repeated.

'Yes,' he whispered, 'like that.'

Olivia's head had come up. Understanding had brought her expression alive. But it was an awareness she refused to accept. She had difficulty in unclenching her teeth. 'Let me see.'

208

Philip was shaking his head. It was not in refusal, it was in rejection.

'Let me see, damn you!' she cried, half out of her chair and with Amelia restraining her.

He turned, and seemed to be on his way to his stool, stumbling towards her. Negligently, disgustedly, he threw the photograph into her lap, then returned to the french window, where he stared out at the water and fumbled with his tobacco pouch.

She grabbed at it, crumpling it, stared and swallowed, blood rushing to her face and then from it. Then she screamed, the sound abrupt and shocking, and threw it away from her. I hauled myself to my feet and bent to pick it up. There was blood on it, from where her clenched hands had forced the nails into her palms.

Shuddering, she fell back, weeping now, muttering and mumbling with Amelia comforting her, and the only thing I could make of it was: 'My little girl.' Over and over. The child she'd never met.

'So tell me, Philip,' I said, standing over him. 'If you didn't see her face to face alive, and she was not recognizable when you found her – how and when did you see her in order to know it was Nancy?'

He shook his head, having run out of answers.

'You say you didn't see her face, that day at Potter Heigham, and you couldn't have known her when you found her. Did you see her dead, Philip, but *recently* dead? Is that the answer?'

There was a clicking silence in the room. Far away, one of the dogs howled. Olivia was silent. I'd been deliberately dramatic, to cut through it and have done with it. Olivia was so still that I couldn't see her breathing. Then Philip, possessing more guts than I'd expected, destroyed the silence with a disgusted laugh, even with a hint of triumph in it.

'You've let yourself get carried away, Richard. I saw her alive and looking like that. Yes. I lied. All right, so I've done lots of lying. I didn't want to make things worse. So now, I'll have to warn you. This room's full of witnesses. What you're saying is plain, downright slander. Do you wish to go on? Make up your mind.'

I heard Melanie whisper, 'For pity's sake.' Amelia was on her feet. I felt a flutter of panic. Was I, after all, completely wrong? I took a deep breath and paused before answering.

The distant sound seemed at first like a noise in my head, then I separated it into distinct shouts, coming closer. I turned, as Malcolm Ruston came charging along the flagstones outside. He stopped. We stared at each other through the glass, then he reached out and jerked open the door. The two dishevelled constables came to an abrupt halt outside. Malcolm had blood on his face. He took two steps inside towards me, and stopped.

Melanie was on her feet. 'Wait!' she snapped at her men. 'Stay there.' Then she turned to watch what was happening.

Malcolm stood with his head down between his shoulders, his eyes hunting the room. He was lost and baffled, licked his knuckles, frowned into the shadows. 'It's Olivia? Livie!' Then he groaned. 'And Philip. I don't understand.'

He turned his eyes to me. I was the one to ask. But he saw the picture, still in my fingers, and snatched at it. Stared at it. 'My Nancy!' A swollen lip forced it out, distorted and high-pitched. Olivia was half on her feet, but she subsided again. Her lips seemed blue. Philip gestured. It could have meant anything, most likely a curt dismissal.

Melanie, not wishing to have any interruption to what I'd been approaching, took charge. 'He can stay. Sit in this chair, Mr Ruston.' Clearly he had to sit somewhere. She meant the one she'd been using. She told the two constables to wait outside. Her voice was harsh. They turned away unhappily, and she went to stand at Malcolm's shoulder. I heard her speak to him quietly. 'You will be silent, Mr Ruston. Hear me?' Then to me: 'Richard, that'll be enough, thank you. I'll take over now.'

And leave me carrying the debt I owed Mark? No! This was mine. I had to carry it through.

For some reason, her calm and unflustered face infuriated me. She was untouched by it, uninvolved. I shouted at that face, and watched the blood run from it.

'No!' I tried to contain it. 'For Chrissake, I've got to finish it.'

She stared at me for a moment, then she turned away. There'd been fury in her eyes.

With no energy left now for Philip, I turned wearily to him.

Amelia stared at me as though I was a stranger, then she walked straight past me and through the open window. I didn't turn to watch her, but heard her footsteps come to a halt.

Philip had been given time to summon his reserves. His eyes were bright.

'Very well, Philip,' I said, 'tell us why you've stalled so long, and when you saw Nancy's face.'

And only the slightest of sounds came from Malcolm.

17

Philip was now sufficiently in control of himself to be able to take out his pipe and fumble with it, to come to his feet and walk round in a proprietorial manner while he did it, and use the pipe for gesturing in emphasis. He made no attempt to light it, though.

'I stalled, as you put it, in order to keep from my wife the unpleasant facts of Mark and his impersonation – his fraud and his deception. I spend half my life fending off these invasions into our lives. They try to get at us. . .' He stopped himself forcibly, then went on: 'Contrary to what you seem to think, I protect Olivia from anything so sordid and upsetting, not as a simple business matter, but because I still love her dearly. I am not demonstrative. She may not believe it, but it's true. So I stalled.'

'All the same – '

He paused in his stride and pointed a finger at me. 'Let me speak for once on my own.'

I nodded, glancing at Melanie. No encouragement. I looked back at Philip, trying to affect patient interest.

'I was at Potter Heigham and around the bridge area all that Saturday. I went early. I thought this young lady might do the same – get there early. And no, she hadn't sent me her photograph. But she came. I saw her first, close to the hotel. I knew her at once, of course. I suspected there was some sort of conspiracy going on, Mark and Nancy, some method being planned for extortion and blackmail. I was protecting my wife, and myself if you like. I watched and I waited. I saw Mark, and I saw them meet. They appeared friendly. She bought a sticker from him.'

'This was in the morning?'

He seemed annoyed. 'Yes.'

'Before he went to lunch with Olivia?'

'Yes. Will you let me speak! I watched her. She went away. I followed. She was merely wasting time. Then I saw them meet again, and I watched them – as I told you – walk away along the river side. And I saw him come back alone. *Now* do you see why I was suspicious? I continued to watch him. Occasionally, he spoke with friends. Still selling his stickers. Then he went to a house, where he apparently unloaded them all. Then he came out of there and went to a pub, and settled in with some mates. I left him, then, and went myself along to Womack Water, and along to the yacht basin. I couldn't see anything. It was dark. No trace of her. Not even her car parked anywhere. I didn't know, at that time, that she'd got a car, but there wasn't one there. So I went back for my car, and returned here.'

He smiled bleakly, but didn't return to his stool. There'd been no sound from Malcolm except his deep, snoring breathing.

'So in effect, you yourself could give Mark an alibi for that Saturday, apart from his walk out of sight along the river?'

'Pretty well all day.'

'So it's in that way that you could've given him an alibi – and taken it away again?'

'Yes.'

'And with no danger to yourself. I mean, you had an alibi for the whole of that day. . . I suppose you did?' I risked a thin smile. 'Even, I remember, for that hour or more you spent at the church. . . waiting. You spoke to the verger, I believe.'

'I resent your suggestion. If I need an alibi. . . shall I write out a schedule? Draw up a time-table. . .'

I shrugged, half turning away. Now that I had him close to the truth, the weariness entered my bones. Malcolm was staring at me, his face haunted, his eyes vacant.

And Philip, now apparently on a flush of confidence, appeared at my shoulder, flapping his empty tobacco pouch.

'Richard. . . if I could just beg. . .'

I looked down into his face, seemingly unstressed, his eyes steady, and wondered at his almost schizophrenic responses.

'Of course.' I offered him mine. I tried not to contact his flesh.

We stood together, then, like old friends. When he spoke, head down and watching his fingers stuffing tobacco into his pipe, it was clear that he thought he could draw me into collusion against officialdom. 'I hope these are no ideas of yours, Richard. What on earth is all this leading to?'

He didn't realize that these actions were only confirming what I now believed, that he was capable of having done what I guessed.

'It's what's been troubling Inspector Poole.' I gestured towards her, where she was standing very still, one hand on Malcolm's shoulder. 'It's what brought us here, really, to try to make sense of it.' It was agony to speak calmly.

He returned my pouch, patted his pockets, found his lighter. All were confident and casual actions. 'I just hope you've managed to do that.'

'Oh, I'm sure I have. You see, when she was found – Nancy – by the police, she hadn't got a sticker on her anorak.'

'I told you what I did.'

'Yes, yes. I know. That's what's so puzzling.'

'Is it?'

He wandered over to the french window, me with him. This, he intimated, was between us, but in fact Melanie was only feet to one side, and Malcolm simmering even closer, and the silence in the room was stifling. I stood beside him.

'They conducted experiments, you see,' I explained. 'It was found that she could not possibly have been wearing a sticker after having been so long in the water. In no way. So you must've found her stickerless, one might say. No, let me go on, Philip. Your intention, you've told us, was to send two photographs to Mark, one indicating she'd been found like that, and one indicating you'd left her wearing a sticker. In fact, to make it very clear to him, you marked the prints 1 and 2. But you actually took the pictures the other way round, the first one *with* a sticker, the second *without*. Now – why was that? There seemed no point why you should not have taken the first one

214

how you found her, stickerless, and then one when you'd put a sticker on. Then the negatives would've been in the same order as the prints you sent to Mark. Am I making myself clear?'

He had his pipe going, and he blew smoke out at the open air, where Amelia stood aloof. 'You're making too much fuss over it.'

'It would have been more natural to do that. But I'd suggest that you particularly wanted the negatives in that specific order, first the one showing the sticker, second the one without. Now I can see why.'

'I wish I could.'

'It's because, if the going got difficult – as it has now – you intended to produce those negatives. With prints, you can't tell the order they were photographed. With negatives, there's no argument about it. They *are* in order, and numbered on the edge of the strip. This means you'd be able to show, with reasonable certainty, that Nancy *did* die on that Saturday, because you'd be able to demonstrate that you'd found her wearing a sticker.'

'Which I do say.'

'That's exactly my point. You were trying to achieve two things with the same photos. You sent the prints to Mark, apparently showing you'd *left* her with a sticker, but you intended to use the negatives, if pushed to it, to prove you *found* her wearing one. One was something to convince Mark – the prints. The other was a fall-back to convince the police – the negatives.'

'This is just words.'

'Words, yes. But for you. . . actions, Philip. Just look what you've achieved by taking those two pictures. You've kept Mark at bay, and you've persuaded the police she died on that collection Saturday. Deeds *and* words, Philip. Your words – and all we've heard is Saturday. Now we hear that *you* have an absolutely solid alibi for the same day. As of course you would. Saturday, Saturday, that's all we've heard. It's *all* come from you, Philip. The day of the appointment – Saturday. The sticker – Saturday. The day you watched Mark's movement – Saturday. The day, you say, you saw the two of them on the river path. Oh. . . what's the point in going on!'

He said nothing. He stared out through the open window.

I turned my head to Melanie. Her eyes were bright, her flush high.

'You said she borrowed a car,' I reminded her. 'You'll know more about it.'

'It hasn't been found,' she said softly.

'But when was it borrowed?' I already knew, but I wanted her answer out in the open air, where we could all look at it.

'From a friend.' Her voice was uncertain. 'On the Friday morning.' And her fingers closed on Malcolm's shoulder.

The air whooshed out of my lungs as I turned back to Philip.

'She borrowed a car on the Friday morning. She wouldn't have done that unless she intended to drive to Norfolk that day. She would not have intended to stay overnight at the Rustons', because that would have involved explanations. If she'd stayed anywhere else. . .'

I didn't need to finish it. Melanie was with me. 'We made enquiries. Nobody. Nowhere. She was not seen.'

'Then it seems more likely she'd have gone straight to her appointment on the Friday. At Potter Heigham, Philip? Most certainly not. You've gone to so much trouble to point our attention in that direction. I'd suggest it was somewhere quiet, where she would not be seen. To here. To the place Nancy already knew. Friday. Were you here that day, Olivia?'

I turned to her. Moaning and incoherent, she could not even move her head, either sideways or downwards. She stared past me.

In a conversational tone Philip said to her: 'That was the weekend you were in London, my love. Agent and publisher.' He shrugged. As well talk to a block of stone. He returned his attention to me.

'I'm getting very, very tired of this, Richard. You're now charging me – '

'Not charging, Philip. I haven't the authority. Accusing.'

'I would have had absolutely no reason to kill Nancy. Mark, yes. Oh, don't worry, I thought about that. But Nancy! Pure fantasy.'

'Is it, though? As you say, you'd been driven to the point where you could consider killing Mark. You'd gone quite a way, you know. Then all of a sudden, there is Nancy on the scene. Another one come to haunt you, bedevil you, threaten you. So even if you killed Mark, there would still be Nancy, waiting to take his place in Olivia's affections. So you'd have gained nothing. You couldn't even get rid of Mark by exposing him as a cheat and a liar, because that would still have introduced Nancy on to the scene. So you were in dead trouble. You'd have to go as far as considering two killings, one after the other. But that would be too dangerous, quite apart from the fact that you wouldn't be able to face that. You're not psychotic, Philip.'

I paused for a moment there. Not psychotic, no, but I suspected he was paranoiac. His persecution complex indicated that, his calmness under pressure, this self-assurance of his superior intellect. I decided to take that no further. He was staring at his hands.

'But I'd suggest, Philip, that by now it'd changed itself into a scenario. Like the plot of one of Olivia's books – not too real. You were thinking only that this was an insufferable intrusion you'd got to fight off. So. . . remove Nancy first. . . and how would that leave things?' Out of the corner of my eye I saw Malcolm's head jerk up. Tony was quietly moving in. 'Nancy first, and you could see how that could be made to achieve two things. It might, of itself, frighten Mark away. But in reserve you'd thought out a way in which you could scare Mark off with the photographs.'

I paused again, to give him time to say something, for somebody to interrupt. But the silence was clammy when my voice ceased to roam round the room, and Philip's face looked back at me with an expression of pity for my continuing stupidity.

With a great effort, I went on. I understood him now. Any moment he would crumble. 'So you would ask her to come here. On Friday. You could arrange appointments for Olivia, and have the house to yourself. And then. . . it would be all welcome and friendly chat, and Nancy loved the water, and you had a boat, so that you could offer to show her a water route out of this very quiet inlet. I suggest she died in the boathouse. Held under. Yes? And her body was taken to where it was found much later, days later, because, to anybody, it is a shattering thing to take a life deliberately.'

217

I could see it in his eyes. He could still fight back. He could have demanded proof, and I had none. But that final description recalled the deed. The memory of what if had cost him drained the blood from his cheeks. With a set face he stared at me. Then he turned on his heel and walked, head high, towards the door, where Tony once again intercepted and refused to move, though this time Tony had no smile. Then, as Olivia had done, Philip turned on his heel and marched back to stand at the open window beside me. But he was facing Olivia now, staring at her, as though hypnotized.

At last she stirred. Shock had held her, but now she emerged from it with a whimper, which shuddered up to the heights of a full-blown scream, breaking through all her resources and her mental energy. With her hands, she forced herself out of the chair and hurled herself across the room at Philip, launching her full weight at him, hands extended, nails, already bloodied, aimed for his eyes. What had been a scream crumbled into insane cries of fury.

He whirled round and flung himself through the open french window. In a second he was in full flight. Melanie threw herself sideways, forgetting Malcolm in her way. He was rising with clumsy but explosive energy, like a wakening bear, and the two of them fell full-length in front of me. I stumbled over them, falling heavily and painfully across the sill. Amelia was shouting out: 'Livia! Livia!' She must have rushed in, jumping clear over me, though I don't remember that. Whatever she did, Olivia didn't reach me. Amelia's voice came from inside the room, and they couldn't have been in Tony's direct line, because in one bound he cleared our tangle of bodies and was away in great strides after Philip.

I got myself to my knees. Melanie used my shoulder to heave herself up, but Malcolm was already thrusting himself forward, his penetrating howl chasing after Philip and Tony. Neither of them stood a chance. The boathouse had an end door, and Philip was inside at a flat run, and had only to shut the door behind him and throw a bolt, and they couldn't get to him. Tony tried splashing into the water beside the shed, but the bank fell away steeper than he'd expected, and he was up to his chest inside six feet, and tangled in weeds. From the open end of the boathouse Philip emerged, hand-paddling his little boat until he was clear.

But Malcolm, slower on his feet but with a few more seconds in which to think, took one great leap from the bank on to the top of the boathouse, three strides across its corrugated iron roof, and launched himself with a yell of triumph at the boat. His fingers caught the stern, just as Philip moved to swing down the outboard motor. Malcolm's hands clasped the stern, and for a second Philip hesitated. Then he slammed down the shaft and propeller into Malcolm's face. The fingers opened, and Malcolm disappeared beneath the water. Philip was snatching savagely at the starter cord as Malcolm's blood-streaming face reappeared. But the engine fired and the water spluttered back into Malcolm's face. His reaching fingers were a foot short as the boat rode clear.

Tony was trying to get back up the bank, Melanie lying full-length and reaching a hand. Malcolm was in trouble, and I shouted out to Tony. By turning, he could reach a free hand to Malcolm, so that Melanie and Tony were a bridge to Malcolm. But his weight was sliding Melanie down the slimy bank.

The two constables had done nothing. They stood at my shoulder. 'Do something!' I snapped at them, then I threw myself down on to Melanie, arms round her waist, toes digging in.

What the constables did was to grab one of my legs each and haul us in, one at a time. Malcolm was close to passing out as he lay on the bank. The constables were the only ones not covered in mud or blood and not soaked to the skin.

I didn't hold out much hope for their futures when Melanie finished with them, but at the moment she showed her strength of character by doing no more than stare at them, then turning to the immediate problems.

Malcolm had a gash across one eyebrow, and was retching up water, Tony merely soaked, Melanie muddied, me uncomfortable.

She walked quickly to the french window, looked inside, then turned and snapped out: 'Ambulance. And fast.'

One of the men ran off. The other was bending over Malcolm as I followed Melanie into the room.

219

Amelia had been unable to lift Olivia into her chair. Olivia had collapsed on the floor, but now Amelia had her sitting with her back against the chair's arm, and was kneeling helplessly in front of her. As we approached, Amelia lifted her face, grey with distress.

'Listen, Richard!' she said softly.

Olivia's face had collapsed. Saliva ran from the corners of her mouth and down her chin. Her blouse was torn apart, where she'd struck at herself, unable to vent her fury on Philip. What she was saying had no meaning, was no more than sound bubbling up from inside. Occasionally, caught on her tongue and spat out, there was the phrase:

'He killed my little girl. My Nancy.'

From time to time it was repeated, only to be submerged again in her bubbling jumbled miseries.

Melanie, on her knees beside her, looked up. Her face was stiff with shock, at the suddenness that had taken her so much by surprise.

'Tony, look for blankets. Get those clothes off. . .'

'And you?'

'It's only mud. Where's Mr Ruston?'

The constable was bringing him in and steering him to a chair. Wide-eyed, the constable said: 'The first aid kit. . . the car. . .'

'Get it,' she said, no force now in her voice.

He ran off. Tony went looking for supplies of blankets, and Amelia again said urgently: 'Listen! Listen!'

As we bent over, Olivia shuddered, then for a few moments her red and streaming face seemed to hold intelligence. But her eyes were dull. When she spoke the words were clear, if lifeless.

'He lied. Lied. He told me it was Mark, and all the time it was Philip.' She reached over and clutched at Amelia. 'Oh, Mellie, help me, help me.'

And my poor Amelia buried her face in her hands and wept for her own distress.

After that, I sat and smoked and allowed it to happen all round me. Amelia, now silent in the other chair, watched me in misery, and also waited.

An ambulance came. I thought Melanie had intended it for

Malcolm, but now, plastered and bandaged, he refused, and was allowed to stump off to his pick-up. But by this time it was clear that Olivia had gone well past the stage where a sedative and a long rest would restore her. So the ambulance took her away.

Tony, blankets flapping, ran Melanie's errands with alacrity, his clothes drying off on a radiator. Philip couldn't get away, said Melanie confidently, coming back from her car. The river banks were too marshy to offer escape on foot, and she had him shut off with police motor boats.

At one point, the Great Dane and the two Spaniels came in to see what was happening, sensed human misery, and slunk out. They gave Amelia something else to worry about.

Eventually we were driven back to the station to pick up our car. Melanie had said not a word. She must have spoken to Tony, though, because he said he had instructions to tell Larry he could go home. I went down to the cells with him, Tony in his now dry crumpled suit, determined to give myself the pleasure of telling Larry he was free.

'I knew you'd do something,' he told me.

'It was touch and go. Come on, there's a police car waiting to take you home.'

'Ma'll love that.'

'You're forgetting your book.'

'Oh, that. A load of rubbish. Women don't understand these things.'

'Then it's up to us to teach 'em gently, Larry, isn't it,' I said solemnly.

'Too right. I've had enough of Lovella Treat.' He chattered on up the stairs. 'Will he use his flasher and his siren?'

'You'd better ask him.'

Tony and I grimaced at each other as he galloped out through the reception area. He didn't even notice Amelia, as she rose from one of the seats.

'Can we leave now, Richard?'

I think they were the first unemotional words she'd said since Olivia collapsed.

'Yes, we can leave.'

But leave-taking absorbs time. We had to say goodbye to

221

Melanie. She was depressed at the outcome, but quietly elated at the success.

'I didn't expect it,' she admitted. 'Did you know where you were heading?'

'The negatives, yes, I thought I could see what those meant. But I had to force him into a dead-end, then he'd produce his alibi. That was the clincher.'

'I didn't expect to get both murders solved.'

'Didn't you?'

'It was obvious it had to be Philip who took the photos, but I couldn't see beyond that.'

'Nor me, really.'

'But it's all so clear now. Philip's obviously unhinged, and removing Nancy *would* have seemed logical to him. What a pity for him that Mark managed to get hold of the negatives! It put Mark right back in the running as principal pest, and when you came along, stirring up the mud. . . that really upset things.'

'It certainly did.'

'And it left Philip with no alternative but to remove Mark as well.'

'I hadn't seen as far as that,' I admitted.

She shook my hand, kissed me on the cheek. 'You're only saying that. Thank you for your help, Richard.'

Then, apart from saying goodbye to Tony, and apart from the two women pressing cheeks, we were free to go.

I drove away. Amelia, emotionally exhausted, was asleep inside the first mile.

18

Aching for news, yet too fearful to enquire because of what it might be, I tried to return to routine. For a fortnight there was nothing but gloom in the house. The evening television news made no mention of an arrest involving Philip.

Then Tony came again. He said he'd waited until there was nothing new coming in, and now he was here to bring us up to date.

Philip had not been found, either alive or dead. His boat, capsized, had been discovered, but no Philip. I said nothing to this. My guess was that Malcolm, whose knowledge of the waterways was no doubt unsurpassed, had beaten the police to it in the search for Philip. I hoped that long submersion would hide any thumb marks on his throat.

'And Melanie's completed her report on it?' I asked.

Tony nodded. 'And been commended.'

'Olivia?' Amelia asked breathlessly.

Tony smiled. 'They sent her home after a couple of days. I don't think she's working yet. But here's a strange thing. The Rustons went and collected the dogs, and have been looking after them, and for some reason it seems to have brought them together, the Rustons and Olivia. Isn't that strange, Richard?'

I cocked my head. No, it didn't seem strange to me. I smiled. 'It's to be hoped they find something to hang on to, together.'

Amelia was looking at me with speculation. 'What does that mean?'

'I'm a little surprised at Olivia, that's all. Maybe a psychologist could explain it.'

'Richard . . .'

I grinned at the warning note in her voice. 'Don't you remember what she said? "He told me it was Mark, and all the time it was Philip." It's just the strange wording. Most people would've said: "all the time it was himself." But perhaps she didn't mean that.'

'Then what?' she demanded, leaning forward in her chair.

'Perhaps the "he" involved wasn't Philip. Perhaps it was Larry. I mean . . . Melanie told us he'd listened to our scene with Mark in his office. Larry himself told me he'd been thinking of a way to kill Mark, but didn't want to see it happen. What better way to do it than to take the whole story to Olivia? With all that to think of . . .'

'Do you mean that she –'

'Killed Mark? Of course. He'd cheated and lied, and he'd killed her Nancy. And how could Philip have told her about Nancy? He wouldn't have dared to mention her. Of course it was Olivia.'

Amelia and Tony sat and thought about that. I gave them five minutes, then I said:

'I wonder if they ever meet, Olivia and Larry, at the boatyard, he knowing it was she who killed Mark, and she knowing he realizes it. And he knowing that he was wrong, and it was Philip and not Mark who killed Nancy. Perhaps that's why she goes to the Rustons. They'd be drawn together, Olivia and Larry.'

Tony slapped his knee. 'I'd better not tell Melanie.'

'Oh heavens no!' said Amelia.

'Not,' I decided, 'now she's put in her report. And I'm just wondering . . .'

'What now?' she demanded.

'Whether Olivia might, in due course, adopt another false son. I mean, they'll never dare to lose sight of each other.'

Then we sat for a long while, silently staring at the fire.